The Secrets of Inishbeg Cove

—

What if your whole life was a lie?

Izzy Bayliss

A Heartbreaking Page-Turner of Love, Loss and What it Means to Belong . . .

I

www.izzybayliss.com

For Mam & Dad, for being my greatest cheerleaders

Prologue

I tried opening my eyes, but the room was spinning in a bright kaleidoscope of colours that made me dizzy, so I closed them again. I just wanted to sleep, everywhere hurt. Somebody stroked my skin, but even the gentlest touch was painful. The cool cloth on my brow was a welcome relief. The voices around me were trying to soothe me as I drifted in and out of sleep. I dreamed I was six years old and running along the beach with the sun warming my skin. Gulls squawked as they soared overhead. Waves were breaking in arcs and hissing up along the biscuit-coloured sand, rushing towards me. In another dream, I was cradling the baby once more in my arms. Then the infant was snatched away from me. I screamed and tried to reach out for him, but all that came instead was a low moan. I had the sensation of being lifted, like they were trying to move me, but it hurt everywhere and I wanted them to leave me alone. Voices called to me frantically. They were calling me back, but I couldn't go to them. They were praying for me not to leave, to fight harder to stay with them. But how could I? They didn't know what had happened. This was the price you paid for what I had done.

Chapter 1

Charlotte, North Carolina

The day he lost his mother was the day he lost everything ...

The slow *drip, drip, drip* of the morphine IV as the clear liquid drained from the bag and entered his mother's veins was the only sound to be heard in the room. Greg was holding her cold hand in his own; cold because her body was too weak to keep her warm anymore. He gripped her papery skin, speckled with age spots, as tightly as he dared—he didn't want to hurt her, but at the same time he wanted to squeeze her hand hard, he wanted to pull her back from wherever she was about to go and keep her here with him forever. He wasn't ready yet to lose her, but he knew that soon he would have no choice. Her body was giving up. He had had forty-two years with her, but now it still didn't seem like enough. He felt greedy; he wanted another year, another ten.

Kimberly, her nurse, had dimmed the lights so the room was filled with a soft glow. He leant in close and listened to her breathing. It was so faint now, barely audible. Sometimes it would catch and gurgle in her throat like water passing over stones, and his heart would pound as he thought, is this it? Is she about to leave this world? He would selfishly think, *please, not now, I'm not ready yet*, and then she would take a shuddering breath once more and he would start to breathe again too. He knew he needed to be courageous, but he was scared.

Kimberly came back into the room to check on her. She fixed her pillows before feeling her pulse. His mother let out a groan, and Greg gently raised a water-soaked cloth to moisten her lips.

'It's close now, Greg,' Kimberly whispered when she had finished. She was kind and sympathetic but in a manner that told Greg this was part of her job. She would go home when her shift had ended and maybe she would tell a husband about the patient who had died during the night. They might talk about it for a few minutes and then the topic would invariably change to taking out the trash or what they would eat for dinner that evening.

Kimberly went to leave the room, but she hesitated at the door and tilted her head to the side. 'Are you sure I can't call anyone to come be with you, Greg?'

He shook his head like he had done all the other times she had asked him the same question.

'I'm okay,' he said.

She nodded before dimming the lights once more and creeping out of the room.

Greg looked back down at his mother's face, creased with pain. The morphine seemed to be losing the battle at keeping her comfortable. He hated seeing her like this and being powerless to help.

'It's okay to go, Mom,' he whispered. 'I'll be okay; you don't need to hang on for me. I'm ready to let you leave—you go find Dad.' He had heard that our hearing was the last sense to depart, and he really hoped it was true.

Suddenly her eyes flickered open and her lips began to twitch. He realised she was trying to speak.

'In—'

'What is it, Mom?' He quickly moved in close to her.

'In—In.'

He racked his brains to think of what she might need. 'Do you need something?'

'Inishbeg—' The word was propelled suddenly from her dry, scratchy throat.

'What is it? What are you trying to say?' He leant in closer to her so that his ear was almost touching her parched lips.

'We . . .' Her voice was liquidy and rasping. 'Inishbeg Cove'—she stopped for a breath—'Ireland.'

4

He slumped back against his chair. She was on a lot of morphine and was rambling now. Kimberly had warned him that this might happen. 'It's okay, Mom, just relax,' he soothed as he traced delicate circles on her skin.

'We got you'—she paused for a breath—'in Inishbeg—' She stopped again for a moment, clearly trying to summon the power to say whatever it was that she felt was so urgent. 'A cottage—I'm sorry—'

Suddenly a rattle sounded deep in her throat. Then she took a few shallow breaths followed by one long exhale as the air left her lungs and her spirit left this world.

Greg jumped up and pressed the call bell, and Kimberly hurried back into the room.

'I—I—think she's gone—'

He stood back in shock and let Kimberly in beside the bed to listen to her breathing. She used a torch to check his mother's pupils before nodding at him to confirm what he already knew. 'She's passed on. I'm so sorry, Greg,' she offered her condolences.

After Kimberly had recorded the time of death and completed her paperwork, she crept out of the room leaving them alone together. As Greg whispered his final goodbyes, tears fell down along his face and onto the bed sheets leaving damp circles.

He woke some time later to the sound of birdsong and early morning light filling the room. He didn't know how long he had been sitting holding his mom's hand for, but it was now cold and stiff in his own. He noticed someone had opened the window, and there was a blanket covering him where he had been sleeping in the armchair.

'I'm so sorry for your loss,' a voice said as they entered the room. Kimberly was gone and a new nurse, full of vigour and energy having only just started on the morning shift had taken over.

Greg nodded, unable to get the words out of his mouth.

'Do you need me to notify anyone?' she asked.

He had texted two cousins and an elderly brother of his dad's, but they weren't close. He didn't think they would even bother to travel to North Carolina for the funeral.

'I've let our relatives know, thanks.'

She pursed her lips in a kindly half-smile before retreating quietly out of the room again. A feeling that he didn't recognise suddenly overwhelmed him. He guessed it was fear. He was scared for the future. They had never had a big circle, it had always been just his mom, dad, and him, and they were content like that. His father had passed away almost seven years earlier, a massive heart attack had taken him instantly as they had been watching the Super Bowl together. Greg still missed him every day, but he always feared the day that his mother passed on because that would be the day he would have no family left.

He had visions of future Christmas dinners sitting alone at the table or not getting a phone call on his birthday. For the first time ever, he found himself longing for a brother or a sister. He imagined it would have been easier to have someone else to go through this with, someone to share the load and your worries about the future. Someone else who knew exactly how much you missed that person, how much the pain of your loss cut right down to the bone. To have somebody who was there for him so he knew that he wasn't alone in the world.

Over the years people had often asked him in a pitying tone how it had been growing up as an only child, as if by not having brothers and sisters that he had missed out on something fundamental in his upbringing. He had always been taken aback by it, his childhood had never felt lacking, they had had each other, it had always been enough, but now he knew what they meant. He envied all those people with a band of siblings. He felt a longing to be near someone, to have closeness. He needed to hold someone or for someone to hold him. It occurred to him then just how few people he had in his life. Sure, he had friends, but they were people he worked with or went to a game with or had a few beers with. They didn't talk on a deep level. And anyway, they had their own lives, careers, wives, and children. He briefly thought about calling Selena, but he knew it probably wasn't a good idea. He would just come away from it feeling worse. He had to remind himself of that, especially now when he was feeling so low.

Selena and Greg were on a break, although technically it had been over two months now, so he wasn't sure you could even call it a break anymore. She had been the one who wanted some time apart; he had wanted to spend the rest of his life with her. They had been together for three years, and he was sure she was 'the one'. He had loved her—he still did. He had hoped to propose to her and one day had delicately tested the waters about how she might react if he did pop the question, but she had blown his tentative actions out of the water with jet-powered propulsion. A few days later she had announced that she needed some time away from him 'to think about their future together'. Greg had respected her wishes and given her all the space that she needed. He guessed she wasn't ready to commit to marriage right then, but he still harboured hope that she might be one day.

Later that day, after Greg had made arrangements for his mom to be brought to the funeral home, he gathered up his stuff to leave. Her forehead was startlingly cool against his lips as he kissed her goodbye.

His bones ached with tiredness, his eyes stung, and his heart hurt as he walked out of the hospice for the last time. He had spent so much time here over the last few months; in a weird way, it was almost bittersweet saying goodbye to the place.

He started driving on autopilot but didn't take the route home to his apartment. Instead he found himself heading in the direction of his childhood home. It was like a force pulling him there. He drove through the familiar streets, feeling detached from everything, like he was watching the world around him through a glass screen. He had just lost his mother but that hadn't even hit him yet. He was still in a dense fog.

He found himself thinking about his mother's last words to him, what had she been talking about Ireland for? She had never even been there; they weren't an Irish-American family. His father's family had been German immigrants who set sail for America in the 1800s, and his mom was second generation Italian. He couldn't help but smile; it would actually be quite funny, if it weren't so sad. It was crazy to witness the delirium that morphine could induce. The bittersweet thing was that he didn't even have anyone in his life to share the anecdote with.

When he reached his mother's house, he put his key in the lock and let himself in. He breathed in that soothing smell that was home. Photos hanging in the hallway greeted him. He usually paid no attention to them, he had seen them so many times, but now as he studied them, they made his stomach sink with the weight of grief. There was one of the three of them at a wedding back when he was about seven. Another one was of his parents beaming the proudest of smiles at his graduation from Duke. They had been a perfect unit. He had felt so happy as a child when he walked along in between them with his small hands cased inside their bigger hands. If he ever had children—and he really hoped he would —he wanted to give them that same love and security that he had always felt.

Greg went through to the living room, and the walls seemed to echo with memories of happier times. Christmas morning opening presents, birthday parties, movie nights with a bowl of popcorn overflowing onto the sofa around them. His swim trophies lined the wall, and pride of place was the rose he had made for his mom out of clay when he was in second grade. He walked over and drew the curtains. He knew his mother would hate the curtains being open at night. Then he opened the doors of the cabinet and pulled out some old photo albums. He pored over the now yellowed pages where a lifetime of memories graced each leaf. There was an album full of pictures of him as a baby. Another one had photos of him on his first day of little league and of his dad teaching him how to fish at the lake on one of their camping trips. He guessed from his toothless grin he must have been about six or seven. He traced his finger over the outlines of their familiar faces.

When he reached the end of that one, he lifted down a different one. There seemed to be an album for every year of his life. He opened it, and his absence from the photos inside told him that these were from an earlier time before he was born. As he turned the pages, he could see his parents looking so much younger than he had ever remembered as they posed in front of the Eiffel Tower or at the Trevi Fountain. He couldn't help but smile at his mother looking so young and girlish and his dad with his wiry sideburns and denim flares. He knew his parents had gone to Europe for their tenth wedding anniversary. They had visited Paris and Rome, and as a kid he had always loved hearing about their trip. On the next page there was a photo of them standing on top of steep cliffs, with foam-topped waves crashing in the background. The image for some reason was familiar to him. He had seen those cliffs before. He tried to place them, and then it hit him —he was pretty sure that they were the Cliffs of Moher. When he was in the fourth grade he had done a project on Ireland, but he was certain that his mom and dad had never visited Ireland. He peeled back the film covering it and pulled the photo out. He turned it over and saw his mom had written 'Ireland, Aug 1976' on the back. It was a habit of hers to date every photo she took. He thought it was strange that they had never told him they had gone there. He had listened to them reminiscing about their trip to Europe so many times over the years, but they had never mentioned stopping off in Ireland. He suddenly realised that he had been born in the September of 1976, so if this photo was taken the month previous, shouldn't his mom be heavily pregnant in it? His heart stumbled; in this photo, she was so slender and her stomach was too flat to carry a baby. She was definitely not almost forty weeks pregnant. Trembling, he brought it closer to his eyes. A memory came rushing back to him then of his dad helping him with the project, and when Greg had said that he would like to visit Ireland one day, he had said, 'We might get there someday, son, it looks like a swell place.' He could remember his words so clearly.

Maybe his mom had got the date wrong, a voice said hopefully. He thought about her dying words, and a cool shiver washed over him. Was it the morphine talking or was there something more here? Greg put the albums away and stood up from where he had been kneeling.

He fished his phone out of his pocket and found himself

typing 'Inishbeg Cove' into Google. He clicked on the first link and was shocked to see it was an actual place. An image on the town's website showed grassy dunes reaching up to high cliffs hovering over a beautiful horseshoe-shaped beach. So even though his mother had been high on morphine in the end, she had still managed to get this village name right? What the hell was going on? The warm, fuzzy feeling was gone, and the watery doubts had now started to crystallise into something bigger inside his head.

Chapter 2

The crematorium was dark and the atmosphere heavy. The pungent smell of incense scratched in his throat. He was trying hard to hold himself together, but like a charcoal cloud ready to spill its rain, he felt as though he was on the brink of falling apart. In the centre of the room stood his mother's casket, and his breath would catch every time he looked at it. It was hard to believe that the mother he loved, the woman who was always so full of life, was inside there.

He was touched to see a few relations had actually travelled from different sides of the country to North Carolina for her funeral. He guessed people surprised you when you least expected it, and their efforts moved him. He knew his mom would have appreciated it too. He spotted a few of his friends as they entered; there were some work colleagues and some guys from the netball club. Some of his mother's friends from her needlework group had come too. They all shook hands with him, and he thanked them for being there. He saw Selena come in next—you couldn't miss her. Tall and elegant, all eyes followed her as she cut through the room. She was immaculately dressed in a navy blue tailored trouser suit. His heart somersaulted; he knew she still had an effect on him.

He had texted her in the hospital to let her know that his mother had finally passed away, and she had sent a nice message back to say she was so sorry and that she was thinking of him. He could picture her elegant fingers typing out the reply, her high cheekbones working upwards to meet her eyebrows furrowing downwards as she carefully chose the correct words and tone: sympathetic but firm.

He hadn't been expecting her to come, but when he

thought about it, of course she had come, if for no reason other than out of a sense of duty. She had met his mother many times over the course of their relationship. Selena gave him a tight smile from across the room. Greg nodded in acknowledgement and was about to go over to her when the priest came out, so instead he took his seat.

The priest began the sermon, and as he made his way through the liturgy, Greg's mind began to drift off to happier times: his mom wrapping him in a fluffy towel after playing on the beach all day. His parents sharing a kiss in the kitchen with watery sunlight streaming in above them, not realising that Greg was watching them.

He heard his name and with a start realised that he was being called on to deliver the eulogy. Nervously, he got up and made his way towards the lectern. His heart was thumping, and his palms were sweaty as he unfolded the sheet of paper where he had tried to put together a few words earlier on. He could write legal briefs and deliver presentations to clients with ease, but when it came to trying to put his own sense of loss onto paper, his words felt deeply inadequate and did nothing to convey how broken he was feeling, so in the end he had deliberately kept it short.

He cleared his throat and began, 'Look, the words I say here today will never do justice to the lady that was my mother, but I'm going to try—' he started. He could feel the paper quivering in his shaking hands as all eyes watched him.

'Those of you who knew my mom knew how important her family was to her, she loved my dad and me, and such was the strength of her love that we never doubted it for a second. When I started kindergarten, I was quite shy and anxious, and Mom promised me that she would wait outside for me. The story goes that at some stage during the day, I opened the classroom door and began walking down the corridor. When my teacher came out after me and asked where I was going, I told her I was going to my mom because she was waiting outside for me. My teacher laughed and told me to come back inside, but just as I was turning to go back into the classroom with her, I spotted Mom through the glass doors at the end of the corridor. She was sitting on the bench outside—she had waited like she said she would. And that sums up my mom. She was always true to her word and was there whenever I needed her. I am going to miss her so much.' He began to choke on his words. 'So thank you, Mom, for the depth of your love, for the security and happiness of our home.' He took a deep breath. 'Sleep tight and now go find Dad and tell him the Panthers beat the Cowboys.' Greg was grateful when people laughed, easing the sadness in the room.

He sat back down and took a deep breath inwards to help steady him as the priest blessed her casket with holy water and it began its retreat behind a purple velour curtain. That was it; his mom was gone.

'I'm so sorry for your loss, Greg. I know how close you were to her,' Selena said, coming up beside him a few minutes later. She didn't move to hug him; instead she offered him her hand, which he shook awkwardly. 'You did great up there,' she continued. 'She would have been proud of you.'

'Thanks for coming.'

'I wanted to be here for you. Your mom was a lovely lady.'

He nodded in agreement. 'She was—' It stung to talk about her in the past tense.

'So, how've you been?' she asked.

'It's been a rough couple of months if I'm honest . . .'

She looked at the floor and nodded. 'I know . . . look I'm sorry—'

Suddenly his mother's death had made him braver. He was able to ask the question that he had been too afraid to ask for the last two months. He was already at his lowest point; things couldn't really get any worse. He took a deep breath inwards.

'I need to know where I stand with you, Selena,' he blurted.

'Greg, I'm sorry, I really am . . . Perhaps we could meet up in a few days and talk then? I don't like doing this, especially at your mom's funeral—'

He exhaled heavily. 'Just be honest with me, Selena.' He was weary and too tired to play any more guessing games.

Her eyes darted down to the floor. 'I don't see a future for us. I'm so sorry, Greg.'

There they were, the words that he had somehow known were coming but had been too afraid to face had finally been delivered. Over the last two months he had naïvely clung to a glimmer of hope that by giving her the space that she needed, she would wake up and see that she missed him, that they were good together.

'It took you two months to tell me?'

'I wanted to tell you—I really did—but then your mom was so ill . . . and I guess I was trying to find the right time . . .'

'So you waited until the day of her funeral?'

She looked up at him, and he could see her squirming, her eyes pleading with him not to make this conversation any harder for her. 'I'm sorry, Greg, I didn't mean for it to happen today, but I think I owe it to you to be honest. You're a really great guy. You'll make another girl very happy—I just know it. You deserve someone who can give you what I can't.'

Her words were patronising and stung like salt on an open wound. He nodded.

She continued, 'I should probably go now . . .' She paused. 'Look, I know you probably don't want me in your life as a friend, but I want you to know that I'm here for you.'

'Sure,' Greg replied, trying to sound indifferent but failing miserably.

He watched her walk off, her elegant silhouette making a quick exit through the small gathering of people.

'Greg, I'm so sorry for your loss,' a voice said from behind, jolting him out of his thoughts. He turned around to see it was from his cousin Francis. He was kept busy as one by one people came over to shake his hand and offer their condolences.

It was a while later when Greg suddenly noticed that everyone was gone, and it was just himself and the crematorium director left. The man was starting to tidy up around him, and Greg realised with a tinge of mortification that he probably wanted to go home and that he was keeping him late. The thing was that Greg was dreading going home to an empty apartment. Even being here with this stranger was company, but he knew he couldn't delay the inevitable, so he thanked the man before saying goodbye and heading out to his car.

Greg didn't remember the journey home, but somehow he reached his block. He parked in the basement and took the elevator up to his floor. A wry smile crossed his lips as he remembered how his mom had always called it the 'bachelor pad,' and then the pain of her loss seared through him once again.

As he went inside the air was cold having been empty all day. He walked over to his drinks cabinet and poured himself a large Scotch. He took a greedy gulp, and it burned its way down along his throat. Soon he began to feel its numbing effects, exactly like he wanted.

He collapsed down onto the sofa and lay back into the cushions; he was exhausted, his body ached with tiredness. He was so tired, but he knew he'd never sleep if he went to bed, and even if he did, he was afraid of the fresh pain he would face when he woke up again and remembered that his mother was gone. It was easier just to stay awake for as long as he could.

He drained his glass and then poured himself another, enjoying the heavy, sedated feeling brought on by the Scotch. His mind kept switching back to his mom's last words and that photo of his parents in Ireland. Over the last few days he had tried to rationalise it in his head, but he still couldn't shake the uneasy feeling. Had she been lucid, trying to empty her mind of a long-held secret before she took her final breath, or was the morphine messing with her head? It was the date on the photo that was bothering him the most. After he had gone home that day, he had walked into his home office and taken out his birth certificate. Next to *Mother* was listed Alice Bianchi, and *Father* was listed as Samuel Klein. They were his parents. The *Place of Birth* was listed as Charlotte, North Carolina. If he had been adopted, wouldn't his biological parents be named on it? He had replaced it back in the filing cabinet, telling himself that he was being ridiculous, but still something about it all made him feel unsettled.

His phone rang just then bringing him back to the present.

'Greg, it's Joel.' Joel Snyder was his parents' attorney. Greg had always refused to do his parents' legal work, believing that work should be kept separate from family. As well as being their attorney, he had also become a family friend over the years. It had been Joel who had given Greg his first job when he was fresh out of law school. Greg thought it was strange that he was calling him; he had seen him at the crematorium just a few hours ago.

'How are you holding up, Greg?'

'I'm doing all right,' Greg said, touched that Joel was checking on him. 'Thanks, Joel.'

'Listen, I need you to stop by my office.'

Greg knew he was referring to his mother's will. He had brought her into Joel's office just six weeks previously when the doctors had first given her a terminal diagnosis. He had waited for her in the reception while she had put her affairs in order and finalised matters. She had been upset when she had come out, and Greg knew it was hard for her to accept that she was dying and to be putting a plan in place for when she would no longer be around.

'Yeah, I'll drop by over the next while,' he said non-committally. He wasn't in any rush; he would do it in a few weeks when he knew he would be better able to face it.

'Greg, I think you should come in soon, there's something that I need to give you.'

Chapter 3

Greg sat in Joel Snyder's reception looking at the office art that decorated the walls. He had always wondered if the artists who created pictures destined to be hung in offices deliberately made their work so bland and meaningless. The very opposite of what you would put up in your home. It had been two days since his mom's funeral and two days since Joel had called asking him to drop by. There had been something in his tone, a hint of worry forewarning him that this wasn't going to be the straightforward meeting about his mother's will that he thought it would be. He couldn't understand it, though, it wasn't like he had siblings to squabble with over who got the silverware. Unless she had bequeathed everything to some crazy cat charity . . . he was smiling to himself at the thought when a door opened and Joel walked out into the reception. A tall, broad man, Greg guessed he was about two decades older than he was.

'Greg,' Joel said, offering him his hand. 'How are you doing?'

'I'm all right. At least she's out of pain now . . .' Greg said. Greg had learnt after his father had died that whenever people asked you that question, they didn't *really* want to hear how you were feeling, it just made the conversation awkward if you were truthful and told them you were broken. People expected you to keep your chin up and to make them feel comfortable by putting a positive spin on your grief.

Joel nodded. 'Come through this way.' He stood to the side to let Greg past.

Greg went into Joel's office with its sombre dark furniture. Bookshelves brimming with legal tomes ran the length of the walls. Joel sat down behind the desk, and Greg took a seat opposite him.

Joel cleared his throat and began talking. 'So your mom was here about six weeks ago to make her last will and testament.'

'Yeah, I brought her to the appointment.'

Joel nodded. 'So as I'm sure you've guessed, her entire estate is being left to you as her sole heir.'

'Well, that's hardly a surprise,' Greg mumbled.

'No, there's no shock there,' Joel conceded, pursing his lips together. Greg noticed that he wasn't meeting his eyes. It looked like there was something more that he wanted to say. 'Greg,' he spoke again.

'Yes?'

'There is something else—'

'What is it, Joel?'

'There is a letter—'

'From who?'

'Your mom—'

'Okay, so where is it?'

Joel slid an envelope across the desk to him.

'What is it?' Greg asked, taking it from him and starting to pull out the paper that was inside. He uncurled the letter and recognised his mom's handwriting instantly.

'I'm going to give you a few minutes alone to read it,' Joel said, standing up from his desk. 'I'll be outside if you need anything.' With that he left the office before Greg had a chance to ask him what was going on. Greg began reading the letter with an unsettling feeling flooding through him.

Dear Greg,

So I guess if you are reading this I have passed on. I want you to know that you are so loved not just by me but by your father too —I use the present tense because love doesn't die. I never knew I was capable of loving another person as much as I love you, Greg, you are our pride and joy. When I held you for the first time as an infant, I couldn't ever have imagined the fun that we had ahead of us. And we certainly did have a lot of fun over the years, didn't we? I want you to know that I'm still with you, on the good days and the bad days too, I'm there.

As I'm sure you've figured out, there is a purpose to this letter, Greg. There has been something weighing on my mind for many years, and now that my days on this Earth are coming to an end, it is time for the truth for once and for all. There are no easy words to call upon to tell you what I need to say, but I will try to explain the circumstances as best I can.

You see, your father and I had spent many years waiting for a baby, but it just never happened for us. We watched as one by one our friends all fell easily into parenthood. We didn't worry; we just thought we were a bit slow out of the starting blocks. Then when the friends who married several years after us began falling pregnant while we still remained childless, I began to think that maybe something was wrong. We went to our doctor, but he had no answers, so I went to a different doctor and still nobody could tell me why I couldn't conceive a baby. In desperation I turned to faith healers, I even went to a lady in a circus tent who made me drink a dark purple drink and promised that I would be pregnant within the month, but a fool is easily parted from their money, especially a desperate one. I borrowed medical books from the library to see if I could find out for myself what was wrong, but we never got any answers. We were just 'one of those couples', and people told me we had to accept it and get on with things. We were lucky that we both loved each other deeply, but there was no denying that there was still a huge hole in our lives where a baby should be.

After ten years of marriage, we had booked a trip to Europe to celebrate our anniversary, so you can imagine my surprise to discover a few weeks before we were due to travel that I was pregnant. Concerned about the flight, I went to our doctor who assured me that because I would be past the first trimester when we were due to fly, that we should go and relax and enjoy our trip.

Paris was our first destination, and we had a wonderful time exploring the city that I had only ever seen in magazines. Then we headed for Rome, to taste such amazing food and feel the history on the streets with every step we took was wonderful. We were having a magical trip, but it was in Rome that I lost the baby. We were devastated. We had already told our friends and families back home that I was pregnant before we had left, and the thought of facing them on our return without our baby was so upsetting; I couldn't face their disappointment layered on top of my own. The humiliation that I had failed to give us a child once again burned deeply.

Your father suggested we could take a couple of months in Ireland to give us the space to grieve before we would have to face everyone back home. He found us a cottage in a remote fishing village on the west coast called Inishbeg Cove where nobody knew us, and it was the perfect spot to repair our broken hearts. We ate good food, walked on the beach every day, and slowly we started to piece ourselves back together again.

One day your father was walking up on the headland when he met a young man who was clearly in distress. He stopped to ask him if everything was okay, and the boy told him that his girlfriend had just given birth to a baby and he didn't know what to do. Your dad ran with the boy to help him. The boy led the way to an old stone cottage, and when he went inside, he saw that there was a young girl sitting on the cold floor, cradling a newborn infant. The girl was wide-eyed with fear and shaking with shock, and the baby was still bloody and crying out to be fed. They were so young, Greg, your father reckoned barely sixteen or seventeen. They were just kids; they were scared and didn't know how to take care of a baby. Your dad felt as though it was a sign. He told them that he knew a couple that yearned for a baby like no couple before. He promised it was a good and loving home and that was how you came to be ours.

When your father arrived home from his walk with this tiny, mewling infant, I thought I was hallucinating at first, and then when he placed you into my arms and I realised from your very weight that you were real, I thought it was a cruel trick. I'm ashamed to say I got angry with him. Why would you do that to someone who has just lost a baby, I cried? But then when he told me the story of what had happened up on the clifftop and that you were our baby, it was the most wonderful moment in my life. You were ours; we finally had the baby we craved.

You were so tiny, Greg. I guessed you were a few weeks early. We got you formula, and you fed well. You were a hungry little thing, God bless you. Now that we had our miracle in our arms,

I was terrified it would be snatched away from us again, so we arranged our flight out of Shannon the very next day. Nobody asked for papers for you, things were a lot looser in those days, but I hardly dared to breathe until we were safely home on US soil.

Back in Charlotte, we registered you in our own name as a homebirth, which is why it is our names that are on your birth certificate. We laid low for a few weeks and didn't tell people we were back, and then after a month, we announced that I had had a baby boy and told them that you had arrived early. Nobody questioned our dates; they were too busy being happy for us. I quit my job to be with you every day and that was the start of the happiest days of our lives.

I like to think it was fate that brought you to us, and I have spent my life praying for your birth parents that their lives turned out well because they gave us the most precious gift of you. I'm sure you are probably wondering why I didn't tell you this before now, but your Dad was always adamant that you were our son and that we didn't need to tell you. I was more torn, but as the years crept past, the truth was buried deeper and it became harder to have that conversation.

When your father passed away, I thought about telling you then, but in the end, out of respect for his memory, I decided to wait until I had passed on and that is why you are only reading this letter now. I'm sorry if this has come as a shock to you, we never, ever intended to deceive you, but I didn't want to go to my grave with any secrets.

It's not too late to find them, Greg—if you want to. We might not be here, but you have a chance to find a new family in Ireland. I'm sorry I don't have more details for you, I don't know their names, I don't know if your father ever got them. If that is the road you decide to go down, then I wish you every blessing and I hope you find happiness.

I pray you can find it in your heart to forgive us, I know it doesn't excuse us, but we were desperate and so were those children in the cottage.

I love you always,

Mom x

The room felt claustrophobic as Greg tried to make sense of her words. The dark wood furniture, the shelves heavy with literature, all felt as though they were closing in around him. He heard the door creak open, and Joel came back into the room.

'What the hell, Joel?' he said, pushing back his chair and spinning around to face him.

Joel sat down opposite him and studied his face, trying to read his reaction. 'So I take it you've read it then?' he broached.

Greg nodded, looking directly at him. 'How long have you known?' he asked.

'Only since she came to see me that day. I was as shocked as you were. I've known your parents for many years now, and I never knew anything about this. As her attorney, I had to respect her wishes and wait until she had passed on before showing it to you, you understand that, don't you, Greg?'

'How could she?' Greg said in disbelief that his mother, the person he trusted the most in the whole world, had deceived him for his entire life. When he was a kid, she had always told him to tell the truth, she said, lies lead to more lies but that if you stick to the truth, then everything will always work itself out no matter what the situation.

'She felt as though she didn't have a choice—your father was completely against you ever learning the truth.'

'Everything that I thought was true has been turned upside down! My whole life has been a lie!'

'She was so torn by what to do; you have to believe me, Greg. None of this sat easily with her, it was weighing heavily on her conscience before she died.'

'She could have told me after Dad died, there was nothing stopping her then!'

'I guess she was scared.'

'I need to go home and try and get my head around all of this,' Greg said, rubbing his hands down along his face. He stood up and began gathering his things.

'Sure,' Joel said, standing up too. 'It's a huge shock to you. If you need to talk, I'm here for you—I don't mean that as an attorney but as a friend.'

Greg nodded.

Joel reached out and gave him a manly clap on the back, and Greg walked out of the room, just wanting to get the hell out of there.

Chapter 4

Greg didn't sleep that night. Midnight became 1 a.m. and 1 a.m. became 2. He watched every hour change on his alarm clock, and eventually after 4 a.m., he gave up. He sat up against the headboard and turned on the lamp. He picked up the letter from his bedside table and began reading it again. He had lost count of the number of times he had read it since Joel had given it to him just hours earlier, as if by reading it one more time, he could find something new to help explain all this heartache.

He was angry on so many levels. For the betrayal. For the years of deceit. For the pain he was now feeling; it was bad enough losing his mother this week, but now he felt as though he had lost everything. All the things that Greg had thought were a constant in his life—his very being—was a lie. He was acutely aware that if his mother's conscience hadn't got the better of her, she could have gone to her grave with that secret and he would never have known that he was originally someone else's baby! Wasn't it a basic human right that everybody was entitled to know where he or she came from?

Greg had always thought he looked like his dad; their noses sloped in the same aquiline way, and they both spent every morning trying to tame a stubborn cowlick above the left side of their foreheads. His mom would swat him playfully on the arm and say, 'Oh, Greg, you're just like your father' whenever he did certain mannerisms. It was amazing how you saw whatever you wanted to see sometimes. Hell, after his dad had died of his heart attack, Greg had gone to get tested because he knew that heart disease was often genetic, and his mother had never even tried to discourage him! Had they begun to believe their own lies? He felt as though he had unwittingly been enveloped into their charade and begun to see things that didn't really exist.

The hardest part was not knowing where he belonged. The place he had thought he belonged; everything that he thought was his truth had been tossed up into the air and was now falling back down around him again into millions of broken pieces. He thought about the young couple that were his birth parents, the people whose genes he carried. His heart broke for them; it was hard to palate that the people Greg knew as loving, kind, and caring parents were capable of taking advantage of such vulnerable young people. He had always been so proud of his parents' kindness, their willingness to help others. They donated money to the Salvation Army every Christmas, and his mom helped to make meals at the homeless shelter every Thanksgiving, but this showed a very different side to them, a side he would never have believed them capable of.

He had so many questions about the young couple that had given him up. He guessed they were probably pushing sixty now, maybe even older. What were they like? How had their lives turned out afterwards? Did they ever think about the baby that they had given up that day? Did they manage to stay together, or did they break up? Did Greg have other siblings? He could have a huge family of brothers and sisters in Ireland that he knew nothing about. There were just so many unknowns that he had to try and get his head around.

In some ways as he read his mother's letter it felt as though she was encouraging him to go Ireland, but did she really expect him to go there and try to pick up where he had left off with a new family, forgetting that essentially forty-two years were missing in the middle? And what if his birth parents didn't want to know him? They might have new families now who didn't know anything about the baby that had been taken straight out of their arms. And besides, he thought bitterly, how was he supposed to trace them when he didn't even know their names!

Greg put down the letter, tossed back the duvet, and got up out of bed. Bleary-eyed, he stumbled into the kitchen and flicked on the light switch. He made himself a strong coffee and then sat down at the breakfast bar with his laptop. He needed answers. He needed to be able to make sense of all of this. He brought up the Inishbeg Cove website that he had looked at briefly the other day. Clicking on the heading 'About Our Village', he read how it was a small village on the west coast of Ireland. He looked at photos under the 'Gallery' heading. There were scenic pictures of the fishing village with small white fishing boats bobbing in the bay. There was a row of traditional stores with old-fashioned fronts that had their owner's names displayed over the door. He spotted a pub called *The Anchor*, a grocery store, a café, and a post office. At the end of the street a simple stone church sat keeping a watchful eye over the town. As he clicked through the photos there was an image of a young fisherman showing off a haul of crabs. There were photos of a St Patrick's Day parade, and Greg found himself studying the faces of people in the crowd, wondering if they could be related to him. It was surreal to think that this village, which looked to be in the middle of nowhere in Ireland, held the key to his beginnings. If things had been different, he might have grown up there. He might have gone into those same stores or cheered on that exact parade from the sidewalk. It was like a peephole had been opened up into a parallel life, and he wanted to see more.

Greg clicked on the photos to see if he could find anything resembling a cottage up on the headland like his mother had mentioned, but he couldn't see anything. He tried using Google Street View but couldn't see anything that way either. He guessed the headland was probably a bit off the beaten track.

It occurred to Greg then that it was possible that one of his parents might still live in the cottage. Or even if they had moved on, perhaps the current owners would be able to put him in touch with them. Then he had a brainwave, he could write to them! Feeling a buzz of excitement at a chance of getting answers, he jumped up, grabbed a pen and some paper, and began drafting a letter. After a few lines trying to explain what his mom had told him in her letter, he realised it was going to be more difficult than he thought. It was hard to put his story into words when he didn't know the exact events that took place on that fateful day. He tore up the page and tried again.

Several attempts later, he found himself ripping up the paper once more. It was pointless, how was he meant to word it? And even if he could manage to spew something onto the paper, other problems began to occur to him—he could hardly just address it to 'The Cottage on the Headland'. There could be several cottages on the headland; how was he going to get the right one? Or what if someone read the letter that wasn't meant to, perhaps a child of his birth parents who never knew about the secret baby their parents had given up years earlier? A letter like this could be like a grenade arriving into someone's life. Greg didn't want to upset anyone; he just wanted to know a bit more about where he came from. He scrunched up his latest attempt and fired it at the wastepaper basket. If he could just pinpoint where exactly the cottage was located on the headland and who was currently living in it, then it would help a lot. Suddenly another idea occurred to him: there had been a post office in the village photos, perhaps if he wrote to it, they could tell him a little more about the village?

He took another sheet of paper and tried again.

Greg Klein
1132 Wainwright Row
Charlotte, NC 28207
USA

Inishbeg Cove Post Office
Inishbeg
Co. Clare

Dear Sir or Madam:
My name is Greg Klein and I am seeking to find out more information about the owners of a cottage set up on a headland in Inishbeg Cove. I am not familiar with your village so excuse my ignorance if perhaps there are several cottages situated up on the

headland or even several headlands . . . In particular, I am trying to trace the occupants who would have lived there in September 1976. I realise this is probably like looking for a needle in a haystack, but I would appreciate any assistance you can give.

Yours Sincerely,
Greg Klein

Greg reread the letter again, finally happy with this draft. He had deliberately kept it light-hearted and informal, but more importantly, it didn't give any secrets away or incriminate anyone. Who knew whether he would even get a response, but he definitely felt better having taken some control of the matter. At least it was a step forward out of this nightmare. He watched the clock until the working world had opened. Then he jumped in his car, drove to the post office, and sent his letter on its journey to Ireland.

Chapter 5

Inishbeg Cove, Ireland

Beyond the window, the grey-green sea swelled and rolled, moody and brooding just like the lead-coloured sky overhead where gulls arced gracefully and the hours moved so slowly on the clock.

The post office had been open for two hours, and Sarah O'Shea hadn't had a single customer through the door in that time. Well, unless you counted Mrs Murphy and Mrs Manning . . . oh, and Timmy O'Malley, and although she loved them all dearly—they were almost like family to her—she knew they were really only there for a chat. Not that she minded, of course, she liked helping people, but sometimes her job was more of a counselling service. Some of them had nowhere else to go and nobody else to talk to—the post office was about far more than just posting a letter. It certainly wasn't the world's busiest, but it was the social hub of Inishbeg Cove, and Sarah loved her role in the village.

She had taken on the post office after her mother had died. Sarah was the fourth generation of O'Shea women to run it. As a little girl she had loved helping her mother behind the counter. She still remembered the thrill of seeing the mail as it arrived in large sacks from all over the world. The letters decorated with colourful stamps with different languages and currencies had all seemed so exotic to her. Her mind would drift off concocting vivid stories about what might be written in them. As soon as the school bell sounded, she would run home to help her mother sort through them and would stay there until closing time, when her mother would take her home to their cottage to do her homework.

She had always known that she would take over the post office one day. Working in the post office was the only job she had ever wanted. It was in her blood.

From her small class in school, most of her friends had gone to live in bigger towns and cities like Limerick and Dublin for further studies or work. More had moved abroad, and now Sarah was the only one from her class that still lived in Inishbeg Cove. She sometimes wondered what her life would have been like if she had travelled or spread her wings a little further afield, but she knew she could never live anywhere else. The remote village certainly wouldn't be everyone's cup of tea. It could be a harsh place—on a cold February day like today when it was at the mercy of the elements, it could be bleak, but to her the village was just as pretty in the depths of winter as it was on a blistering July day. There was nowhere else she'd rather live.

Of course, the post office had been much busier in those days. Sarah could remember how long queues would trail out the door as her mother worked quickly to try and serve all of her customers. This was before the Internet had arrived and changed everything.

It made Sarah sad that people didn't need to make an effort anymore. It was all too easy now. People barely put a greeting on their emails these days. Back when she was a child, people had to sit down and write their letters by hand and then go to the trouble of visiting the post office to send them on their way. She knew technology brought a lot of benefits, but a small, nostalgic part of her longed for the days of letter writing, when people spent time crafting words into exquisite letters. She could still remember watching her mother taking her time choosing stationery and then carefully thinking over her words before putting them down on the paper. When you received a handwritten letter, you knew that so much thought and effort had gone into it. Opening an email didn't hold a candle to the excitement of opening a letter that was addressed to you. Sarah knew she was a soppy, old romantic but that's just the way she was. So when a letter had arrived to her post office out of the blue one day, brandishing a blue airmail sticker and US postal stamp and addressed in inky handwriting to her, Sarah had felt a little jolt of excitement that had transported her back to her childhood. With a fizz of pleasure, she had picked up her pen straight away and began writing her reply.

Chapter 6

Charlotte, North Carolina

Over the next few days Greg flitted in between waves of anger and utter desolation at how much his world had been uprooted since he had first read his mom's letter. Initially it had felt as though he was standing on a sandy seabed, sinking further downwards, but he was finding that once he had got over the initial shock, he was slowly coming to the bottom and was starting to accept his new normal.

Despite his anger at all that he had learnt, he still missed his mother desperately. He felt a strange, hollowed-out feeling sitting in the pit of his stomach. The more he thought about it, he realised it was actually loneliness. It was the first time in his life that he had ever felt like this. The colour had been washed out of his world, and it now existed in shades of grey. He felt broken and could not see how he would ever be pieced back together again.

He was just about able to function. He would get up in the morning, eat something or more times he wouldn't. Then he would run over to his mom's house to open her curtains. Her house wasn't too far from his apartment. When he had started work in the law firm and was buying his first home, he had deliberately chosen an apartment just a short distance from them. The heavy feeling of his feet pounding off the pavements and breathing the fresh air deeply into his lungs helped to clear his head and gave him clarity to think through it all. He liked the routine of having somewhere to go, and he found comfort in being in his childhood home. Sometimes he would take down the old photo albums again and study those photos of them on vacation in Ireland to see if he could find some new clue in them to his heritage, but he never did.

He hadn't been able to summon the energy to return to work. When he had told the partners that he needed some time off, they were understanding, if a little surprised, and had told him to take as long as he needed. Greg was a work-aholic and was usually one of the last people to leave the office in the evenings. His mother had always urged him to work fewer hours and have a little more balance in his life, but he loved his job. After his father had died, he was back in his office again the day after his funeral, keen to bury himself in his workload and take his mind off his grief, but it was different this time. He had been floored since he had read his mom's letter. Greg knew he wouldn't have the mental concentration needed to do his job. His mind was constantly thinking about the other life he could have had. He would drift off into his imagination to another place where he was a child living in a tiny stone cottage with an army of brothers and sisters, blissfully happy as they played around on the sandy beach outside. If he had been raised in Inishbeg Cove, his childhood probably wouldn't have been anything like the rose-tinted images in his head, but it was hard to stop his head getting carried away with what might have been.

One day on his way home from his mom's house, he entered the lobby in a breathless, sweaty mess. He headed straight for his mailbox and quickly scanned through the en-velopes like he had been doing since the day after he had posted the letter to Inishbeg Cove's post office. He would scan through the envelopes that usually just contained con-dolence cards or bills with suspended breath, hoping that today would be the day he received a response. As he flicked through the mail, a simple white envelope with neat handwriting caught his attention. His stomach somersaulted when he saw that the letter had an Irish stamp. He quickly jumped into the elevator and headed upstairs, clutching the envelope tightly. Once inside his apartment, he stuck his thumb underneath the gummed flap and took out the letter from inside. His heart was thumping wildly in his chest as he unfolded the paper and read down through it.

Inishbeg Cove Post Office
Inishbeg
Co. Clare

Greg Klein
1132 Wainwright Row
Charlotte, NC 28207
USA

Dear Greg,

My name is Sarah O'Shea and I am the postmistress here in Inishbeg Cove. I must say it was a lovely surprise to get your letter—it wouldn't be every day that I receive post from North Carolina! I am intrigued by your unusual request. Inishbeg Cove is a small fishing village where we all know everyone else. The cottage that you are referring to is now derelict, although some of the older people in our village tell me that nobody has lived there since Famine times. So to answer your question, nobody would have lived there in 1976, although from time to time ramblers may have sheltered there in harsh weather. In recent years, the roof has fallen in, though, and the walls are crumbling too. It really is a sorry sight.

Should you ever travel to Ireland to find out more about your roots, we have a local man named Danny Walsh who is a keen historian, and he has helped many people like yourself to put your family tree together, or you will always find me at the post office anyway. Please let me know if I can be of any more help to you.

Wishing you all the best with your research,
Sarah O'Shea

Greg read the letter and then read it again once more. There was something about Sarah's description of the village that made it leap from the page. He could already see there was a warm sense of community there. She seemed so friendly and eager to help. It hadn't dawned on him that she would think he was another American of Irish descent trying to trace his roots. He knew in a way he was, but his story was different because his ancestors might still be alive.

Greg immediately thought about writing to this Danny Walsh man or even calling him to see if he could help, but he knew from trying to write the letter the first time around that it was difficult to put what his mother had told him into words. Also, he didn't want to upset anyone. If the village was as small as Sarah had suggested in her letter, then it was inevitable that word could spread to the people he was looking for and something deep within told him that he needed to be subtle with his investigations. A letter arriving out of the blue like this could open a Pandora's box that someone had long ago thought was firmly shut. His gut told him that he needed to take his time, prod gently. He didn't want to poke too hard at the clam and risk it closing up altogether.

He made himself a coffee and then read the letter again. It seemed that this tiny village in the West of Ireland held all the answers to the puzzle of where he came from. Forget writing letters, he could go there, he realised. He could go and meet these people for himself. What was stopping him? He could do it delicately, tread carefully, and try to discover the truth about his past without upsetting anyone. He needed to get a feel for the place and the people in it and to judge their reactions face to face. He had nothing to lose. He could take a month out to clear his head; a change of scenery would do him good anyway. Work would understand; they knew he was grieving. He was caught up in anxious excitement when suddenly his phone rang, bringing him back to the present. When he picked it up, he saw that it was Joel.

'Greg, how've you been?'

'I'm doing all right.' He paused. 'Actually, Joel, I was thinking of heading away for a while.' He wanted to sound it off someone else and make sure that he wasn't completely crazy.

'Oh, on vacation? That's a good idea, Greg, a little R and R is just what you need right now. Are you going to go anywhere nice?'

'Well, I was thinking of going to Ireland actually.'

There was silence on the other end until eventually Joel spoke again. 'Are you sure that's a good idea, Greg?'

'Why not?'

Joel paused. 'I don't know . . . it might not be the right time for you to embark on something like this. I know you've had huge shock and you're trying to figure it all out, but are you sure you're ready for it? You've just lost your mom, you're not in a good place.'

'Come on, Joel, what do you take me for? I'm a big boy, and besides, I only want to see the place. I'm not expecting to find a new family lined up and welcoming me with open arms!'

Joel laughed nervously. 'Of course, Greg, sorry, I didn't mean to patronise you. You do what you gotta do, just'—he paused—'just look after yourself.'

Greg knew Joel was just looking out for him. He wanted him to be careful and not get his hopes raised.

'I will. And look . . . thanks, I appreciate you watching out for me.'

After he had hung up from Joel, he flopped down onto the sofa. Was he crazy? Was flying over to Ireland like an episode of *Long Lost Family* a hare-brained notion? The conversation had unsettled Greg and made him start to doubt himself. Then the other side of his brain told him it was only for a few weeks, he just wanted to see the village where he was born; there was nothing more to it than that.

Chapter 7

Early the next morning, Greg laced up his gym shoes and began running in the direction of his parents' house. He breathed out clouds of white onto the cool morning air and enjoyed the feeling as the blood began to warm up and pulse through his veins.

He hadn't slept well and had lain awake thinking about what Joel had said all night. In the cold light of day, he was starting to think that he was probably right. Greg knew he was vulnerable right now, and he shouldn't be making rash decisions. He knew Joel was coming from a good place—he just wanted to protect Greg from any more heartache. Greg had decided to put on his rational hat and to take some time to think it through properly. He would give himself a month or two, and if he still wanted to travel to Ireland, then he would. The last thing he needed was to go on some crazy crusade and end up being crushed once more.

He stopped running to let a reversing lorry down an alleyway before continuing on, and it was then that he saw a figure that he recognised up ahead in the distance. Selena was on the sidewalk coming in his direction, but she wasn't alone. She was holding hands with someone else. Another man. He stopped dead as if his legs had forgotten what to do. He watched as she suddenly threw her head back in laughter before leaning in to cuddle against the man's shoulder. He reached across and stroked her face lovingly with his free hand. It was surreal seeing her like this; doing the things they used to do, being the way they used to be, but instead of being with Greg, she was doing them with somebody else. He was frozen to the spot as if stuck in an awful horror movie that he couldn't escape from. They hadn't seen him yet, but they were getting closer, and he knew it was only a matter of seconds before they would. As they got nearer, Greg realised that he knew the man—Selena worked alongside him. Greg had met him at a few social evenings that her firm had put on. John something-or-other was his name. The last remaining fragments of his heart were shattered into tiny smithereens.

Suddenly Selena and John were standing in front of him and there was no way he could avoid them. A sickly mixture of mortification and awkwardness snaked its way down his body.

'Greg!' Her face read shocked, and her mouth hung open. She untangled her hand from John's, letting it fall limp by her side. 'How are you doing?' Her voice was concerned but in the same kind of patronising tone that you would use for a child.

Silence fell between them.

'You know John, don't you?' She spoke quickly trying to fill the gap.

Greg nodded. He was unable to find words to convey just how much this hurt, how broken his heart now was. Did their three years together mean nothing to her? How had she been able to move on so soon? He couldn't even look at another woman right now.

'I'm sorry, Greg,' she started.

'Look, it's fine.' He put his hand up to stop her and went to move around them on the sidewalk.

'Greg, wait—'

'Please, I get it—'

'I'm sorry, I was going to tell you.'

'I said it's fine, okay?' His tone was harsh, and she stepped back from him.

She nodded. 'All right, Greg . . . well, um . . . look after yourself.'

Greg watched their backs as they walked away from him. They didn't reach for one another's hands. He knew they were probably cringing over how awkward that had been. Who knew, maybe when they got home, they might even laugh about it.

It dawned on him then that this had probably been going

on for a while. John was most likely the reason why she had broken up with him. How had he not seen it? It seemed so obvious now. Of course, there was a reason for their break-up. These things never just happened out of the blue. There was always a reason, and it appeared Greg's reason was John.

Greg kept on walking over the old city streets. He didn't have the heart to run anymore. He walked around in circles under the watch of Charlotte's silver-scaled skyscrapers until he lost all sense of time and direction.

In the space of a week he felt as though his whole world had ended, he had lost his mom and Selena, then the letter had wiped out his entire sense of belonging, and now Selena had taken a battering ram to the last remnants of his self-worth too. It seemed there were new hurts waiting for him everywhere he turned.

The hardest part of all was having no one to turn to. A few weeks ago he had been Mom's son and Selena's boyfriend, there was an automatic sense of belonging to someone, now he had no one. He felt a deep yearning just to *belong* somewhere. The impulsive, crazy thoughts of going to Ireland were calling him again. He needed to get away from this place, and for the first time in his life there was nobody other than himself to think about. There was nothing keeping him here now. It was suffocating not knowing about his past. He wanted to see for himself the place where he was born and try and get his head around it all. He needed to go there and put his feet on the same soil that his parents had all those years ago. There was a lack of fear that came when you had already lost everything; you realised there was nothing left to lose.

*

Greg didn't know how long he walked for, but it was starting to grow dark and the streetlights were casting a shadowy glow around the city when he decided he should probably head for home.

He let himself into his apartment and felt a gnawing pain in his stomach and realised he hadn't eaten anything all day. He opened the refrigerator to see if there was something to eat, but it was empty, so he shut it again.

He picked up his cell phone and called his boss to re-

43

quest a month off, which he gave with no questions asked. He just assumed Greg needed some more time to get his head together. Greg didn't mention anything about his plans to travel to Ireland—he wouldn't even know how to explain everything that had happened over the last few weeks—and so, with the first hurdle successfully crossed, he sat down at his breakfast bar and opened up his laptop.

He studied a map of Ireland and saw that Shannon Airport in Co. Clare on the west coast of Ireland was the nearest international airport to Inishbeg Cove. He checked flights from Charlotte to Shannon and saw that he could get on a flight the next morning via Boston if he wanted to. Could he really go that soon, he wondered. But once again that voice inside his head reassured him that having already faced his worst fears, there was nothing stopping him.

He booked a flight with Aer Lingus for the next morning. He would hire a car in Shannon Airport, and then from there, he reckoned it was a little over an hour's drive to Inishbeg Cove. He did a search for hotels but soon found there were none in the village. A small guesthouse called *Cove View* was the extent of the tourist accommodation in the place, so he booked a double room for a month. He had no idea if he would even stay that long, but it felt like a good amount of time to get a feel for the place. Then he ordered a car to collect him and take him to the airport in the morning.

When he was finished on his laptop, he went into his room and took his case out from the wardrobe. He would need clothing for all sorts of weathers, because from his brief knowledge of Ireland, you could sometimes get four seasons in one day. He moved around folding raincoats and thick knit sweaters, packing them into his case.

Suddenly it was all very real. This was happening. For the first time in weeks, he was emerging from the fog and felt a tiny spark of excitement grow inside him. The decision to go to Ireland had put a temporary seal on the pain and given his mind something else to focus on. If he was completely honest with himself, he knew a small part of him harboured hopeful thoughts of having a potential new family. He imagined tearful reunions and smothering hugs, but then he would feel guilty, like he was betraying his parents. He had to remind himself to stop thinking that way. To protect himself from any more rejection, it was safer if he didn't allow himself to hope and dream. At least that way, if it all came crashing down, he couldn't fall any lower. Maybe he would get some answers, but if not, at least he would see the place where he came from and even the knowledge that he was breathing the same air and feeling the same wind on his face that his birth parents might be feeling too was a comfort.

Chapter 8

A voice woke Greg with a start somewhere over the Atlantic. The cabin air was chilly, and he pulled his duvet closer around him. The pilot was announcing that it was thirty minutes to landing, and Greg's heart started to hammer. This was it; he was nearly there. There was no going back now. Never before had he done anything as impulsive as this. He had grown up with two conservative parents who had brought him up to be controlled and measured in his actions. He wondered what they would think of him now heading off on a wild goose chase to Ireland?

Soon tall cliffs being mercilessly beaten with wild waves came into view. Beyond them mossy, velvety hillsides ran down to meet rich fields of emerald green grass, the patchwork sewn together by seams of evergreen hedges. Now he could see why Ireland was always associated with the colour green—there were so many different shades, some he had never seen before.

It wasn't long before the pilot was guiding the plane down onto the runway, and he listened to the sound of what he guessed was *Gaeilge* over the tannoy as the passengers were welcomed to Ireland by the cabin crew. He looked out the windows, where rivulets of rain ran down along the plastic glass. Heavy clouds hung low and thick above the wet tarmac.

Greg made his way through passport control and customs, and then he collected his luggage. It wasn't long until he was sitting in his hire car and keying Inishbeg Cove into the sat nav. The map had said the village was only sixty miles from the airport, and he had guessed it would take about an hour and a half. As he set off on his way, he was feeling a strange mixture of excitement and nerves and part disbelief that this was actually happening.

It wasn't long before he was off the smooth motorway and driving along narrow, country roads. The roads twisted and turned through the countryside, edged by colourful hedgerows decorated with pretty orange flowers like something from a postcard. A sheepdog guarding a thatched cottage ran out onto the road after him, barking at the tyres until he grew tired and gave up the chase.

Greg followed the sat nav obediently, even when it instructed him to turn right onto a road with grass growing up the middle. It was no more than a dirt track, and he was driving painfully slow. He was already feeling nervous driving on the opposite side, but these roads were a whole new experience for him. He met a car coming against him, and as there was no room for both of them, there was a standoff. After a few moments, Greg knew that the other driver wasn't going to budge, so he had no choice but to reverse his hire car back down along the road until he found a gateway to pull into. Then after he had got past that hurdle, he got stuck behind a tractor for several miles. He soon realised that on these twisty, windy, bouncy, grass-growing-up-the-middle roads, he would be lucky to arrive in the village before nightfall.

Just when he thought the road couldn't possibly get any narrower, it did, and he began climbing upwards over mountainous terrain where the glow of cadmium yellow furze popped against the cloak of rich green. High hedgerows encroached on his car, and brambles scraped against the paintwork. He winced thinking of the hire car damage excess. He was starting to doubt that he was going the right way. He had been driving for almost two hours, and there was still no sign of the village. He wondered if he had taken a wrong turn somewhere. He found a field gate and stopped the car to check his directions. The sat nav was telling him that he was going the right way, but he wasn't so sure. He hadn't seen a signpost for miles, let alone a house. Suddenly out of nowhere he saw a flock of sheep on the road up ahead. He slowed the car and saw a man herding them through a field gate using a stick. He wore a flat cap and a dirty brown overcoat over brown rain boots. Once the last one was through, the man closed the gate, and Greg stopped the car beside him and rolled down the window.

'Excuse me, sir, but I'm trying to get to a place called Inishbeg Cove. Would you happen to know how I could find it?'

Without saying a word, the man walked over towards the car, leant forward onto his stick, and narrowed his eyes suspiciously at Greg. He eventually opened his mouth to speak, and Greg could see his teeth stuck up like tombstones in his gums, well, the ones that were still there.

'And what has you out this way?' Greg's question was met with a question.

'I'm visiting the town on vacation.'

'But why would you want to go there?' The man was clearly bewildered.

'Well, I'm looking for someone there.'

'You won't find that place too easily.' He straightened up and shook his head.

'Well, if you could point me in the right direction to a nearby town, and I could try and find my way from there. I would be really grateful.'

'Do you know Ballymcconnell?'

Greg shook his head. 'No, sorry, I'm not from round here.'

'Well, if you go to Ballymcconnell, it's not far from there.'

'Well, how do I get to Ballymcconnell?'

The man stopped to think for a moment. 'Well, you could go by Tirgorman either—'

'How do I get there?'

'Well, it's not far from Ballymcconnell.'

'Right—'

'Where are you from?'

'North Carolina. USA.'

'My God. And are you tracing your roots?'

'Something like that . . .'

'Well, good luck to you, once you find Ballymcconnell, it's only ten minutes on from there.' Then he banged hard on the car roof to send him on his way. Greg started to laugh; he had spent five minutes talking to the man but still was clueless about where he was headed.

He drove on again and followed the sat nav as the road continued to climb higher still. He imagined his parents driving these roads back in the seventies. They looked like they hadn't changed since then. Had they found them as perilous as he did now?

Eventually the road began to dip downwards, and in the distance, Greg could see the sea shimmering. He was relieved at last to be heading in the direction of the coast. Soon the fields changed from emerald green to grey-grassy dunes as they sloped off towards the sea. Finally, he saw a signpost saying 'Inishbeg Cove 6 km', and he breathed a sigh of relief. He was almost there. Then it hit him; *he was almost there.*

He drove out along on a narrow peninsula with the sea on both sides of him. Sand lined the road and in places had gathered into ridges causing the car to bump along over them. After a few minutes the road snaked around a corner, and Greg saw a small sign saying 'Welcome to Inishbeg Cove'. A beautiful horseshoe-shaped bay with pretty white fishing boats bobbing in the foreground came into view.

It was a picturesque village with a short row of stores fronting out onto the sea. In the middle of the village an old shipwreck stood beached on rocks making a roundabout of sorts. He saw the same church that he had seen on the website, neat but imposing, at the end of the street and that was pretty much it. His first impression was that the place was small, much smaller than he had realised from the website.

He drove on until the stores turned into houses, and he realised that one of them was his guesthouse. *Cove View* was a two-storey whitewashed house with hanging baskets on either side of the door. Greg parked the car on the street, took his case out of the trunk, and went inside to a small lobby. There was a desk, but nobody was behind it. He saw a bell and rang it. A moment later a small, neat lady came rushing out from a room beyond.

'Hi, I have a reservation,' Greg said politely.

'Sorry, I was catching up on my soaps. So you're the Yank then?' she said immediately. She had a downturned mouth, which gave her face a square appearance.

'Sorry?'

'You're the one from America?'

'Oh yes, that's me.'

The lady smiled a satisfied smile. 'I thought as much. I'll put you in the peach room so.' She reached up to the wall behind her and took a key off a hook.

'Great,' Greg said, not knowing whether this was a good or bad thing.

'So what has you here?'

'I'm on vacation.'

She nodded in a way that made him think she knew there was something more to his arrival in the village. 'Fancy choosing Inishbeg Cove, it's hardly a tourist destination! It's so far off the beaten track.' She leaned forward onto the counter and eyed him suspiciously. 'But maybe that's what you're looking for?'

'A friend vacationed here a few years ago and recommended it to me,' he lied in a bid to end the conversation. It was late, and he was tired now after the journey.

'I see . . . Right, I'll bring you up to your room.'

Greg lifted his case once more and followed her up a narrow stairs. She unlocked a pine door and showed him inside. As the name suggested, the walls were painted a warm peach colour and peach bed linen clothed a pine bed frame.

'This is the peach room,' she announced without a hint of irony. 'Breakfast is served in the dining room between nine and eleven or you can take it in the bar next door if you prefer. My husband, Jim, runs it. They serve good food. My name is Maureen and if you need anything during your stay just ring the bell.'

'Great, thank you, Maureen.'

'Well, I'll let you get settled.'

Once she was gone, Greg looked around at the room that was to be his home for the next month. It was a clean but basic room, with a double bed and an en suite bathroom. He opened the window to let in the fresh sea air and breathed it down into his lungs. It was different to the air at home without any exhaust fumes or pollution. Also, it was so quiet —everything felt so still here, there were no sirens blaring or horns honking that was his usual backdrop at home, just the screech of seagulls piercing the air. He felt exhausted from the flight and then from driving on those kamikaze roads too. He walked over and lay down on the bed. Instantly he felt the weight of tiredness pulling his eyes closed and decided he would have a quick nap first before heading out to explore the village.

*

When Greg woke again, sunlight was creeping its way around the edges of the blind and spreading out across the ceiling overhead in a fan. He looked at the alarm clock on his bedside table and realised with a start that it was after eight the next morning. He had slept all night. He had obviously been more tired than he had realised. He was ravenous, not having eaten anything since the flight. He got out of bed and dragged himself into the peach-coloured bathroom.

Greg felt much better after he had showered. He dressed quickly and after nine o'clock headed downstairs for breakfast. He opened the door of the dining room that Maureen had shown him the day before. There was nobody in there, so he sat down at a table and waited. It seemed as though he was the only guest staying here.

After ten minutes there didn't seem to be anyone coming. He listened for noises in the house, but it was deathly silent. She had definitely said breakfast was between nine and eleven, so he headed out to the reception desk and pressed the bell before heading back in to his table to wait. After a few minutes, a flustered Maureen came running through the door.

'I suppose you're looking for your breakfast?' she barked, her tone was almost accusatory.

'Well, yes,' Greg said, feeling confused. 'I thought you said it was between nine and eleven?' He wondered if he had misheard her yesterday.

'Well, we *say* nine, but nobody actually comes for *nine*. It's nine for nine thirty, like?'

Greg was confused. He felt like asking her why she didn't just tell him it was at nine thirty in the first place if that's the time she wanted him to come at. Perhaps it was some strange Irish custom that he didn't understand.

'Oh, I see, sorry . . .' he found himself apologising. 'I'll wait until nine thirty tomorrow.'

She nodded. 'Yes, that would be better. So is it the full Irish you'll be having then?'

'Sounds great!' He would have eaten the hind legs off a donkey at that stage.

While Maureen headed into the kitchen to make breakfast, Greg walked over to the window and pulled back the lacy net curtains to have a look around the village. It was a calm, sunny morning, and the sea gently lapped the shoreline. He could see a headland towering over the bay in the distance. If he had to guess, he would say that the cottage that his mom had told him about was up there. It was strange to think he had once been in this village before, albeit as a tiny infant. He imagined his mom and dad in this very place many years ago, cradling him in their arms, hardly daring to believe their luck. He had spotted the post office amongst the stores when he had drove through the village the previous day and decided that that would be his first port of call. Then perhaps he would take a walk up on the headland afterwards to see for himself the place where he had been born.

Chapter 9

Later that morning after a hearty breakfast of sausages, bacon, eggs, and something Maureen had told him was called black pudding, Greg left the guesthouse and stepped out into a beautiful spring day. Wispy clouds were pulled across the sky like stretched cotton wool. His first impressions of Ireland were of a riot of colour; blue skies clashed with green grass. It was unlike anything he had ever seen in America. Everything was on a miniature scale, and it all seemed so quaint. He thought about his parents. It looked as though nothing had changed in the village since they would have been here.

He had only glanced quickly at the stores as he drove through the village the day before, but now as he walked along the main street, he could see all of the shopfronts still had the name of the original owner overhead, the grocery store had the name *'O'Herlihy's'* above the door, and further along the street, he passed a shopfront with *'Tubridy's Victuallers'* over the door, but it looked as though it had been closed for many years. There was a coffee shop with a blue and white striped awning with the name *'Ruairí's Café'* overhead. There were a couple of tables and chairs outside, but Greg guessed there wasn't much call for *al fresco* dining at this time of year. The buildings were all whitewashed, their stone uneven and lumpy from a time when they were painstakingly built by hand. It was as though time had stood still for this place. There was only a basic complement of stores; there was no pharmacy or bank. There was no public transport either, and he guessed if you didn't own a car here, you were in trouble. His phone signal wasn't great, and when Greg had asked Maureen at breakfast earlier whether the guesthouse had Wi-Fi, she had laughed at him, so he had taken that as a no.

He realised now just how remote the village was. It was one thing seeing it on the Internet but another thing actually being here and seeing just how cut off it was from everywhere. Initially it had felt strange not having access to his emails, but already, after only a few hours, he found there was actually something liberating about it. He felt totally cut off from the trappings of his life back home, which was what he needed right then.

Greg passed the pier where fishermen were gathered at the harbour to begin unloading their catch and send it on its way to stores and restaurants around the country, and he kept going until he reached the green sign saying 'Inishbeg Cove Post Office' that he had seen as he drove through the village the day before.

He pushed open the door to hear a bell overhead give a pleasing *trrring*. An elderly lady was standing leaning on a stick as she chatted to the woman behind the counter. Despite her advanced age, she had her hair set in curls and wore brightly coloured lipstick. She was carrying a small box covered with a check cloth in one hand.

'You're looking well, Mrs Manning. That was a nasty fall you had,' the woman behind the counter was saying.

The elderly lady moved closer and leant in conspiratorially against the glass screen. 'I thought I was on the way out,' she said dramatically.

'You're made of stronger stuff than that!' the woman behind the counter replied kindly.

'They're making me use this thing to get around.' The older lady nodded in disgust to her walking stick. 'I look like an old person!'

'It won't be for long. I'm sure you'll be back whizzing around the place before you know it!'

'Hmmh, we'll see . . . anyway, I brought you a little something to say thanks.'

Greg watched as the younger woman behind the counter opened a door to the side and the older lady handed the box in to her.

'You shouldn't have done that, Mrs Manning!'

'It's just some eggs from my hens, Sarah. You were very kind to bring my post up to me every day when I couldn't get out.'

Greg realised with excitement that this must be the same Sarah who had answered his letter.

'Ah, you don't need to be doing that! Sure, it was on my way home anyway,' Sarah replied.

'It's only a few eggs—my ladies are laying them faster than I can eat them,' Mrs Manning said with a wave of her hand. 'I know I always say it, but we'd be lost without you.'

Greg noticed that Sarah had begun to blush. 'Well thank you, Mrs Manning, I'll look forward to these for my breakfast in the morning.'

After the old woman had left, it was his turn, and he was strangely nervous as he stepped up to the counter. He hadn't really given much thought to what he was going to say to her.

'How can I help you?' Sarah said with a smile that stretched right up to the sides of her eyes. Even though she was sitting down, Greg could see she was very petite. Blonde hair framed a heart-shaped face where big blue eyes shone out. She was younger than he had expected; for some reason the title 'postmistress' had conjured up an older woman in his head, but he guessed Sarah was in her late thirties. She had soft features, the sort of face that told you she was a kind person.

'Hi,' Greg said at a loss for words.

'So how can I help you today?' she repeated.

For some reason his throat felt dry and scratchy and his heart was hammering.

'Um . . . my name is Greg Klein,' he began. 'You might remember I wrote to you a few weeks ago?'

'Greg that sent the letter from North Carolina?' she asked in amazement.

'That's me, the one and only!' he said, giving a nervous laugh afterwards. He really hoped she didn't think he was strange.

'You were trying to trace your ancestors, isn't that right?'

'Yes.' He nodded.

'What was their surname? We don't get many *Klein's* around these parts.' She laughed.

'Well, that's the thing, I don't know . . .'

'Oh, I see . . .' She was clearly too polite to state that it would be impossible to trace them without knowing their name.

There was something about her face, her eyes were honest and told Greg he could trust her.

'Would I be able to meet you somewhere to get your help with something?'

Her brow furrowed downwards, and he knew she was wary of this unusual request, but he was relieved when her features relaxed quickly again and she said, 'I'm on my lunch break at one. I could meet you in Ruairi's for a coffee?'

*

Although Sarah had enjoyed writing her reply back to Greg and sending the letter on its way across the Atlantic, she didn't think much more about it until the bell over the door had tinkled and a tall, handsome man entered. It was his clothes that she had first noticed; he was nicely dressed, wearing a long woollen coat over a roll-neck jumper. Her curiosity had been piqued. There weren't many young men in the village. In fact, there weren't many young people at all, so he definitely stood out by virtue of the fact that he didn't have grey hair. The majority of people living in Inishbeg Cove were over the age of sixty. And Inishbeg Cove never got tourists in February—even in the height of summer, the village was a little too far off the beaten track to be frequented by holidaymakers. The tourists that they did get normally had been recommended the pretty village by a friend or stumbled across the place by accident. When he had asked for her by name, alarm bells had set off in her brain. She knew then that he wasn't an ordinary tourist, but she was certainly not expecting him to introduce himself as the American from the letter. He was younger than she had imagined him to be. He was well built too with tanned skin that showed a love of the outdoors. He had long, dark wavy hair that fell over his forehead. When he had asked her to meet him, initially she had been wary. Although she didn't want to be unwelcoming, she couldn't help feeling a little cagey. She didn't know this fella from Adam and here he was with his American accent and fancy clothes—she couldn't help but feel suspicious. Her first instinct was to make an excuse, but there was something about him that made her think twice. There was something about his eyes that caught her off guard—beyond their cool, sage green shade, she was sure she could see sadness pooling in their depths. She decided that she would meet him in the café and hear what he had to say.

Chapter 10

At five minutes before one, Greg opened the door to the café and took a seat inside. It was small and homely, and the delicious smell of fresh baking filled the air. There were only a handful of customers in the place. Colourful maritime-themed paintings were displayed around the walls, and when Greg looked closer, he saw they were available for purchase. An open fire roared through a chimney in the centre of the room radiating heat. A glass counter displayed home-made treats. His mouth watered as he looked beyond the glass to the scones bursting with sultanas, an apple tart with layers of juicy looking fruit, and a pear and almond pie topped with flaky pastry. He soon saw the man he guessed was the eponymous Ruairí as he steamed milk into a mug. With his mass of long frizzy red hair, which he had wrapped up into a man bun, and his thick wiry beard, Greg couldn't help thinking he looked like a poster boy for Celts everywhere.

'Can I get a coffee please, and I can't possibly resist that pear and almond pie,' Greg said when he reached the counter. Jars of chutney, jam, and honey all with home-made labels were displayed for sale beside the till.

'Coming right up. Take a seat and I'll bring them down to you.'

A few minutes later, a breathless Sarah came running through the door.

'Sorry, I'm late, Greg.' She paused to catch her breath. 'I had to drop something in to Mrs O'Sullivan up the street. She's isn't very mobile these days—the poor thing is nearly a hundred!'

'You really go above and beyond for the locals,' he said. He had only been in this village for a day and already he could see there was something special about it. There was a sense of community that he had never seen before. It made you want to belong. He noticed Sarah had started to blush.

'Ah, I like doing it,' she said modestly with a wave of her hand. 'Some of them have no families near them, so I like helping them out if I can.' She began unwinding her scarf from around her neck and slid her arms out of her raincoat.

'Hiya, Sarah.' Ruairí waved out from behind the counter.

'How are you doing?' she called back to him.

'I'm good, my lovely. The usual, is it?'

'That'd be great, thanks, Ruairí.' She beamed a smile at him and sat down at the table opposite him.

After Sarah had been served, Greg took a bite of his pie. The buttery short-crust pastry melted on his tongue followed by a sweet burst of fruit as the pear hit his taste buds. It was divine. It had that same home-baked goodness that transplanted him back to his mom's kitchen, and suddenly he felt a desperate yearning for her. Despite everything that he had learnt over these last few weeks, he still missed her so much, especially now when he found himself so unsure of everything.

'This is so good,' he said through a mouthful.

'Ruairí makes it all himself, he even grows the fruit in his garden and everything! You won't find anywhere better. It's pure soul food.'

Greg nodded in agreement as he savoured another bite.

'So what is it that you want me to help you with?' Sarah asked, jerking him out of his thoughts.

He took a deep breath. 'Well, where do I begin . . .'

'At the start is usually good.' She smiled kindly, and the sides of her eyes crinkled. He knew he could trust her.

'Okay . . .' He smiled nervously. 'So my mom passed away a couple of weeks ago—'

Her hands flew up to her mouth. 'I'm so sorry to hear that, Greg.'

Greg nodded. 'Thanks. It's been a roller coaster.' He paused before saying the next bit. 'In her will she left a letter for me—' Sarah nodded reassuringly as he continued, 'in that letter she told me that I was born here.'

'You were born in Inishbeg Cove?' Sarah was wide-eyed as she digested that he wasn't just the American tourist that she thought he was.

Greg nodded and lowered his voice. 'My parents were on vacation here in 1976, and one day while my dad was out walking he came across a young couple in distress. The boy told him that his girlfriend was after giving birth to a baby in a cottage up on the headland, which was me, and my parents ... well—' He broke off. Even though Greg was angry with his parents, he couldn't bear for anyone else to think badly of what they had done.

'Go on, Greg,' Sarah encouraged.

'Well, they were desperate for a baby ... and somehow I came to be theirs,' he finished.

Her eyes were wide with the shock of what she had just heard. 'Oh, Greg, you poor thing. What must you be going through?'

Besides Joel, Greg hadn't felt able to confide in anyone about it, and it felt good to have offloaded this burden and shared it with somebody else.

'It's been a rough couple of weeks, I won't lie. My whole world has been turned upside down by that letter.'

'Of course, it has, what an awful shock to get,' she soothed. He noticed her eyes were brimming with tears. 'Sorry,' she apologised, wiping them away quickly, 'I don't even know you! I'm a daft fool! People are always telling me that I'm too soft!' She started to laugh then, and he laughed too. He decided that he liked Sarah, she was a nice person, and it felt good knowing that she was on his side.

'I really believe that if I can find my parents, then maybe something good can come from all of this heartache.'

Sarah nodded. 'I wasn't born in 1976, so I don't know what Inishbeg Cove was like back then, but I will try and help you as best as I can.' She paused then and narrowed her eyes.

'What is it?' Greg asked.

'Well ... it's just that this village ... don't get me wrong, it's the best place in the world but it is very small. Everyone knows everyone else, and most people go back several generations, so my advice is to tread gently, Greg.'

'I get that, I really do. The last thing I want to do it upset anyone.'

Sarah nodded. 'I promise I'll do all I can to help you, let me have a think about it and I'll see what we can do.'

'I appreciate your help, thanks, Sarah.'

They chatted some more until Sarah looked at her watch suddenly and realised it was almost time for her to reopen the post office. 'Sorry, Greg, I have to run but call into me tomorrow!' She went up to the counter to pay.

'Please, let me,' he said, jumping up after her. 'It's the least I can do.'

'Well, thank you, Greg,' she said. 'I'll see you tomorrow then.'

They said goodbye, and then he paid Ruairí for their food before heading back out onto the street.

*

Sarah went back to work but found she couldn't really concentrate for the rest of the afternoon. Greg's story was spinning around inside her head. She had been embarrassed when tears had begun to fill her eyes as he had recounted his mother's recent death and then the letter she had left for him. It was seeing the pain so clear in his eyes that had got to her. She was finding it hard to believe that this had happened in Inishbeg Cove—the only place she had ever known, the only home she had ever had. She felt a deep protectiveness towards the village, but she also knew she couldn't turn her back on him. Not now. His story had pulled at her heart, and she needed to do all she could to help him. She knew everyone in the village. It was hard to believe that one of them—somebody in her village—harboured a deep, dark secret. The question was who?

Chapter 11

The blue sky had changed to steely grey, and threatening clouds hung overhead. Instead of going back to the guesthouse for the afternoon, Greg decided to risk the weather and head for a walk up on the headland. He wanted to try and find this stone cottage that his mom had mentioned and see for himself the place where he was born.

He followed the curve of the bay and continued on as the land climbed higher until the sea began to twinkle far below him. Frothy waves crashed off the rocks relentlessly. The wind roared past his ears, leaving him lost inside his thoughts. Sarah's words were ringing in his ears; he couldn't help but feel a sense of unease, and then he realised it was trepidation. Now that he was actually here in Inishbeg Cove, the doubts in his head seemed to be bigger. It was easier when he was at home in North Carolina to plan a visit to Ireland to try and learn about his birthplace and maybe even find his biological parents, but now that he was actually here, dealing with a real village and its real people, the reality was different. Was he ready to do this? Was the *village* ready for him to do this?

He kept climbing higher, to where the grass was longer and the village seemed like a tiny model behind him in the distance. It was so isolated up there; it really felt like he had reached the edge of the world. He could see why if you were young and desperate, this would be the place to come and hide while you birthed a baby.

Greg walked on for a while, and then he saw it up ahead of him in the distance; well, he assumed it had to be it. An old stone ruin that looked as though it once might have been a dwelling house stood right on the edge of the cliff face. It was built from the smooth, round stones that were scattered in the fields there, but the walls were crumbling down now. The roof had fallen in, and there were holes where the windows should be. It had to be the cottage that his mom had mentioned. Excited that another piece of the jigsaw had fallen into place, he quickened his pace the rest of the way.

Greg had almost reached the cottage when suddenly a person appeared from inside the ruin, startling him. He jumped, and when they saw him, they jumped too. Clearly neither of them was expecting to meet anyone else up there. The person was wearing a long, dark overcoat, so long it was almost sweeping off the ground, and was carrying what looked to be a staff in one hand. The hood was pulled up so it was hard to tell if they were male or female, but they were small in stature, which lead Greg to think it was a woman.

Greg's heart began to hammer, but he told himself to calm down. What was he afraid of? He was six foot two inches tall and well built, nobody was going to mess with him too easily, but he was still nervous.

'Oh, excuse me, I'm very sorry. I didn't mean to frighten you,' Greg said, stepping backwards to show them that he wasn't a threat. As the person left the protection of the walls and stepped out into the full force of the wind, the hood was blown back, and he realised that it was indeed a woman. She looked at him head-on, her cool blue eyes meeting his, unflinching. She didn't say a word, instead she just stared at him for the longest time. There was something unnerving about her eyes as if they could see right through him. Her behaviour was a little odd, but he guessed being confronted by a strange man in the middle of nowhere would be unnerving for anyone. Then she turned away from him and hurried away down the headland without saying a word.

Greg waited until the black shape had faded into the distance. His heart rate started to slow down, and he breathed in deeply. He stepped over a stone that would have marked the threshold and stood down into the centre of the cottage. He looked around at the tiny space. It was hard to believe that these crumbling walls had been the very first place he had been in the world. It was eerie to think that he was here once before in such difficult circumstances. He imagined his hooded newborn eyes slowly opening in this room, taking it all in. He pictured his birth parents, scared and alone, relying on these walls for their protection. Greg could imagine their confusion upon meeting his dad and his solution to their problem. Had they felt sadness to lose their baby, or was it a relief? He didn't know which feeling he would find easier to bear.

The walls began to feel claustrophobic, and he stepped back out of the cottage and onto the headland. He breathed the salty air in deeply and let it fill his lungs. Grey clouds were now rolling in, spreading darkness across the land underneath. The light had changed to dusk and a soft mizzle had begun to fall. The village below had vanished, cloaked under the heavy grey mist. It was a reminder of just how on the edge of the world the place was and how much it was at the mercy of the elements. Greg felt exhausted; the events of the day were weighing heavily on him. Somehow in his preparations to come here, he hadn't taken the emotional toll of it all into consideration. He made his way back down again using the yellow lights of the village to guide him home.

Chapter 12

February 1976

I waited until the whole house was sleeping before creeping out from my bed. I stole down the old flagstones along the passageway, their centres hollowed from the feet of generations, and crept into the kitchen where the red light of the Sacred Heart lamp cast a carmine glow around the room. I held my breath as I felt around in the drawer underneath the sink of the back kitchen to find the keys. At last I felt the cool metal under my fingertips. I opened the door as delicately as I could, wincing as the heavy wood creaked.

I stepped out into the night. The yard was bathed in silver moonlight. I whispered for our dog Toby to come so he wouldn't startle and set off barking. I quietly made a fuss of rubbing his silky ears before heading into the shed to get my bike. I hopped up on it, leaving Toby looking after me in the confusion. I breathed a sigh of relief as I cycled through the stone pillars and turned onto the road. I kept close to the trees, where it was darkest, and cycled quickly, my feet pushing hard on the pedals. Jagged shadows jumped out of the hedgerows, and I held my breath praying that I wouldn't meet a car or a person out walking.

We had been meeting like this for a few weeks now, since our paths had first crossed. His father drove the school bus, and sometimes he came along to give him a hand with the fares. I was always the last stop on the way home, and we had got talking over the last few months, and somehow it had grown into something more. He had slipped me a note one day asking to meet me that night and that was how it had started. I lived for seeing him. Every time I saw him, my stomach flipped and was filled with thousands of chaotic butterflies careering around inside me.

I knew Mother and Father would never approve of our relationship. How would they when even the few friends that I had dared to confide in thought him too common for me? I knew our love was doomed, but still, there was something almost romantic about that because I knew we would make our love endure to prove them all wrong. You couldn't stop love; it was too powerful a force. If I could, I would because I knew that being in love with him was creating trouble for myself, I wasn't stupid. Oh, but I couldn't stop it, no matter how many times I told myself that I needed to end it before Mammy discovered what was going on. He was a good person, that was the thing, but I knew Mammy and Daddy would never give him the chance to prove that to them.

We had a plan though; on my eighteenth birthday we were going to leave Inishbeg Cove together, and I was counting down the months. I would sit in class listening to Ms Didion conjugate French verbs and my mind would drift off to the life we would have once we had left this place, when I could do whatever I wanted without Mammy and Daddy's approval. My dreams of our future together were the only thing keeping me going.

It wasn't long before I reached the village. The sea was calm that night, and the moonlight rippled a path across the water. There wasn't a soul around; everyone in Inishbeg Cove was safely tucked up for the night. I saw him in the distance, waiting for me by the shipwreck. My heart soared with anticipation. He grinned, showing his teeth, white but slightly overlapping. I liked that about him, he was rough and ready, and it made him all the more endearing to me. I threw down my bike and ran to be in his arms. I had decided that tonight was the night.

Chapter 13

After his *faux pas* the first morning, Greg decided to wait until it was nine thirty before going down for breakfast. As he descended the stairs, the delicious smell of fried bacon greeted him.

'The full Irish, I presume?' Maureen said, greeting him as he came into the dining room.

'You presume right. Thanks, Maureen.'

She went into the kitchen, and he took a seat at a table by the window. There was an older couple at another table. From their accents, he guessed they were from mainland Europe. He listened to the intricacies of the accent but couldn't place it.

'So how are you getting on?' Maureen asked, coming back into the dining room with his breakfast a short while later. 'Mind you don't touch it now, it's hot.' She used a tea towel to set down the plate down in front of him.

'Great, it's a beautiful village.'

'I saw you in the café with Sarah yesterday.'

'Oh yeah?'

'A lovely girl is our Sarah . . .'

'She certainly is,' he agreed, cutting into a juicy sausage. 'I'm going to be booking two seats on my flight home if I keep eating these breakfasts, Maureen.'

'Nonsense, a good breakfast will set you up for the day. So have you any plans today?' It was clear she was fishing for information, but he wasn't going to bite.

'Not really,' he said.

When it became obvious that Greg wasn't going to give her an explanation for being here, she gave a snort before busying around the place leaving him to tuck into the delicious food.

*

After breakfast, he left the guesthouse and stepped out into a bitterly cold February morning. His ears were stinging from the biting wind, and the cold air burned his nostrils as he inhaled. He headed straight to the post office to see Sarah.

'Good morning, Greg,' she sang as he came through the door. There was nobody else in there, and he went straight up to the counter.

'How are you?' he asked.

'I'm good thanks. So I had an idea, Greg, and I was thinking why don't we go to see Dr Fitzmaurice? He was the village doctor here for decades; he only retired a few years ago. He would have birthed a lot of babies around these parts back then because people often didn't get to the hospital in time, if at all, and even if he wasn't there for the delivery, he would have cared for all the pregnant women around here for their antenatal check-ups. He's very elderly now and suffers a bit from dementia, but he has some lucid moments, so you might be lucky.'

'That's a great idea! Thanks, Sarah,' Greg said. He felt more positive that they were on the right track. It was as though he had pulled the end of a ball of wool and the secrets of his birth were finally starting to unravel. He had already found the cottage where he was born, and now Sarah was steering him onto the right track to find his parents. Finally, he was close to solving the mystery.

'Right, well, meet me here after this place closes at five thirty, and we'll call down to see him then. He only lives at the top of the street.'

*

That evening Greg waited for Sarah as she locked up the post office, and then they walked down the street together. As they passed the guesthouse, he noticed the curtains twitching from the inside. He thought he caught a glimpse of Maureen at the side of the window, but the shadow darted away quickly again.

'So how are you finding Maureen's place?' Sarah asked,

noticing the shadow in the window too.

'It's nice. I'm sleeping really well since I got here ... Maureen seems okay, but she's a bit ...' he paused.

'Nosy?' Sarah finished for him.

'You took the words right out of my mouth,' Greg said with a smile.

'People say that the post office is the place to go to get information about the village, but I sometimes think Maureen knows more than anyone.'

They both laughed until Greg noticed that the strange woman from the headland the day before was up ahead of them on the path. She was wearing the same long overcoat, and she was still carrying the staff. He felt the hairs on his arm stand to attention. He turned to Sarah. 'Who is she?'

'Who?' Sarah asked, following his line of vision until her eyes landed on the figure. 'Oh, that's just Ida.'

'What's with the staff?'

Sarah shrugged her shoulders. 'She's a bit odd, but she's harmless. She likes to keep herself to herself.'

'I saw her up on the headland yesterday.'

'She was probably gathering herbs and stuff. She's always concocting lotions and potions. They say she's a healer; she has the gift passed down from her father. My mother told me the story that when she had warts on her fingers as a child, my grandmother brought her to Old Leamy. He gave her a cream, and would you believe they had all vanished within a day of using it and never returned again! Funnily enough, Ida never treated anyone, though, I'm not sure why.'

Greg didn't know what it was, but there was something about this woman that made him feel uneasy. They continued walking towards the end of the street.

'Here we are,' Sarah announced when they had reached the last house before the church. It had an impressive two-storey facade with large steps leading up to a painted red front door. They climbed the steps, and Sarah rapped on the fish-shaped brass knocker.

'His daughter Hilda has recently moved back in to take care of him,' Sarah whispered as they waited. Soon the door was being pulled back, and a comely lady, who Greg guessed was in her fifties, greeted them.

'Sarah, how are you?' she said, taken aback to find them on her doorstep.

'Hilda, I'm sorry to call unannounced. This is Greg.' Sarah gestured to him. 'He's over from North Carolina on some business, and we were hoping your father might be able to help him.'

'Certainly, we can try. Dad is having a good day today. Will you come in?'

They followed her into a room she referred to as the parlour. An elderly man was sitting in an armchair. His lap was covered with a blanket, and an open book was lying face first down on the table beside him.

'I was just in the middle of reading to him,' Hilda said.

'Hello, Dr Fitzmaurice, how are you today?' Sarah asked, leaning in close to the old man.

'I'm very good thank you. Is that you, Joan?'

'Dad, it's Sarah from the post office,' Hilda reminded him.

'Oh yes,' he said. 'Did you get my letters?'

'I've nothing for you today,' Sarah said.

'And who are you, young man?' He turned to Greg then.

'I'm Greg,' he said, offering him his hand.

'Greg is here from America, Dr Fitzmaurice,' Sarah said. 'He was wondering if you could help him with something.' She turned to him, urging him to tell his story.

Greg took a deep breath. 'I was born in this village in 1976. I believe it was in the abandoned cottage up on the headland. My birth parents were a young couple, and they were in distress. My parents were staying in this village, and somehow my dad came across them, and they agreed to give their baby to my parents. I'm here in the village to try and track them down.'

Hilda's eyes were wide with shock, and Dr Fitzmaurice listened thoughtfully as Greg recounted the story.

'Greg was wondering if perhaps you can recall a young girl that gave birth in the cottage in 1976?' Sarah encouraged.

Greg held his breath as he waited for Dr Fitzmaurice to speak. The old man's eyes closed, and it looked as though he was going through his memory to recall all the women he would have dealt with over the years. Suddenly his eyes flickered open again, and Greg's stomach somersaulted.

'Where's Joan?' he said.

Greg and Sarah looked over at Hilda in confusion.

'No, Dad,' Hilda guided gently. 'Joan isn't here. Sarah and Greg were asking you about a young girl having a baby in 1976, can you remember her, Dad?'

'Did Joan have a baby?' he asked, suddenly making to get up from the armchair.

Hilda shook her head sadly. She signalled for them to come out to the kitchen. They followed her down an elegant hallway with black-and-white chequered floor tiles.

'I'm sorry,' she said once they were in the kitchen. 'I thought he was doing okay today but perhaps not . . .' She sighed. 'Unfortunately, his good days are few and far between these days. I don't think he will be able to help you.'

'Don't you be apologising,' Sarah said. 'I just hope we haven't upset him. It must be heartbreaking to watch him slipping away from you like that.'

'It is, every day I lose another little piece of him,' Hilda said sadly.

'We'll go and let you get back to your reading,' Sarah said. 'Thank you for your help.'

They followed Hilda to the door. Even though Greg had known coming here was a long shot, he couldn't help feeling deflated.

'Good luck with your search, Greg,' Hilda said as they left her home.

They climbed down the old granite steps wordlessly. 'I'm sorry, Greg,' Sarah said when they reached the pavement.

'Well, it was worth a try!' He was trying his best to sound upbeat, but in truth he was desperately disappointed. They began walking back down the street towards the village.

Suddenly they heard a voice calling from behind.

'Sarah, wait!'

They turned around to see Hilda coming down the street after them. 'I've just thought of something,' she said. 'Follow me.'

Chapter 14

Sarah and Greg hurried back towards the house with Hilda and climbed up the steps once more. This time she led them into another room on the opposite side of the hallway to the parlour. The room was chilly and had an almost musty smell, and they guessed it hadn't been used in a while.

'This was once Dad's study,' Hilda said. Medical certificates hung proudly behind an old mahogany desk, and shelves brimming with old books lined the walls. She looked up at a shelf where leather-bound diaries stood. 'He kept meticulous records. He had a book for every year.'

Hilda reached up and lifted down a black book with the date 1976 embossed in gold along its spine. The leather was cracked with age, and she ran her finger along the top, wiping off a thick settling of dust. 'If my father treated your mother, Greg, then it will certainly be in here,' she said, tapping the book before handing it to him.

'I'll leave you two to get on with it. I'll be in with Dad if you need any help.' Then Hilda slipped out of the room leaving them alone.

Greg nervously opened the book, and as he flicked through the pages, he saw handwritten entries with dates, patients' names, symptoms, treatment plans, and prescriptions. He read through the first few pages and quickly saw many children being treated for coughs and colds, there were cancer patients too, and a man with pneumonia. They saw that he had assisted at a birth in February. From the notes it seemed the woman had been delivered of a baby boy, her fourth child, at home by Dr Fitzmaurice. There were women for antenatal care, but their dates of birth put their ages as women in their twenties, and they were listed as couples like 'Mr and Mrs Murphy' and 'Mr and Mrs Jones'.

As Greg scanned through the months, there was nothing there that described a teenage girl. He guessed if his mother had been young and naïve, she probably didn't learn that she was pregnant until she was quite far along, probably around the summertime. He continued to read through all the entries for the summer months, but nothing seemed to fit with the story his mother had told him.

'To be honest, Greg, she probably didn't even receive antenatal care at all,' Sarah said as she read over his shoulder.

Greg nodded, guessing she was right but feeling heartbroken thinking of the lonely road his mother had faced.

They kept reading until they got to September's entries, and Greg found himself holding his breath hoping that perhaps in his birth month, his mother had finally turned to Dr Fitzmaurice for care. His heart stopped as he turned the page onto his birthday, but there was no record of a birth that day. He checked the days following it in case there had been a mistake with dates, but there was no record of a birth at all in September and certainly no entry that described a young, single girl.

'I'm sorry, Greg,' Sarah soothed as he closed the diary. 'Try not to be too disappointed; it was unlikely a young girl like that would have sought help from a doctor anyway. She would have been terrified that he would have gone straight to her parents.'

'I just hate the thoughts of her being all alone, giving birth, and being so afraid for what was going to happen.' He sighed.

Sarah nodded. 'I know, it's hard to imagine what the poor thing went through or how she must she have felt.'

Greg closed the diary and replaced it back on the shelf. Then they thanked Hilda and said goodbye before heading back into the village.

They walked along by the seawall and stopped to look out over the cove. The sea was deadly calm, almost ominous. He noticed a few hardy souls were swimming. He was shivering just looking at them.

'They're brave,' he said, nodding towards them.

'They're the Inishbeg Cove sea-swimmers. They meet here every morning come hail, rain, or snow to get their vitamin sea,' Sarah said.

Greg saw a surfer lying on his board using the swell to carry him back towards the shore. They watched him as he jumped up when he reached the shallow water and used one hand to flip the board up under his arm. He emerged from the surf with water dripping from his dark hair and scanned the shoreline with brooding eyes. It was only then that Greg realised he was holding a crab by the shell in his other hand. He walked up the beach while it wriggled its pincers and dropped it into a bucket. As the man got closer to the seawall, Greg recognised him from the Inishbeg Cove website when he had first researched the village—his moody eyes and stubble were instantly recognisable. The man stood up straight, unzipped his wetsuit down to his waist.

'What's he doing?' Greg asked as the man ran his hands back through his long hair sending a shower of droplets flying through the air.

'That's Tadgh,' Sarah said, waving back to him. 'He owns the restaurant. He paddles out into the cove; there is a shelf there where the crabs like to gather. He picks them up and then comes back to shore with them and puts them in his bucket to bring them back to the restaurant. Then he serves them that evening. You've never tasted crab claws as fresh.'

'But isn't that kinda dangerous?'

She shrugged her shoulders. 'Probably, but he's been doing it for as long as I can remember. His father used to do it too and his grandfather before him. They've passed the skill down through the generations. You have to taste his food. You won't find seafood like it anywhere in the world.'

'A surfing fisherman, I think that's a first for me.' He laughed.

'Tadgh is unique!' Sarah grinned back at him. 'He can be a little . . . intense, but it's just because he is so passionate about what he does.'

Tadgh scanned the beach with narrowed eyes, but he waved up to them when he saw them. They waved back before turning and continuing to walk down the main street. 'Come on,' Sarah suggested. 'Let's go to *The Anchor* for a drink. I don't know about you, but I could use one.'

'Well, only if you insist,' he joked. Even though it was next door to *Cove View*, he still hadn't managed to get there since his arrival in the village. He had felt a bit too self-conscious to go in alone.

'I do!' She linked his arm and pushed open the door.

Greg followed Sarah into the pub that was run by Maureen's husband Jim. They were hit with the same beery smell that greeted you in pubs the world over mixed with wood smoke. All heads turned to look at them as they came in. A few people sat at tables while others sat on stools at the bar. The floor was covered with traditional flagstones where worm-like fossils had worn intricate grooves over time. A fire burned invitingly in the grate, and a sheepdog lay toasting in front of it.

'That's Jim's dog, Skipper,' Sarah said. 'He always nabs the best seat in the house!'

They made their way up to the bar, and Sarah introduced him to Jim. He was a portly man with a friendly, open face.

'I was wondering how long it would take you to find us here,' he said. 'So are you having a nice stay?'

'Yes, thank you, I'm really enjoying it. Maureen has been feeding me well,' Greg said patting his stomach.

'And I see you've already made friends with our Sarah,' Jim said with a wink. 'You don't hang around!'

Greg found himself blushing at the man's teasing.

'Jim, you're a divil!' Sarah said, throwing her head back in laughter. 'Never mind him, Greg.'

'So what'll you have, Greg?' Jim asked with a playful smile lingering on his lips.

Greg ordered a pint of Guinness, having wanted to try it since he had arrived in Ireland. Sarah had a glass of wine, and they sat down into a cosy nook close to the crackling the fire.

'I'm sorry our visit to Dr Fitzmaurice didn't throw up anything,' Sarah said as she took a sip from her wine.

'Well, even if I'm still no further along, I have to say thank you, Sarah,' Greg said. 'I really appreciate it.'

'It's no bother, I'm glad I can help. Sure, what else would I be doing? It beats sitting at home watching *Fair City*,' she laughed.

He took a sip from the pint and screwed up his face as the stout hit his tongue. He wasn't expecting it to be quite so bitter.

'It's an acquired taste,' Sarah said, laughing at his reaction. 'Look, Greg,' she continued, 'just because today didn't throw up anything doesn't mean we're at the end of the road. We can still try Father Byrne,' she suggested.

'If she didn't go to the doctor, she hardly went to the priest!' he said hollowly.

'Maybe not but it's worth a try. You have to realise that the church had a powerful hold on society back then, it's hard to imagine it now as people turn their backs on organised religion, but back then the Catholic Church ran everything. A young girl getting pregnant outside of wedlock would have been a big taboo; people would remember it. If your birth mother told her parents that she was pregnant, they may have gone to Father Byrne for help or perhaps your mother went to the priest for forgiveness in later years. People carried shame about things like that around like a millstone in those days.'

'I don't know much about the Catholic Church, but I've seen enough movies to know that what happens in the confessional box has to stay in the confessional box,' Greg said.

'It does, but I was thinking ... and I know it's a long shot ... but perhaps if Father Byrne knows who your mother is, he might be willing to act as an intermediary without her having to reveal herself just yet?'

There were definitely a lot of *what ifs* and *maybes* in Sarah's plan, and although he didn't feel too hopeful, right now it was the only avenue open to him. 'It's worth a shot, I guess.'

Chapter 15

St Brigid's church took pride of place at the very end of the street. It had the best view in the whole village perched up on a rocky ledge looking out onto the ocean. A slate pitched roof sat above a nave built from dove-grey limestone. A double-height bell tower climbed into a steeple at the front, and gothic-shaped windows filled with colourful stained glass ran the length of the walls. In reality it now seemed much larger and more intimidating than how it had looked on the Inishbeg Cove website.

They climbed the steps, and Sarah blessed herself with holy water from a font inside the door, and although he wasn't Catholic, Greg found himself doing the same. Dust motes danced in the beams of light that flooded through the stained-glass windows. Rays of bright colours were spread across the varnished benches where an elderly man sat with his head bent fervently in prayer.

'Father Byrne should be in the sacristy,' Sarah whispered to him as they walked down the aisle. 'Don't let his age put you off, he is as sharp as a tack, he remembers everyone! There aren't any young priests coming through the ranks. Young men don't want to join the priesthood anymore, which means the likes of Father Byrne have to keep working when they probably should be long retired.'

Greg followed Sarah up the steps of the altar and through an arched doorway at the side, which lead into a small room. They were greeted with an elderly priest, dressed in white vestments. He sat hunched over a desk, writing something. Age spots covered his bald scalp where a tiny thatch of wispy white hair grew. Greg guessed he must have been nearly eighty. He didn't hear them come in, so Sarah cleared her throat noisily to get his attention.

'Ah good morning, Sarah,' he said, raising his head.

'Good morning, Father. This is Greg, he's visiting our village from North Carolina.'

'Pleased to meet you,' Greg said, rushing in to shake his hand.

'You're very welcome to Inishbeg Cove. What can I do for you both?'

'Well, Father, Greg is trying to trace his birth parents. He was born in the village in September 1976.'

'Ah, you want to look back on the baptism records then. Let me get them for you.' He made to get up from the desk but with considerable effort. 'My arthritis means I'm a bit slower than I used to be,' he said, his tone full of apology. He took a moment to ease himself up, and Greg noticed that he had a stoop.

'Actually, I don't think I was baptised,' Greg said.

'Oh, well, is it the marriage records you're looking for so? What were your parents' surnames?'

Greg shook his head and began filling him in on the story.

'You've been with our parish a long time, Father Byrne, and Greg was wondering if you can remember anything from that time that might help him?' Sarah said softly when he had finished.

The old man sat back down again. 'September 1976 you say?'

'I know it's a long shot, but I believe my parents were a young couple from the village here, and I was wondering if you can recall anyone coming to you for help back then?' Greg said.

'There were a few young girls over the years that found themselves in trouble, some would have come to see me themselves, but usually it was their parents that brought them to me. Often times the couple would have married quickly to avoid a scandal or some families would have asked me to place the baby with a family for adoption and the girl would have been sent away until the baby was born. But to be honest, the cases were few and far between over the years.'

'Did you ever come across an American couple?' Sarah asked hopefully.

Father Byrne shook his head. 'Anyone I dealt with was always Irish, we had one couple who lived in England, all right, but the wife was from the village. I would have remembered someone from America.'

'Maybe you were approached by someone looking for forgiveness in later years?' Greg pushed, remembering what Sarah had said in *The Anchor*.

Father Byrne looked shocked by the suggestion and shook his head. 'I have a duty to keep secret everything confessed to me, but even if I didn't, I can tell you that I haven't come across anyone seeking forgiveness for giving up their baby. You have to understand that in a village the size of this, there were only a handful of women who needed my help over the years in relation to those sorts of matters. We've had several American tourists holidaying here from time to time, but I can tell you for certain that I never placed a baby with any of them. Of course, I could look through the records, but without a surname … well, I don't have a lot to go on. I'm sorry I can't be of more help.'

Greg nodded as the sheer size of the mountain that he was up against began to hit home. None of the pieces of this puzzle seemed to fit together. Every door that opened up to allow a chink of light to shine through was then slammed shut in his face. It seemed like his birth parents had birthed him without anyone's knowledge, but how had that happened? Surely the girl's family had realised that she was pregnant? There was so much that he didn't know. He was making so many assumptions without having enough pieces to put together. It felt futile.

'We'll think of something else,' Sarah said softly as they walked back to the post office after.

'I can't believe nobody knew she was having a baby, surely someone must have known?' He turned to Sarah.

'She wouldn't have been the first woman to try and conceal a pregnancy. I know it might seem unbelievable to you, but to find yourself pregnant out of wedlock was probably the worst thing that could happen to a young girl in 1970s Ireland. Thankfully things have changed for the better and society supports unmarried mothers now, but back then, being a single mother wasn't a nice situation to find yourself in.'

'She must have been so afraid,' he said sadly.

Sarah nodded in agreement. 'I can't imagine what she went through and all the other unmarried mothers in Ireland back then. I could subtly ask the historian Danny Walsh? He might remember. What would you think? I'll be delicate—'

'Sure,' Greg said, feigning enthusiasm.

As they drew up near to the post office, they noticed a woman standing on the path holding a clipboard. She was dressed in a dark grey skirt suit, and her hair was neatly pulled back off her face and twisted elegantly on top of her head. She was looking at the post office and then writing something down on her clipboard.

'Who's that?' Sarah asked, turning to him.

'Eh, you're asking the man from America who has been in the village for a few days?' Greg said deadpan.

Sarah laughed, and they continued on closer. They watched as the woman turned around and began looking around the village. They stopped where they were to observe her for a few minutes. Whenever someone entered a shop, she wrote something on her clipboard and did the same whenever somebody exited.

'It looks as though she is counting the people,' Greg said.

Sarah narrowed her eyes. 'Hmmh,' she said, walking on leaving him no choice but to follow her.

She walked up and introduced herself, 'Hi there, I'm Sarah. I'm the postmistress here.'

The woman smiled but revealed nothing.

'Is everything okay?' Sarah tried again.

'Everything is perfect,' the woman said, flashing them a smile before turning and walking away. They watched her make her way down the street, tottering along the bumpy path in her high heels.

Sarah narrowed her eyes as she watched the distance grow between them. 'I don't like the look of her,' she said to Greg.

She was just putting her key in the lock to open the door

of the post office when Mrs O'Herlihy stepped out from the grocery store. She was wearing her usual old-style apron over her clothes.

'Who was that?' she asked Sarah with worry lines creasing her forehead.

'I'm not sure to be honest, Audrey.'

Mrs O'Herlihy folded her arms across her chest. 'I hope she's not from one of them supermarket chains. I'll never survive if they come to Inishbeg Cove.'

'Oh, I'm sure it was just a traffic survey or something,' Sarah said, giving her arm a little squeeze to reassure her.

Mrs O'Herlihy nodded. 'Let's hope you're right, dear,' she said, pulling her lips together tightly before going back inside her shop.

Sarah turned to him once Mrs O'Herlihy was gone. 'I'm not sure why, Greg, but there was something about that woman that makes me feel uneasy . . .'

Chapter 16

At the end of his first week in Inishbeg Cove, Greg was amazed at how much he had already settled into village life. He had a routine where he would usually go for a long run after breakfast to work off Maureen's excellent cooking. She insisted that he eat everything on his plate and took offence if he left a sausage or a small bit of bacon behind. As a result, he had noticed the waistband on his pants had grown a little snug. He would take a different route along the twisty roads every day to explore the village and its environs. His calves would burn the whole way as he climbed the sandy hillocks that surrounded Inishbeg Cove, but the view of the pretty village set in front of the twinkling sea down below was worth it. Then he would loop back towards the beach and run along under the towering clifftops that surrounded the cove, where waves skimmed over the sand left flattened by the outgoing tide. He would keep going until he reached the sea caves down the far end that Sarah had told him had once been used by smugglers to store their loot. Then for his warm down, he would walk up the path through the dunes that lead back to the village.

By the time he returned, there were usually fishermen docking at the pier ready to unload their haul, and seagulls and gannets would swarm above them making a cacophonous racket.

He ate lunch most days in Ruairí's. The food was so fresh and all home-made. He could taste the goodness in every bite. He had grown partial to the leek and potato soup that Ruairí served with Guinness bread slathered with creamy butter. He had even gone into the bar for his dinner by himself on a couple of evenings. Greg had got used to Jim's jokey manner and would chat to him as he served pints to the locals who were usually men that were several decades older than Greg.

He had still made no headway on finding out who his parents were though. His visits to the doctor and the priest had yielded nothing. Sarah had spoken to Danny Walsh the historian, but he hadn't been able to shine any light on it either, and Greg couldn't help but feel deflated. At that moment in time, he couldn't see any other doors open to him, and he was starting to grow frustrated.

When he was sitting in the pub in the evening time, he would find himself looking around at the older men sipping pints beside him wondering if one of them could be his father? The time was going quickly, and as much as he was enjoying the break away from his home life, he had to remember the real reason why he was here. He didn't want his trip to be a complete waste of time; he needed to get some answers from it.

One evening Sarah and Greg had arranged to go to the pub for a bite to eat after she had finished work. Sarah had told him there would be a *céilí* band playing, and it was always good *craic*, which Greg had learnt had a very different meaning to what it meant in America and was the Irish word for 'fun'.

He waited for her after work, and when she had locked up the post office, they headed down the street to the pub together. The sun had started to set in a blaze of red over the cove setting the trees aflame.

'Red sky at night, shepherd's delight,' Sarah remarked.

'Red sky in the morning, shepherd's warning,' Greg finished.

The sound of sweet evening birdsong filled the air as they trilled melodies before they would settle down for the night. Greg had noticed in the short time that he had been there that the spring air was beginning to push out the last days of winter, and there was a definite hopefulness in the air of better weather to come.

'So, did you manage to find out any more about your parents?' Sarah asked as they walked along.

Greg shook his head despondently. 'Nada,' he said. 'I can't help but feel they don't want to be found.' The truth was that little doubts were starting to grow in his mind. He was starting to wonder if his mom had got the details wrong. Perhaps he was in the wrong village or she had got the wrong date? But the cottage on the headland was exactly as she had described . . . and he was sure his birthday was accurate, give or take a few days. It was all so frustrating.

'Well, maybe it's time to leave the softly-softly approach behind,' Sarah said gently. 'Perhaps it's time to push a bit harder and tell people the real reason why you are here. Who knows, maybe it will throw up some clues.'

Greg sighed. 'I think you're probably right. I don't want to ruffle any feathers, but I need to get some answers, or else this whole trip is going to be a complete waste of time . . .'

When they reached *The Anchor*, Greg pushed open the door and they went inside. The pub was dimly lit, and a few old men sat on stools at the bar. Otherwise the place was empty. The band was setting up in the corner. The accordion player was warming up while another man was strumming a banjo. A young girl tuned a fiddle.

'Wait 'til you see it in an hour, the place will be packed,' Sarah said. 'They come from far and wide for this music.'

Greg was glad to see Jim had the fire lighting, and the peaty smell of turf filled the air. Skipper was in his usual spot on the rug in front of the fire.

'Hi, Greg, hi, Sarah, what can I get you both?' Jim asked.

'A pint of Guinness and eh . . . a white wine?' he said, looking at Sarah for confirmation that he had ordered correctly for her.

She nodded. 'I see you've got a taste for the black stuff now,' she said, elbowing him as Jim pulled his pint.

'I'll have a bowl of the chowder as well, Jim,' Sarah said, reading the chalkboard menu that hung behind the bar.

'I'll go for the line-caught sea bream,' Greg said. He had ordered it a few days ago and had never tasted fish so fresh.

'This is Mr Farrell, Mr White, and Mr Murphy,' Sarah said, introducing Greg to some of the men who were sitting at the bar.

'Are you on holiday here is it?' Mr Murphy asked. 'We don't usually get many tourists out this way, we're a bit too far off the beaten track.'

'That's the way we want to keep it!' Mr White said with a cheeky wink. 'This village is Ireland's best kept secret.'

Sarah gave Greg a look, encouraging him to tell them. He guessed there was no time like the present and took a deep breath before beginning. 'Well, actually . . . I'm here because I'm trying to trace my birth parents. I was born in the cottage up on the headland and given to an American couple who brought me back to North Carolina with them where I was raised.'

Their faces read shocked. 'By God,' Mr Farrell said eventually.

'Can you remember anything from that time that might help Greg to find out who his parents are?' Sarah asked.

Mr White paused thoughtfully. 'There were stories around this place for years that there was a baby born up on the headland, but nobody ever knew who it was or if it was even true. I always thought they were just rumours, but maybe there was some truth to them after all . . .'

Finally, it felt as though a chink of light was shining through a crack in the door.

'Can you remember who you would have heard those rumours from?' Greg asked quickly. He could feel his heart start to thump at the chance of being close to finding out some more details. He knew he had to stop getting his hopes raised for every little piece of information that he heard, but it was so hard when his whole identity was on the line.

'Aragh, there would have been whispers around the place over the years,' Mr White continued. 'I can't remember exactly who I heard it from . . .'

'Right,' Greg said, feeling himself slump down again.

'Well, if you think of anything, will you let Greg know? It would be nice for him to get some closure on this before he goes back to America,' Sarah said. Then she linked Greg's arm. 'Come on, let's get a seat.'

They sat down at a table beside a window where beyond

the sunset had bled into dusk and a velvety cloak of darkness had fallen on the village. Yellow lights shone out across the bay as far as the eye could see.

'Mmmh,' Greg said, tucking in after Jim placed their food in front of them. It tasted just as good as it had been the first time he had tried it.

'So how long have you left here?' Sarah asked.

'A little less than three weeks. Work gave me a month off, but they'll be expecting me back then, all fired up and ready to go.'

'Do you know something?' Sarah said. 'I feel like I know everything about you and nothing at the same time. I don't even know what you work at! Tell me some more about yourself, Greg.'

'Well, I'm an attorney,' he began. 'I work for a large firm in Charlotte—that's the city where I live.'

'And are you married? Kids?'

He shook his head quickly. 'No . . . sadly not,' he said. He paused. 'Sorry, it's a bit close to the bone. I just broke up with my long-term girlfriend before I came here actually . . .'

'Oh, I'm sorry, Greg,' Sarah gushed. 'I'm forever putting my foot in things . . .'

'Don't be sorry,' he said, taking a sip from his pint. 'Would you believe she broke up with me on the day of Mom's funeral?'

Sarah gasped in horror, and Greg nodded to confirm it was indeed true.

'That was great timing!' she said with heavy sarcasm threading her words.

'It gets worse. I met her with her new boyfriend a few days later . . .'

Sarah was wide-eyed as Greg filled her in on the rest of the story.

'That's part of the reason I decided to come here. I had just lost Mom and read her letter, and then when I saw Selena with him . . . I felt as though my whole world had ended, I didn't know who I was or where I belonged anymore. I needed to escape my life and clear my head.'

'It might not seem like it now, but she did you a favour in

the long run,' Sarah said softly.

Greg didn't know what it was about Sarah that made it so easy to open up to her. He was by nature normally reserved and coy about his feelings, but she had such a kind face; he didn't feel exposed or vulnerable as he talked about what had led him to come here.

'What about you?' Greg asked.

'What do you mean?' She began fiddling with a beer mat on the table. It was clear that she wasn't comfortable when the spotlight was cast back on her. 'Sure, I'm young, free, and single! Well . . . maybe only two of those things are true.' She laughed.

'I hope this comes out the right way and you won't take offence . . . but you're a good-looking woman . . . I'm sure you could have your pick of men!'

'You'd think so, wouldn't you? Funnily enough, there aren't any men beating down a path to my door!' She paused, and her joviality faded as her face darkened. 'Ah look, I might as well tell you . . . I was engaged before to a fella from the village.'

'What happened?' Greg asked. 'Well, I guess this place wasn't big enough for him . . . He wanted more, so he went to Australia for a year to travel, but my mam was sick at the time. Her cancer had come back again, and she had just been told it had spread. She had the post office to look after, so someone needed to help her do that. I couldn't just up and leave, so I stayed behind. We did long distance for a while, but eventually the phone calls stopped coming.' She paused for the sting of the old wound. 'I believe he married an Australian girl, and they have three kids together now.' Her voice was tinged with sadness as she reminisced over past hurts.

'And you haven't met anyone else since?' Greg probed.

'No, I'm afraid not.' There was a heavy sadness in her eyes. 'There aren't many men here to choose from, although the village does a good line in the over-seventies.' She nodded up towards the bar, and they both laughed. 'I think it's time to accept that it's unlikely that I ever will meet anyone, and I'm okay with it. It's better to be on your own than to spend your life with the wrong person. I firmly believe that.'

Greg nodded in agreement. 'Do you ever regret not going with him?' he asked.

She shook her head with certainty. 'Mam died three months later, and I'm glad I had that time with her. I wouldn't have been able to care for her if I was in Australia. And besides, I could never leave Inishbeg Cove. No, Greg, I believe everything happens for a reason.'

They both fell quiet, marauding over one another's revelations. Greg noticed that the pub had filled up since they had arrived. He had never seen so many people in the place.

'Are they all here for the céilí?' he asked.

Sarah nodded. 'I told you. Nothing beats céilí night in *The Anchor*!'

Soon the band started to play lively, traditional Irish music. Tin whistles squealed, and the fiddle player deftly moved her bow back and forth across the strings while the accordion player squeezed the box so fast that beads of sweat glistened on his brow. The low beat of the stick against the goatskin of the bodhrán drum formed a steady base. A couple took to the floor and started to dance. Soon several more followed.

'Come on,' Sarah said, pulling him up to dance.

'No way! I can't dance!' Greg said, feeling panicked as he quickly tried to sit back down again.

'Come on, Greg,' Sarah coaxed. 'You'll enjoy it; it's a bit of craic.'

'But I've never done any kind of folk dancing,' he protested.

'Don't you know you never refuse a lady a dance,' Mr White shouted over to him with a wink.

'Well, in that case . . .' Greg stood up and took Sarah's hand with trepidation. 'Now, I'm warning you that I've two left feet, and I've never done Irish dancing before—it won't be pretty!'

Sarah laughed as he linked her arm, and soon she was swinging him around the pub. They moved in and out in a chain of people, then, just as he thought he was getting into the rhythm of it, she would pull him off to the left and they'd be doing new steps. At one stage, he even stood on her toes. 'Sorry, I'm like a baby elephant,' he mumbled, but she just giggled, which set him off too. He felt stiff and clumsy and always seemed to be two steps behind, but he had never laughed so much in his life.

'There, you see!' Sarah said breathlessly as they collapsed back into their seats while the band took a break. 'Just what the doctor ordered for both of us! You weren't too bad actually,' she said, giggling as she took a sip from her drink.

'Maybe it's genetic. Who knows, my parents could have been Irish dancers,' Greg said, and they both creased over, laughing some more until he had a pain in his side and his mouth ached.

He noticed that Sarah's cheeks were rosy, and her hair had come loose around her face. When she laughed, her eyes shone too. He found himself thinking about Selena; she was always so elegant and poised. She would never let loose like this; he wouldn't normally either, but there was something about this place that had crept under his skin. He had only been here for a matter of days, but it kept pushing him out of his comfort zone. He had a feeling when it came to returning home to North Carolina that he would be going home a changed man.

Chapter 17

Greg was sitting at his usual table beside the window in the dining room as Maureen put yet another legendary fried breakfast in front of him. He was practically drooling as he looked at the sausages, rashers, poached egg, black-and-white pudding, and a thick slice of home-made soda bread oozing with golden butter on the plate. He was slightly seedy from the céilí the night before, and this breakfast was exactly what he needed to quell his queasy stomach.

'Did you sleep well, Greg?' Maureen asked.

'Never better.'

And it was the truth. He had fallen into a deep sleep, like he had every night since he had arrived in the village. He had never slept as well in his life, and he guessed it was from the fresh sea air. He would lay his head on Maureen's plump pillow every night and not wake again until the sunlight filtered around the edges of the blind the next morning. There was something calming about being in Inishbeg Cove. It was like a soothing balm had been applied to his wounded heart. Being on the very edge of Ireland's rugged coastline really helped him to feel disconnected from his life at home and all the problems and hurt he had left behind him there.

'It's a lovely day out there,' Maureen continued as she poured a mug of coffee for him.

'It's beautiful,' he replied simply, not wishing to keep up the conversation with her. His stomach was growling, and he just wanted to get stuck into his food.

'So how are you finding our village?' she continued. 'You seem to be settling in well.'

'I'm really enjoying my time here, although I think I'm enjoying your food a bit too much,' he said, biting into the bread, savouring the salty taste of the butter. He had never tasted butter as creamy as what Maureen served every morning.

'I like to take care of my guests.' She smacked her lips together proudly.

He cut down into his sausage and took a bite.

'So, are you getting to see everything you wanted to?' Maureen went on as she cleared off the table beside him. Obvious curiosity laced her words. Ever since Greg had arrived in Inishbeg Cove and set off to meet Sarah, Maureen's interest had been piqued. She was sharp enough to realise that he wasn't just an ordinary tourist, and Greg knew she had been trying to deduce his reasons for coming to the village. Maybe now was the time to put her out of her misery, Greg decided. As Sarah had said, he needed to cast his net a little further if he wanted to catch something. Who knew, Maureen might actually be able to help him. He lowered his knife and fork down onto the plate.

'Actually, Maureen,' he began. 'The reason that I'm here is that I'm trying to trace my birth parents.'

Her arms jerked suddenly, and the plate she had just been loading onto the tray landed with a clatter.

'Were your parents from around here?' she asked as she managed to recover the plate.

Greg filled her in on the story, and as soon as he had finished, she began shaking her head. 'Oh, I don't know, Greg . . . I never heard of anything like that happening around here,' she said. 'I think you've been watching too many movies!'

He was taken aback by her reaction. Was she accusing him of lying? 'I—I—can assure you that it did; my mom wouldn't have made something like that up. A lot of the details she gave me were very accurate, like the cottage up on the headland, how would she have known about that if it didn't exist?'

'Sure, people can look up anything on the Internet nowadays!' Maureen snapped. She narrowed her eyes and spoke in a strange voice, 'People won't like this, Greg,' she warned. 'The past should be left in the past.'

Greg sat back in his chair, lost for words. 'I—I—I don't

want to upset anyone . . . I'm only trying to find my birth parents,' he ventured, suddenly feeling unsure of himself. 'Don't I have a right to know who they are?'

'Don't people have a right to be left in peace?' she retorted before lifting his plate from the table and putting it onto her tray even though he wasn't yet finished. She turned on her heel and headed back into the kitchen.

Greg was stunned by the vitriol of Maureen's reaction. Anger swirled red-hot through his veins, and he knew he needed to get out of the guesthouse before he said or did something he might regret. Pushing back his chair with a screech along the tiles, he got up from the table. He headed out to the lobby and through the front door. He slammed it shut and stepped out onto the sidewalk.

As he stormed down the street, Maureen's words looped inside his head. Her tone had been cutting, and he was hurt by what she had implied. He wasn't trying to upset anyone —that was the last thing that he wanted. He just needed to know more about where he came from. He didn't think that was too much to ask.

When he had read his mother's letter, his whole existence had been turned upside down. It felt like he didn't belong in North Carolina, it was as if the mould he thought he had come from had altered shape and no longer fit, and now according to Maureen, he wasn't welcome in the village of his birth either. He couldn't help but feel it like a fresh rejection all over again. If the truth was told, he was beginning to question why he ever came here in the first place.

Greg found himself calling in to the post office to see Sarah. He needed to see a friendly face. He pushed open the door and went inside, but instead of being in her usual place behind the desk, she was standing out in the middle of the floor clutching a piece of paper in her hands. A few of the locals were gathered around her. As he got closer, he could see she looked stricken.

An older lady that he knew as Mrs Manning banged her stick off the ground. 'We'll not let that happen!' she was saying, her voice full of vitriol.

'What's wrong?' Greg asked, looking around at all the

mournful faces.

'Oh, Greg, I just got some terrible news,' Sarah said with tears brimming in her eyes. 'They want to close the post office!'

She handed him the letter to read, and as he scanned down through it, he saw that it was unambiguous; due to cost-saving initiatives, plans were being made to gradually withdraw postal services from Inishbeg Cove.

'Did you know anything about this?' he asked.

She shook her head. 'This is the first I knew of it!' Suddenly she looked up at him. 'The woman that we saw last week—you remember her, Greg—she had the clipboard? That must have been why she was here. I knew there was something suspicious about her!'

'We won't stand for it, Sarah,' a man piped up. 'Somebody is sitting in an office up there in Dublin doing sums and plugging figures into a computer, but they don't understand what it's like to live in rural Ireland. This place is more than just a post office; it's the heart of the community. Inishbeg Cove needs its post office!'

'It certainly does,' the rest of the group echoed.

'I'm sorry, Sarah,' Greg said when everyone had left and they were alone.

She shook her head sadly. 'It's such a shock. I know my post office doesn't have the highest turnover in the country, but that doesn't bother me. I am happy just being of service to the village. The elderly people collect their pensions here every week or come in to pay their bills. They even use this place like a counselling service sometimes—it means more to them than just buying a few stamps. The nearest post office is over ten miles away, how are they meant to get there when they don't drive and there is no public transport?' Suddenly she broke down crying, and the tears spilled down her face.

'Oh, Greg what am I going to do?' she sobbed. 'Running the post office is the only job I know.'

Greg felt useless and had no words of comfort to offer her. There was nothing he could say or do to help her, so he found himself doing the only thing he could do, he wrapped his arms around her, pulled her in closely, so close that he could feel her hot tears against the skin on his neck as she cried it all out.

Chapter 18

The next day it rained biblical amounts. Greg ran along the winding boreens, trying his best to dodge the puddles, but there was just no let up as it kept spilling down. As the road climbed higher, he could see thick clouds of mist had rolled in from the bay and were settling over Inishbeg Cove for the day. It was in such contrast to the day before, which had been a beautiful spring day. Greg could see why Irish people were obsessed with talking about the weather—it changed so fast.

He looped around the village and took the path leading through the dunes down onto the sandy cove. The cliffs loomed above him like watchful giants as he ran, and the sand, normally washed smooth by the outgoing tide, had instead been left puckered by the raindrops.

Suddenly he saw a dark figure hunched over near the sleek black rocks up ahead. As he got closer, he realised it was Ida. She was wearing her usual cloak with the hood up to shield herself from the onslaught of the wind and rain, but there was no mistaking her. He noticed she had left her staff leaning against a barnacle-studded rock. She bent to collect fronds of brown seaweed that were strewn across them before putting them into a wicker basket. The wind was roaring, and the crash of the waves meant she didn't hear him. It allowed him to observe this strange woman for a while. When she was finished collecting the seaweed, she picked up her staff and righted herself before surveying the beach. Her eyes found Greg then, and she stared over coolly. He found himself looking away from her gaze. He turned away and decided to head back up to the village. He couldn't figure it out, but there was something about her that made the hairs on his arm stand on end.

Greg was drenched to the skin and starving as he walked along the main street. Having skipped breakfast in the guesthouse to avoid seeing Maureen, his stomach was growling for its usual morning fare. He was still upset by her reaction the previous morning. He decided to call into Ruairí's. He pushed open the door, and the delicious smell of freshly baked bread filled the air. The room hummed with the low buzz of chatter as he made his way up to the counter and read the chalkboard menu hanging behind it.

'I guess you heard the news?' he said to Ruairí after he had ordered the smoked salmon on Guinness bread.

'What's that?' Ruairí asked.

'About the post office.'

Ruairí nodded solemnly. 'Yeah, I did. It's all anyone has spoken about this morning. They'll turn this place into a ghost town if they keep going this way. There'll be nothing left here anymore. The world is changing, they want us to do everything online these days, but sure most people here don't even own a computer. And even if you do, there's no broadband out this way anyway,' Ruairí grumbled as he ground beans to make Greg's coffee.

Greg took a table beside the radiator, keen to dry off. While he was waiting on his breakfast, he heard two older ladies chatting worriedly about the post office at the table beside him. He knew the news was a big blow to the village.

After he left Ruairí's he decided to pay a quick visit to see how Sarah was doing before heading home to shower. She had been on his mind the whole way as he had climbed the grassy dunes and dipped down into valleys on his run that morning. He still hadn't told her about his conversation with Maureen the previous day; she had enough on her mind without him burdening her with that too.

He stopped off in *O'Herlihy's* grocery store to grab a box of chocolates to help cheer her up. He was browsing through the aisles when he overheard Mrs O'Herlihy talking to a customer that she was serving at the counter.

'Did you hear the news?' she was saying to the lady.

'What news?'

'About the post office?' Mrs O'Herlihy said, handing the woman back her change.

'No, what's that?' the other woman asked.

She dug her hands deep into her apron pockets. 'They want to close it.'

'They can't do that!' the woman said in horror, dropping her coins onto the floor. She bent down and began fumbling around for them, and Greg noticed her hands, which were furled with arthritis, were trembling.

'Where would we go to post our letters and parcels or even to pay the ESB?' she continued when she stood back up. 'I don't drive! And we've no buses coming out this way . . .'

Mrs O'Herlihy nodded in agreement. 'It's a disgrace the way they can do these things to rural communities—the only lifeline we have connecting us, and they want to cut us off completely!'

'Poor, Sarah, she must be so upset. She works so hard for us all.'

'She does, she doesn't deserve this,' Mrs O'Herlihy said, shaking her head. 'It's a sad day for our village.'

It seemed that everywhere he went in the village there was concern about the post office. He was starting to see just how big a loss this was to Inishbeg Cove. Greg was from a different generation; a different world where he had technology and fast Internet connections at his fingertips, but to these people here, losing their post office was a very real threat. They were losing their link with the rest of the world. They weren't able to swipe across on an iPad or use a smartphone to do things online. Modern technology was a language that they didn't speak, but it was more than that. They still relied on the human connection.

Even though he had only been in the village for a short time, he could already see that the relationship that the villagers had with Sarah was more than just one of service; it was a social outing as much as anything. They enjoyed the chat they would have with her and whoever else they might meet there. The villagers liked the physical act of collecting their pension money and then dividing it up for their weekly groceries and bills. They didn't want it paid into a bank account somewhere. Sarah had told him that most of them didn't even have bank accounts. The post office was the heartbeat of the community.

After Greg had paid for the chocolates, he left the grocery store and headed next door to the post office. As he arrived at the door, he noticed a handwritten poster taped onto the glass, which read:

Save Our Post Office
Meeting Tonight at 7 p.m. in the Parish Hall,
All Welcome.

He pushed open the door, his ear waiting to hear the little jingle of the bell. There was no one else in there, so he went straight up to the counter.

'Hi, Greg,' Sarah said when she saw him. She looked tired. Her eyes were pink rimmed and her face puffy. He guessed she hadn't slept well.

'How are you doing?' he asked.

'I've been better.'

'Here,' he said, holding the chocolates up to the glass screen. 'I thought you could do with some cheering up.'

She broke into a smile that lit up her whole face, and he felt his heart soar. 'Thank you so much, Greg, that's so thoughtful of you.' She paused momentarily. 'I want to apologise—'

'For what?'

'Well … for … em … well … crying on you like that.'

'Please, don't—you have nothing to apologise for—'

'It was just such a shock, you know?'

'Well, I'm glad to see you're not going to take it lying down,' he said, nodding towards the poster in the window.

'Oh, I can't take any credit for that, it was all Mr Murphy's doing. He's organised everything. Once again, this village has shown me why it is the best place to live in the world. Will you come tonight, Greg?' she asked him.

'Of course, I will.'

'Thanks, I need all the support I can get.' She sighed.

*

That evening Greg watched as queues of people filtered into the parish hall. He guessed there were over two hundred people in there. They were mainly older men and women, but some younger people had turned out too. They hadn't let the heavy downpours outside put them off, and he was glad for Sarah's sake to see how much support she had behind her. She was sitting up the front beside Mr Murphy. He waved up to her, and she smiled nervously back at him. Ruairí had set up a table at the back of the hall serving free tea and coffee and some of his delicious honey and lemon curd buns. Greg noticed that even Ida had come along. She was lurking near the back of the hall, still wearing her cloak, but he was glad to see that she had left her creepy staff at home for once. She didn't sit down, though, and remained standing the entire time. She kept her head bowed and didn't speak to anybody.

When everyone was seated, Mr Murphy called out '*whist*' and then he stood up, took the microphone, and began to speak.

'As you are all aware, our post office is under threat. We have called you here tonight to get support and to show our government and politicians that Inishbeg Cove needs its post office. We will not become another casualty of urbanisation towards the cities and large towns. As you all will know, the village lost its Garda Station five years ago, if we lose our post office too, what will we have left? Where will it end? We are not just numbers on a spreadsheet, our village is full of real people with real needs who rely on our post office as part of their daily life. Enough is enough; we need to make a stand. We are writing to Irish Post to outline our concerns and total disagreement with the proposed plans. We are demanding that our post office be left alone, and I'm calling on you all to sign the letter.'

'Hear, hear,' the crowd echoed when he had finished as a large applause rippled around the hall. A few more people spoke about their concerns and outlined why the post office was important to them. An elderly lady was almost in tears when she described how since her husband had died that there were many days when her trips to the post office were the only time she got to talk to a person for the whole day. It wasn't just a post office to her, it was her lifeline.

As Greg listened to the voices speak about what the post office meant to them, he couldn't help but think how bizarre life was sometimes. A few weeks ago he had never even heard of this tiny, dot of a village on the very edge of the world, and now here he was sitting in the parish hall trying to help save its post office!

When everyone had finished speaking, a long line formed at the table that Mr Murphy had set up as people queued to put their signature on the letter.

'You have the whole village behind you,' Greg said to Sarah as they stacked the chairs in the hall after everyone had left to go home.

She put the chair she had just started to lift back down onto the floor and turned to him. 'I just wish those accountants could see this place and the people in it. The villagers deserve to have their post office based on their generosity alone.'

'Unfortunately, accountants don't measure things like that when they put these proposals together.' He shook his head sadly.

When they were finished, they locked up the hall and Greg walked Sarah home. He was glad to see the rain had finally stopped. The navy blue sky was studded with stars, and a full moon lit a silver path across the bay as they walked. The air was calm and still, almost as if the torrential downpour hadn't happened. Greg had never seen as much rain as he had since he had come to Inishbeg Cove; whenever he thought it couldn't get any wetter, another shower would push in and wash them out. The village really was at the mercy of the elements. He could see now why the area along the west coast of Ireland was called the Wild Atlantic Way.

Sarah's house was set right on the edge of a small headland just above the sea, so close that you could feel the droplets from the sea spray as it broke and taste its salt on your lips. It was a very old two-storey cottage built from roughly hewn sandstone that Sarah had told him had been passed down through the generations. Higgledy-piggledy slate tiles covered a roof, which had sunk in the middle over time, and two chimneys sat at either gable end. A narrow path led up to a carnation pink door where a pretty wreath decorated with wild flowers hung.

'You did great tonight,' he said as they stood listening to the sea beating the coast in the background.

'I really appreciate everyone's efforts . . . but, well . . . what if I can't save it, Greg?' she said in a small voice. Her shoulders sunk downwards as if she had already lost the battle. 'Four generations of women in my family have kept this post office open and served our village through the years, and now I'm going to be the last. I feel as though I've let everyone down.'

'No, you haven't, Sarah, I've seen how much you do for this community, it can't be measured on paper! We just have to find a way of letting them see this.'

She shook her head sadly. 'They don't care about any of that stuff. It's all metrics and targets these days.' She turned to face him, her linen blue eyes saucer-like with worry and fear. 'Oh, Greg, what will I do if I don't have the post office?' she said. 'Who'd employ me? I'm almost forty. I never went to college and have no other experience; this is the only job I've ever known!'

'Try not to look too far ahead yet,' he soothed.

A cat came out of nowhere and rubbed along between their legs, startling Greg. Sarah laughed. 'That's a stray kitten I've been feeding.' The cat looked up at Sarah with intense eyes and gave a loud meow. 'Looks like she is hungry again,' Sarah said. 'Here, I'm being very rude, do you want to come in for a coffee?' she asked him.

Greg wasn't sure if she was just being polite or if she really did want him to come in. He didn't want to impose on her or to overstay his welcome. She had already been so kind with her time by helping him with his search.

'Actually, I . . . eh . . . should probably head on,' he said.

'No worries,' she said. If Greg had looked quicker, he would have seen a flicker of disappointment in her eyes.

They said goodnight to one another, and then he continued on down the street towards the guesthouse. He hoped it was late enough to avoid Maureen. Her words were still racing through his mind since breakfast the previous day. He put his key in the lock and opened the door as quietly as he could manage. He planned on hurrying up the stairs and straight into his bedroom. He had just placed his foot on the third step when he heard a voice calling him from behind.

'Greg—'

He felt his body still as he braced himself for whatever onslaught she was about to unleash on him.

'Maureen,' he said, turning around to face her. He was surprised to see she looked tired and pale. Her normally perfectly coiffed hair was falling down over her eyes, and she wasn't wearing her usual brightly coloured lipstick. Her mature skin looked tired, the creases deeper.

'Were you down at the meeting?' she asked.

'I was,' Greg said, feeling relieved that he wasn't facing another dressing down.

'I couldn't make it myself.'

'Well, there was a great turnout,' he said before turning back around to continue up the stairs.

'Look . . . I just wanted to say that I'm sorry about what I said to you yesterday—'

He stopped and turned back to her. 'Well, I didn't mean to make you angry—'

'I know you didn't . . . I'm just thinking of the elderly people in the village, this could really upset them, you know; some of them are very . . .' she paused for the right word before settling on, 'traditional. They wouldn't like to hear about things like that going on around here.'

He nodded. 'Sure,' he said.

'Just take it easy,' she cautioned.

He felt anger rise within him once again. It was none of her business what he did.

'I'll keep that in mind,' he said, turning away from her and continuing up the stairs.

He unlocked the door to his room and flopped down onto the bed. It felt as though the walls were closing in around him; the shade of peach made him feel sickly. He was hurt by Maureen's reaction. It was as if she wanted him to deny his past. He wasn't intentionally trying to upset anyone; he just wanted to know the truth. He knew the village mattered to people, but she had made him feel unwelcome. Sarah's opinion of the village was one of loyalty and kindness, it was of a village that cared for its people, but according to Maureen, it was closed-minded and traditional. Both versions were diametrically opposed to one another, and he wasn't sure which version of the village was the correct one. He was starting to think that maybe he had underestimated just how big a challenge he had ahead of him.

Chapter 19

A mixture of stubbornness and pride made Greg decide to brave breakfast in the dining room the next morning. He still had a little over two weeks left in Inishbeg Cove, and he knew he couldn't avoid Maureen every morning. However, he was pleasantly surprised when she greeted him politely as he took his seat. She seemed to be back to her usual smiling self. Even if it was just for appearances' sake, Greg was relieved.

'Good morning, Greg,' she greeted, 'it's a lovely day out there today. It makes up for yesterday's washout.'

She was acting as if nothing had ever happened between them. There were a few other guests staying in *Cove View*, so she was kept busy running in and out of the kitchen with trays, and Greg was glad that her focus was off him.

After breakfast he headed out for his run. The rain the day before had washed the sky clear, and now fleecy clouds were pulled loosely across its azure blue backdrop. They seemed to blow across the sky so fast they looked like someone was pressing a fast-forward button.

On his way back, he called into the post office to see how Sarah was doing. He was happy to see that she seemed a bit brighter than she had the previous day.

'I've done enough feeling sorry for myself,' she said. 'Me moping around won't help anyone. I need to fight to save this place.'

'That's the spirit!' he enthused.

They were chatting when the bell sounded and in came two older people.

'Hello, Sarah,' they said.

'Mr and Mrs Murphy! How are you both?'

They were soon followed by several more elderly people. 'Mr McKay, hello!' Sarah said in confusion as they all piled in. 'Oh hi, Mrs Dunne and Mrs O'Meara—' A few more came in behind them. 'Oh, and Mr Ward too. How are you all?' They kept crowding in until soon the small post office was full. Sarah looked around at the gathering in puzzlement.

'We're good, Sarah love, but we'll be a lot better when that shower leave our post office alone,' Mrs Murphy spoke with fierce determination. 'We have all the signatures.' She gestured to the thick pile of paper that she was clutching in her hands. 'We're going to tell the government that we need our post office and that we won't take this lying down. Everyone over the age of two has signed it.'

Sarah took the pages from Mrs Murphy and looked through them in amazement. 'You weren't joking,' she said, pointing to a child's scrawled signature.

'We need to make them see how valued you are in our community.' The woman reached out and clasped Sarah's hands in her own and brought them to her chest. 'I'm just glad your mother isn't alive to see this, Sarah, she would be heartbroken.'

Sarah smiled sadly. 'She would, Mrs Murphy, this place was her life—as it is mine too.'

'We won't let them do it, Sarah. We'll show them that Inishbeg Cove is not to be messed with!' Mr Murphy chimed in.

'Well, thank you . . . everyone . . . I am blown away by your support.' Her voice was full of emotion as she looked around at the gathering. 'I really do appreciate your efforts.'

Greg could see tears glistening at the sides of her eyes.

'Oh, Greg, I feel as though I'm letting everyone down,' Sarah said as soon as the crowd had left. 'How am I going to save this place? I can't hold back governments and corporations!'

'I know it must seem like an epic battle that you're facing, but you're not on your own, Sarah. The community of Inishbeg is behind you, and I know they will fight with you every step of the way.'

'You're right, Greg, of course, I'm not on my own—you can't be on your own in this village. Listen, I'm going to take an early lunch, do you fancy getting a takeout from Ruairí's and going for a walk? I could do with clearing my head.'

'You're on.'

*

After they had ordered sandwiches in Ruairí's, Sarah and Greg climbed up the headland. They were eating their food as they trampled over the toughened grass. The view from the clifftops was unobstructed; no trees were able to withstand the onslaught from the Atlantic winds. The wind roared around them and it felt fresh on their exposed faces. Greg loved how it would suck your breath away. It definitely was just the thing to help shake off the cobwebs. In the distance, gulls and terns swooped down from the cliffs and cast a predatory eye over the water.

'I'm sorry I haven't been much help with your search,' Sarah said as they walked.

Greg shook his head. 'Don't be crazy. You've been great, and besides, you've enough of your own problems right now.'

'I take it you've found nothing more then?' Sarah asked.

'I had a bit of a setback actually—'

'Oh yeah?'

'Well, I told Maureen the reason why I'm here over breakfast the other day. I was hoping she might try to assist me, but she accused me of making it up!'

'She did not!' Sarah turned to him in shock.

'I thought people would be willing to help me, but according to Maureen, it's the opposite. She warned me not to go upsetting people!'

Sarah looked pensive as she chose her words. 'It's a tough one, Greg. This is such a small, close-knit village, and people are very protective of it, so I can see where Maureen is coming from. No one wants to upset anyone, but the people here are good people. I know in my heart of hearts that they would do anything to help you if they could—you can see that for yourself with all they've done to save the post office.'

'So what do you think I should I do? I've only got two and a half weeks left!'

'Don't be disheartened, Greg. We'll keep trying.' She linked her arm through his and they continued on.

Although he knew that Sarah was doing her best, he couldn't help but feel crestfallen. He realised that no one was going to creep out of the woodwork and hand him the answers, and without any leads, he didn't know what path to go down.

Soon they saw the crumbling walls of the old cottage where Greg was born up ahead of them in the distance. 'If only walls could talk.' He sighed. 'Somebody must know something. 1976 wasn't that long ago, there are people in the village who would—'

'Look, there's Ida!' Sarah said, cutting across him. He looked up, and sure enough he saw her shadow standing in the old doorframe looking out over the village into the distance below her. They were approaching her from the side, so she hadn't seen them yet. They continued uphill until the ground started to level off. Soon she spotted them. Sarah waved at her, but she didn't wave back.

'Hello, Ida,' Sarah called out when they got closer.

She didn't reply, instead she just stared at them through narrowed eyes. The air felt thick. Menacing.

'Is she doing a spell or something?' Greg asked.

Sarah began to giggle and swatted him on the arm.

'I'm not joking!'

'We should leave her be, I don't want to disturb her,' Sarah whispered. 'I need to get back to work anyway.'

They turned around and headed back down the hillside again, trampling over spiky tufts of grey-green grass. The pretty village lay before them like an illustration from a fairytale pop-up book. Greg could feel Ida's eyes burrowing into his back the whole way.

'She's so odd,' he said when they were further down. 'That' the second time I've seen her up there.'

'She's a bit strange, I'll admit, but that's just Ida.' Sarah shrugged. 'She's always been like that. Ever since I was a girl, I can remember her acting the same way.'

Despite being warm from their walk, Greg felt a shiver flow through him. A sense of unease crawled along his skin, causing each tiny hair to stand to attention. What was it about that woman that had such an effect on him?

Chapter 20

June 1976

The packets of pads that Mammy bought for me every month remained unopened. They were piling up on the shelf in my wardrobe. After the fourth month that this had happened, I began hiding them deep down in the bin so Mammy wouldn't notice that they weren't being used. The nuns in school were always warning us about sins of the flesh, and now all the signs were there that I was a fallen woman.

As silly as it sounds now, I guessed I just hoped that the problem would disappear. I denied what was happening to myself and continued on as normal. My body colluded with me, and I felt fine for the most part, a bit queasy now and then but nothing that I couldn't hide from Mammy. But then when my belly began to push forward and my clothes started to get tighter on me, I knew I couldn't pretend anymore.

I racked my brain for a solution. I couldn't ask Mammy or Daddy for help because I knew they would be devastated. They would accuse me of bringing shame on the family, and I couldn't bear to do that to them. I wanted to ask my friends what I should do, but I wasn't sure if I could trust them. I knew they would probably tell their parents, and they in turn would just tell Mammy.

You see I was afraid they would send me off to one of those Mother and Baby homes, and everyone knew that awful things happened there. I remember walking past one before, and as I looked through the railings, the poor girls were on their hands and knees with swollen bellies scrubbing the yard outside with brushes. Mammy had told me not to look at them, as if their con-

dition was contagious, but I couldn't help it. I remember one girl in particular caught my eye; she seemed so young, too young to be in somewhere like that. Her body was so petite, almost childlike, except for her pregnant tummy. Her eyes locked with mine and were full of fear; it was almost as though she was begging me to help her. I couldn't get her frightened face out of my head. I always wondered what had happened to her.

So even though it was one of the hottest summers on record, I was still wearing my big woollen jumpers that Mammy knitted for us every winter to try and disguise my growing tummy. One day when I asked for a second helping of apple tart after dinner, Mammy remarked that I had got a bit pudgy and that maybe I should stick to one slice. I think Mammy thought that the reason why I was wearing the jumpers was because I was conscious of my weight, which was true in a way but not for the reason she guessed. Nobody seemed to suspect that I might have been pregnant.

I had decided that I needed to tell him; I couldn't deny it any longer. No matter how much I wished it would, the problem wasn't going to go away. It was happening whether I liked it or not, so I wrote to him and told him to meet me in our usual place the following Monday.

That night I sneaked out on my bike after dark. There was no moon to guide me, so the road was eerier than usual, the shadows darker. I saw him when I came around by the shipwreck in the village. He was sitting up on the harbour wall, swinging his legs idly. We hid our bikes behind it like we did every time we met and quickly walked up towards the derelict cottage so nobody would see us. Soon the village became tiny yellow lights with fuzzy halos in the distance as we climbed up the headland.

When we reached the cottage, we went inside. He switched on his torch, casting a beam around the room. The straw roof was damp, and patchy grass grew up through the floor, but that didn't matter because it was a place for us to be together.

He instantly took me into his arms. 'God, I've missed you,' he whispered as he kissed the skin along my neck delicately.

I pulled back from him.

'What is it?' he said. His brow furrowed with concern. 'Did I do something wrong?'

I shook my head. I needed to tell him; it was time. 'I'm preg-nant,' I whispered. It was the first time I had said those words out loud. All the worry over the last few weeks about what I should do, my uncertainty at how he would react when I told him my news and what it meant for our future came tumbling out as tears began to stream down my face. I searched his features for his reaction, I watched the emotions flit from shock, to disbelief, to horror, but after a moment they settled back to calm again.

'How long have you known for?' he said eventually.

'Only a few weeks.'

'Why didn't you tell me before now?'

'I hoped I had got it wrong, but I don't think so,' I said, putting my hand on my tummy. 'I can feel it moving in there.' I pulled up my jumper to expose the bare skin of my stomach, and under the torchlight, we both watched as the taut skin gave a lit-tle shudder as the baby kicked inside me.

His eyes were filled with wonder. 'Wow,' he said. 'There's really a baby in there.'

I nodded. 'I know; it's crazy. Sometimes when I lie in bed at night, I can see it poking its little legs or arms out of me!'

'This is a huge shock, I won't lie,' he said, 'but I love you, we will make it work somehow.'

Relief washed through me; it was all going to be okay. He would take care of me and together we would work it out.

He continued, 'We have to get out of here, though, or they'll try and send you away to one of those homes. I won't let that happen to you. My mother was in one, did you know that?'

I shook my head in horror.

'She and my dad had a baby before me,' he continued. 'Her parents went to the priest for help, and he arranged for her to go into one. After she had the baby, it was taken off her after three days while she was in the bathroom. She didn't even get to say goodbye. She was allowed to come home to her family then. They couldn't understand why she couldn't just forget about it and move on with her life, but she wasn't the same person anymore.

She and my dad married soon after, but Dad always said that she never recovered from it. She took to the bed every July, which was the month she gave birth; I'll never forget it. It still makes me angry that she died not knowing where her baby went.'

Suddenly I was scared. 'Please, don't let that happen to me—I couldn't bear it.'

'I never would. I don't know how I'll do it, but I promise you, I will get enough money together, and we will run away and get married before the baby is born.' He paused. 'Have you been to Dr Fitzmaurice yet?'

I shook my head quickly. 'I don't trust him not to tell Mammy and Daddy.'

'When do you think it's due then?'

'I can't be sure, but I think it could be around October.'

He grimaced. 'We don't have much time then, but what else can we do? We will go somewhere that nobody knows us. We will start over as a young married couple with a baby who have moved to the area.'

My heart soared. I loved this plan. As dire and all as our circumstances were, it would all be worth it in the end. I just had to get through the next couple of months, and then as soon as we had enough money saved, I would get to be with him—we would marry. I would be a wife. I would free of the claustrophobic restrictions of Mammy and Daddy's home. I would have my own home where I would make my own rules. It was all I ever wanted. I didn't know much about babies, but I was sure I would learn quickly, and I wouldn't be alone, I'd have him by my side too.

Chapter 21

Sarah busied around her cottage. She had invited Greg over for something to eat that evening. Her home was small, with just two bedrooms, a bathroom, a kitchen, and living area, but it was cosy, and it was the perfect size for her. She had been born here; it had belonged to her parents and her grandparents before them. It was the only home she had ever known. With its views of the sea from every room, she loved watching how the light changed the colour of the water depending on the weather. At night she could lie in bed and hear the waves crashing off the rocks beneath her.

She walked over to the window where the stray cat was curled up on the ledge and drew the curtains on the lights twinkling across the bay. No matter how much she tried to coax the cat to come in to the warmth of her cottage, it was too frightened. It seemed there was a wildness in it that just couldn't be tamed.

She began setting the table and then wondered if it was too formal? She didn't want it to appear like she had asked him here on a date . . .

Sarah wasn't sure when exactly it had happened, but lately she had realised that something had changed between them. Greg made her feel confused. They had become very friendly over the last two weeks—she was so at ease in his company it was almost as if she had known him for all her life, but somehow he had crossed the line from being a friend into something more, and it scared the life out of her. She was trying to work out her feelings for him, but no matter how much she thought it over, she always arrived at the same conclusion: she had really grown to like him.

She knew nothing could ever happen between them, after all he would be going back to America soon, but her heart couldn't seem to get that message and infuriatingly soared every time she was near him no matter how much she tried to tell herself that falling for Greg was a bad idea. Whenever she was with him, she felt equal parts happy and terrified—but terrified in an exciting way. He was so handsome, well built, and tall, but the most attractive thing about him was that he didn't realise it all. The way his unruly, dark hair fell down over his eyes and he would have to brush it off his face made her breath catch in her chest. He was completely unaware of how good-looking he was, and that made him all the more endearing to her. She didn't want to like him; he was going home next week, so it could only end one way. Every time her heart skipped, she told herself to stop, but it was futile. 'If only it were that simple.' She sighed. 'If only the brain could overrule the heart.'

She had spent the whole day in the post office deliberating what to cook for him. She wasn't a confident cook; she was used to just cooking for herself. She was worried that his American palate would be used to more sophisticated foods. In the end she had decided on a beef and Guinness stew from one of her mother's old recipe books, served with creamy mashed potato.

She heard a knock on the door soon after and felt her heart skip a beat as she let him in. He handed her a bunch of flowers, and she smiled at the gesture. It had been a long time since anyone had given her flowers.

'It smells heavenly in here,' Greg said, breathing in the aroma of the hearty stew.

'It's almost ready,' she said, checking the pot that was bubbling on the Aga.

She opened a bottle of red wine and poured them both a glass. The stove cast an orange glow around the room. Usually when she was home alone in the evenings, she would light a few tea lights, and she had deliberated for far too long earlier about whether to light some tonight or not, but she didn't want Greg to think she was trying to 'set the scene', so she decided not to. Instead she had turned off the main light, so the warm glow of the stove made the place cosy. She knew she was overthinking everything. God, she hated this feeling of liking someone, of being vulnerable. She felt as though she was falling through space and she had no idea of where the bottom was. The feeling of being out of control frightened her. It had been a long time since she had allowed herself to feel like this and look how that had ended the last time. The man had moved to Australia for Christ's sake!

'Cheers,' Greg said, clinking his glass against hers as she handed him his wine.

'So no more leads?' she asked.

Greg sighed. 'I'm running out of time, and I feel like I'm going around in circles.'

'Don't give up now, you're so close, I can feel it,' Sarah encouraged.

The timer sounded on the cooker, and Sarah got up to serve their food. She was relieved when the rich stew folded into the creamy mashed potato. At least it looked edible. She watched anxiously as Greg tasted a mouthful.

'This is delicious, Sarah,' he said, savouring it.

'Really? You can be honest with me.' She lifted a forkful to her mouth and was pleasantly surprised when it actually tasted okay.

'You're a great cook,' Greg said through a mouthful.

'Oh, I'm really not. I followed the recipe to the letter. I was almost counting out the grains of salt,' she said, laughing.

They chatted and laughed the whole time as they ate their food.

'I'm stuffed,' Greg said when they were finished. 'That was the best meal I've had in a long time.' He lowered his cutlery down onto his plate. 'It reminded me of Mom's dinners.' His face took on a sadness as he reminisced on happier times sitting around the table with her.

Sarah reached out across the table and squeezed his hand. She felt a shiver of excitement wash through her. 'I've a Baileys cheesecake for dessert.' She held up her palms to face him. 'Now hands up, I didn't make it myself, I bought it in Ruairí's earlier. I hope you've room for it?'

'Go on,' he said. 'How can I resist one of Ruairí's cakes?'

After the first bottle of wine was finished, Sarah opened another one. They sat down onto the sofa in front of the stove.

'Life is funny,' Greg said. 'If you had told me a month ago I'd be here in this tiny little village in the West of Ireland sitting on a stranger's sofa drinking wine, I would have laughed at you.'

'I'm hardly a stranger,' she said, laughing. 'It just goes to show you, though, that nobody ever knows what life has in store for us. We really just have to live in the moment and enjoy the journey.'

'To the journey.' Greg raised his glass to hers in a toast. 'Thank you for all your help, Sarah, you've been amazing. Let's hope I get some answers before I go home.'

She felt a stab of disappointment at the mention of his return home, and she wasn't sure why. She knew he would be returning back to his life in North Carolina soon, but still, every time he mentioned it, she felt her heart sink. What was it with men hopping on a plane whenever she allowed herself to grow close to them? She could probably pay a therapist to analyse it—actually, scratch that, she didn't want to know.

'Don't mention it,' she said, feeling embarrassed. She could feel the heat creeping up along her face, which only served to make her feel more self-conscious.

She felt as though he was peeling back her layers until soon her very core would be exposed and vulnerable. She needed to stop these feelings from developing into anything more. It was never going to go anywhere. She knew she needed to quell her feelings for him, but it was oh so hard.

Chapter 22

Greg felt as though he was walking on a cloud of marshmallows the whole way home. His feet seemed to bounce along the pavement, and everything seemed a little bit brighter after the evening spent in Sarah's house. Something had changed between them tonight. It was as though the air was electric around them; it was laden with feelings. The charge between them was so strong that Greg was sure if he reached out his hands, he could almost touch it, he wondered if Sarah had felt it too?

The truth was that he was falling head over heels for Sarah, and he was completely powerless to stop himself. After everything that had happened over the last few weeks, he didn't need any more emotional turmoil in his life. He knew he shouldn't jump into anything, but he never could do casual relationships. Despite his best intentions, he always found himself diving straight in, heart first, swept up in the romance of it all, and inevitably, after the initial flames had fanned down, it always came crashing down. But there was something about Sarah that he just couldn't help himself. He really liked her—really, *really* liked her. She was fun to be around, her sunny outlook was infectious, and when you were near her, you couldn't help but feel lifted. He adored her caring nature and the way she was so generous to everyone she met. She always wanted to help people, and nothing was ever too much trouble for her. Selena had been much sharper around the edges, she didn't have Sarah's inherent kindness; Selena only ever did a good turn for somebody if there was something in it for her.

The night sky was jet black, and without any moonlight

to guide the way or streetlights to soften the darkness as he walked, Greg realised just how dark it actually was here compared to back home.

When he reached *Cove View*, he put his key in the door and climbed the stairs to his room. From the landing, he saw that his bedroom door was open and the light was on inside. He was sure he had locked it like he always did when he had been leaving to go to Sarah's earlier on. He hurried inside and got a fright when he saw Maureen was standing at the chest of drawers with her back facing him. She didn't hear him come in.

'What are you doing in here?' he asked.

She startled and dropped what she had been holding. Greg saw the blue cover of his passport falling back down into the open drawer.

'Sorry, Greg, I—I—I was doing a bit of dusting, and I accidentally dropped something in the drawer—'

'Dusting at eleven o'clock at night?'

'I didn't think you were coming home. I thought you might be staying in Sarah's—'

He recognised the deflection tactic for what it was.

'And even if I was, you still have no business in my room!' he said, annoyed by her audacity.

'Well, I'm awfully sorry,' she said in a tone that was anything but. 'Next time I'll ask you for permission before I enter for cleaning!' She stormed out past him in a huff.

He was outraged. She was the one snooping through *his* stuff, and she had the cheek to get snooty with him? He shook his head in despair. The woman was infuriating.

Suddenly he was feeling tired and unable to fight any more battles with her. Even when she was wrong, she never backed down.

'Goodnight, Maureen,' he called angrily after her.

He waited until he heard her footsteps on the stairs before going over to the drawer and checking inside. When he had been coming to Ireland, he hadn't brought any valuables with him, just his passport, kindle and phone charger. His wallet was with him in his coat pocket. He checked through everything, and all of his stuff seemed to be where he had left it. So what had she been looking for then? He didn't think Maureen was a thief, the woman was just plain nosy. She was definitely strange, there was no doubt about it, but when did strange cross over into snooping through somebody's possessions?

Greg climbed into bed and looked at shadows crossing the ceiling. He couldn't sleep as he thought about the strange business of catching Maureen in his room. He lay in the darkness with his mind whirring and worries charging around his head like a murmuration of starlings all night long.

Chapter 23

September 1976

June changed to July, and July changed quickly to August, and soon the long, heady days were being pushed out by the cooler air of September. I didn't get to meet him very often. He was working all hours to get enough money together for us to leave. He had got a job on the fishing boats and was often gone for days on end, but we wrote to one another.

I had taken my savings out of the post office; my communion money and confirmation money had all gone in there as well as any other money I had got over the years, and it had added up nicely. We almost had enough money together and had chosen September 18 as the day we would leave the village. I had marked the date with the tiniest heart on the calendar in my bedroom so Mammy wouldn't notice. I was living for this day. My mind had switched off in school because I knew I would be gone in a few weeks. What would Catechism or theorems matter to me then?

I took great care to make sure my rounded stomach remained hidden; the last thing I wanted was for my parents to discover my secret at the last hour. I was using a safety pin to close my school kilt, but my bump was quite small thankfully.

On the morning of September 17, I woke up feeling achy in my back. When I refused breakfast, Mammy noticed that I was feeling off and asked if I wanted to stay at home that day, but I gritted my teeth together and told her I was fine. If I was hanging around the house, I was worried that she would start to notice something. I was better off away from her watchful eye.

In school that day, the aches grew into a burning feeling, it felt as if there were lots of little fires gathered around the bones of my pelvis. I couldn't bear to sit on my chair, and after the third time I had asked to be excused from Domestic Science to use the toilet, Mrs Dalton began eyeing me suspiciously.

When the bell finally sounded at lunchtime, I sneaked out of the schoolyard and hurried for his house. I knew it was dangerous territory. If Mammy or Daddy happened to be passing through the village and saw me, they would be asking questions, but I needed to see him. I continued along as fast as I could, but I kept stopping with the pain my back.

Eventually I reached his front door, a narrow two-storey house in a terrace. I rapped hard on the knocker. I knew his dad would be at work in the bus yard.

'What are you doing here?' he said as he pulled back the door.

I shook my head. 'I'm not feeling well.'

He quickly brought me inside before any of his neighbours saw us. I stepped into the hallway. It was my first time in his house. I followed him into a basic kitchen with a TV sitting atop the fridge and a battered sofa against the wall. The tiles were dated, and the walls looked as though they hadn't seen fresh paint in years. It was the kind of room that missed a woman's touch.

'Do you want a cuppa?' he asked.

I shook my head. A cup of tea was the last thing I wanted. Suddenly the fire in my back began burning from the centre, spreading out around the sides of my waist before wrapping back around again. I had to grip onto the table until it had passed.

'Do you think it could be the baby?' he asked when I straightened up again. I noticed his eyes were wide with fear.

I shook my head. From the little bit that I knew about labour, you had pains in your stomach. 'I don't think so, it's too early . . . but my back is so sore.'

'Do you think you should go to the doctor just in case?'

'No way!'

'Okay, but I don't think you should stay here—won't your parents be looking for you if you don't get off the school bus today?'

I felt panicked; I knew I couldn't go home in this state. 'Can we go now? Do we have enough money?'

He looked shocked. 'Now? But the plan is to go tomorrow. I'll be collecting my last pay packet in the morning, and we'll go after that. You know the plan—'

Suddenly I was gripped by another vice-like pain across my abdomen.

'What is it? What's wrong with you?' he said, hopping up. 'You're scaring me!'

'I don't think the baby is going to wait until tomorrow,' I said, grimacing.

He grew pale. 'Oh God.' His hands flew up to the back of his head, and he began pacing around the kitchen. 'What are we going to do?' He was panicked. 'Should I get my dad? I know he'd help us!'

I shook my head. 'Please, no, I don't want anyone to know, they'll just tell—ahhhh—' I gasped as I was assailed by another pain. 'I just want us to be together,' I continued when the pain had subsided.

'We will,' he said calmly, 'but first you are going to have a baby, and we need to be ready for that.' He spent a few minutes gathering towels and food.

'Let's go to the cottage,' he said when he had finished. 'It's the only place where no one will find us.'

It was only then that I realised that although we had had a plan to run away together, we had made absolutely no plans for the baby. We hadn't bought any blankets or clothes, let alone a pram. Where was I going to give birth? Neither of us knew anything about birthing babies. I had presumed I would go to the hospital in our new town, but we hadn't given it enough thought. Suddenly I felt ashamed for myself. I was only realising the mammoth responsibility that lay ahead of us, and frankly I wasn't sure if we were ready for it.

Chapter 24

Greg must have fallen asleep eventually as he woke to the mournful cry of seagulls as they soared over the cove. He remembered what had happened the night before and groaned internally. What had Maureen been up to?

He climbed out of bed, opened the curtains, and looked out onto the beautiful Inishbeg morning. He thought about skipping breakfast in the dining room, but then he thought, no, why should he? He had done nothing wrong. He was going to stand his ground and eat his breakfast in the dining room whether Maureen liked it or not.

He entered the dining room and took his usual seat by the window. When Maureen blustered into the room, there was none of her normal chitchat. An awkward atmosphere prevailed as she poured his coffee and he found himself pretending to read something on his phone. She didn't meet his eyes when she placed his plate down on the table.

After breakfast, he decided to call to see Sarah. He was longing to see her. He knew he shouldn't let himself fall for her. After everything he had gone through with Selena, the last thing he needed was more heartache, but he couldn't stop it. It was like he was surfing a wave and he couldn't get off—he didn't *want* to get off. He had never been one to put his head before his heart.

He was glad to see the place was empty as he made his way up to the counter. 'Hi, Sarah.'

'Greg—' She immediately started to blush, and he found his heart soar. God, she was so beautiful. He wanted to squeeze through the hatch and take her into his arms.

'Thank you for last night, I really enjoyed it,' he said.

Her face broke into a smile, which stretched right up to the corners of her eyes. 'Oh, I'm glad. I did too.'

'You'll never guess what happened after I went home?'

'What?' she asked, leaning forward onto the counter.

'I found Maureen in my room going through my stuff.'

'Maureen?' she said in disbelief. 'But why would she do that?'

Greg shrugged his shoulders. 'I'm not sure . . . she said she was cleaning, but it was very odd. There was nothing missing, so I don't think it was anything like that . . .'

'That is so strange. I've known Maureen a long time, and she's a bit nosy all right, but I've never heard of her doing anything like that!'

'I'm starting to think she might know more than she's letting on. She gets funny whenever I mention my search for my birth parents. It's like she's trying to hide something—'

Sarah looked at him wide-eyed. 'You don't think it could be her, do you?'

'What?'

'Well, that Maureen might be your mother—'

'Nah . . .' Greg said, shaking his head. Then he realised that Sarah could be right. Maureen was the right age profile. 'But I don't look like her—' he added, knowing instantly it was lame.

'Sure that doesn't mean anything! It would explain her behaviour.'

He didn't like what Sarah was suggesting. In his head he had images of a tearful reunion, with someone warm and loving, somebody who wanted him, not somebody manipulative and secretive who would go to desperate lengths in order to keep the truth concealed. Maureen wasn't what he wanted in a mother at all.

'Of all the people it could be, I really hope it's not Maureen -'

Sarah began to laugh. 'As the saying goes, "you can choose your friends, but you can't choose your family."'

Suddenly he realised that Sarah was right. There was a very real possibility that Maureen could actually be his mother. And if she was, well that presented a whole new set of problems for him. She clearly wanted nothing to do with him, which didn't bode well for having any kind of relationship with her. It hit Greg then that even if he was successful in finding his birth parents, there was no guarantee of a happy-ever-after ending. He needed to prepare himself for the fact that they might actually be people that he had nothing in common with or, worse still, didn't even like. But there was one fear bigger than all the others, what if his birth parents didn't want to know him? He wouldn't be able to bear the feeling of rejection all over again. There was so much at stake in his search for them, and he was only starting to realise what a lottery it was. His shoulders slumped downwards.

'Look, forget I said anything, she's just nosy,' Sarah said.

Greg knew she was trying to reassure him.

'Yeah, you're probably right,' he said with assurance that didn't really ring true.

'Look, the reason I dropped in was I was wondering if you would like to come to Tadgh's restaurant with me tonight? I've heard such good things about it, and I've been meaning to try it since I've arrived . . . and well, I was wondering if you were free later . . .' He found himself stammering for words. 'I mean, if you're not too busy that is—'

For God's sake, Greg, stop waffling. Get it together! What was the big deal, it was just dinner, but his heart said otherwise as it thumped louder with every word that left his mouth. He didn't want Sarah to think he was asking her on a date, even though he kind of was.

'I mean, if you've already got plans, then I can go another night,' he continued. He was cringing for himself. He sounded like a high school kid asking a girl to go to the prom with him. 'I just wanted to check it out before I go home,' he added as he finished making a fool of himself. He wanted to turn around, walk back out the door, and forget the whole thing.

'Sure, Greg, I'd love to,' she said with an amused smile on her face.

'You would?' He felt himself wash with relief.

She laughed. 'Of course.'

'Okay, great,' he said, trying to recover. 'Will we say

around eight?'

    'Eight is perfect, see you later.'

Chapter 25

September 1976

The walk up the headland was gruelling. The pains were getting closer together now, the urgency emphasised with every one. I would stop to lean on him until it passed, and then we would continue on again, but we were making slow progress, and I was starting to worry that the baby would be born on the hillside.

'Come on,' he urged. 'Just a little bit further, you're nearly there now.' He was trying to be encouraging, but all I could hear were the undertones of panic in his voice.

About halfway up the hillside, I was gripped by a particularly harsh pain, and I felt a flood of water between my legs. It quickly soaked through my clothes, leaving me feeling damp and soggy. The pains instantly ratcheted up a level. They shook my whole body from within, and my teeth chattered together with every one. I heard a noise like a farm animal would make, and I realised with a shock that it was coming from me. I felt pressure bulging between my legs. I was terrified. I wanted to stop it; I wanted to push the baby back inside, but I was powerless. I said a silent prayer for Our Lady to help me. The nuns in school said she always looked after anyone in trouble and boy did I need her help right now.

'Almost there now,' he soothed. He was practically pulling me up the hill at this stage.

I was so relieved when the cottage came into view. My whole body was on fire, I had never felt pain like it; I actually thought I was going to die. Eventually the ground levelled out in front of the cottage, and I stopped to catch my breath. I could see the village sitting under a soft grey mist below us. It had started to drizzle, and little rivulets ran from my hair and spilled down my face.

We reached the threshold of the cottage and stepped inside. It was strange to see it in the daylight instead of under the glow of torchlight. I saw it for what it really was; no more than a dirty hovel. I was gripped by another pain, starting in my back and burning like a white-hot poker all around until it moved in a wave across my stomach. I cried out as I held on to the wall to steady myself.

He began quickly to spread the towels out on the floor, and then he guided me onto them. I felt a hardness pushing between my legs, a burning and an urge to bear down to relieve whatever was causing it. 'I can see the baby!' he shouted in amazement.

I had no choice but to listen to my body and do what it told me to do to make this pain stop.

'You're okay,' he calmed me.

The pain was back again, and I heard myself emit a frightening roar as I pushed. Suddenly the baby slid out, all slippery and warm, and he lifted it up into his arms. I sat forward and saw a tiny blue thing that didn't look like any baby I had ever seen.

'It's a little boy,' he whispered. He rubbed him down with the towel to warm him up, and soon his blue colouring changed to pink as he took his first breath and roared.

My whole body was shaking uncontrollably. I couldn't believe this was happening. He wrapped the baby in a towel and then placed another one around my shoulders. I tried to sit up but noticed crimson blood soaking the towel underneath me. I had seen plenty of calves and lambs born growing up, and this reminded me of those births. I felt like an animal. This whole thing had been shocking, never in my wildest dreams would I have imagined that labour would be this brutal. The crimson pool beneath me was starting to spread. Was this meant to happen? I didn't know what was normal. I was exhausted and just wanted to sleep.

Suddenly we realised we had nothing to cut the cord with.

'I'll go get help,' he said.

'Don't leave me,' I begged. I tried to reach out to him, but my arms were too weak and wouldn't do what I wanted them to. My teeth were chattering, and my body was shivering despite the *blankets he had put around me.*

He leant over and placed my son delicately into my arms.

'I'm sorry,' he said. Then he ran out of the cottage leaving me alone.

Chapter 26

A narrow path wound the short distance from the village out towards the cliff ledge where Tadgh's restaurant was perched. A rickety rail was the only thing separating Greg from the perilous drop below where waves crashed and rolled beneath him, battering against the cliffs. There were no signposts, and only for Sarah had told him where to go, Greg never would have believed there was a restaurant situated up there. The sky was ablaze with the glorious setting sun, and he couldn't help but feel awestruck by the beauty of the place. It was a timely reminder that we are but a dot on time's storybook.

He was a few minutes early so decided to wait outside the door for Sarah. He saw her approach soon after, and as she came down the path towards him, he had time to take in her beauty. The dusky light caught her pretty face, highlighting all its angles and contours.

'Hey,' he said as she got nearer to him.

'Hi there—'

'After you—' He held back the door for her to enter before him.

When Greg stepped inside, he was instantly speechless as he looked around the restaurant. It seemed to be set into a cave. 'Wow!' was all he could manage to say as he took in the natural stone cavity where candlelight sent shadows dancing across the walls.

'It's Inishbeg Cove's best kept secret!' Sarah said with a proud smile.

Oh, how he loved her smile. It made him want to do everything he could to make her smile every hour of every day.

They removed their coats, and Greg saw she was wearing a long silk skirt with a sweater tucked into it. Her hair was tied back in a simple but elegant ponytail. She looked beautiful, he thought, as he cast his eyes down along her body.

The funny thing was, she wasn't his usual type of tall, assertive woman. In fact, she was tiny beside his six-foot-two-inch frame and would fit neatly under the crook of his arm. He normally was attracted to the kind of woman who made you take notice when they walked into a room—not for their beauty but for their innate sense of self. Greg had always thought it was their brash confidence that he found attractive, but Sarah wasn't like that; her confidence was more gentle, more understated, and took a softer approach. She hated being the centre of attention and much preferred when the focus was on other people. She was confident enough in herself not to need to take over a room, and he loved that about her.

'You look amazing,' he whispered.

'Ah, I guess I'm a little bit different to what you normally see me in ...' she said, blushing and looking down at the floor. 'It's amazing what a bit of make-up can do!'

She was self-deprecating as usual, and it made her all the more endearing to him.

A waiter came over and led them towards their table. They followed him through several chambers softly lit just by lanterns and candlelight. Some caverns were so small that they could only sit two tables, and they had to duck their heads as they passed through another one.

Eventually the smaller chambers lead to a larger chamber at the rear of the cave that seated six tables, and their table was tucked into a natural hollow in the wall. It was both intimate and atmospheric—the perfect setting for a special dinner. Greg knew he shouldn't be thinking romantically, but how could you not in a place like this?

'I hope this will be okay for you both?' the waiter said.

'It's perfect, thank you, Senan,' Sarah said, her voice echoing under the low-vaulted ceiling.

They sat down, and Senan handed them the menus before leaving them alone to choose.

'You have to try the crab,' Sarah said straight away before Greg had even opened his.

'Well, after seeing the lengths Tadgh goes to catch them, how could I not?'

'Apparently when Grace Kelly visited Ireland in 1961, she asked to be brought here to try it! Tadgh's parents used to own the restaurant in those days, but they died in a bad car crash.'

'That's awful,' Greg said, feeling for the man.

'It was,' Sarah agreed, 'but even though Tadgh was only eighteen at the time, he stepped up, took it on all by himself, and put his own stamp on it. He's very proud of his food and sources all his ingredients from farms and suppliers around the village. It's quieter here during the winter months, but during the summer the place is booked solid, people come from miles around.'

Senan returned to take their order, and it wasn't long before he brought out a plate of mouth-watering crab claws with golden butter drizzled over them.

'These are amazing,' Greg said, licking his lips. The meat was sweet, juicy and was perfectly complemented with the garlic seasoning. He had never tasted seafood so good. Literally plucked straight from the sea onto his plate. The food was deliberately simple, and Tadgh let the flavours do the talking.

The crab claws were followed by steak for Greg, and Sarah had ordered the turbot. He watched as she brought a large forkful close to her mouth. She enjoyed her food, and it was good to see. She wasn't obsessed with working out and avoiding sugar like Selena had been.

'Did you know one of the Michelin reviewers called here last year and Tadgh ran them out of the place?' Sarah said.

'What?' Greg asked in disbelief. 'He kicked them out of his restaurant?'

Sarah nodded. 'He said he didn't want to get caught up in any of that business. He doesn't need the foodies of the world beating down a track to Inishbeg Cove. He wants this place to stay small so he can give every customer attention to detail. If it went in one of those guides, he's afraid it would lose that intimacy and it would be a very different kind of restaurant to what he wants. His restaurant is all about wholesome—and I quote—"natural food not bird-sized portions dressed with fancy foams."'

'Sounds like he's a man of principle!'

'He's very passionate about what he does,' Sarah said, raising a forkful to her mouth.

'You can taste it in the food he cooks,' Greg said, savouring another mouthful.

The waiter came over and topped up their wine glasses.

'Thanks, Senan,' Sarah said.

He was several years younger than Tadgh, but their likeness was uncanny. 'Is he Tadgh's son? They're so alike one another.'

'No, that's his younger brother. Tadgh has been looking after him since their parents died. Senan was only six at the time.'

'So even though Tadgh was only a teenager, he raised his kid brother and ran a restaurant?'

Sarah nodded. 'Uh-huh. There was only the two of them, and Tadgh was adamant that Senan was staying with him and that he would raise him. And that's what he did. The village rallied around them, of course; there was a rota drafted up for dinners, to help with laundry, to collect Senan from school or babysit him when Tadgh was in the restaurant. Everyone did their share, but all credit to Tadgh, Senan has grown into a fine young man. He's in fifth year now, but he helps Tadgh out in the restaurant in the evenings and weekends. You won't find a more helpful or polite teenager around.'

From what Greg had heard of Tadgh, he was definitely the brooding intense type, but maybe his past explained the reason he was like that. Being in this village had made him realise that everyone had a story to tell. It was easy to let your head get caught up in your own problems, but you could be guaranteed that everyone had their own worries. Sometimes you just had to ask them.

'So anyway, did Maureen say or do anything else?' Sarah

asked as they tucked into dessert.

Greg shook his head. 'She was a bit off at breakfast but no . . . I can't stop thinking about what you said to be honest.'

Greg had left the post office earlier feeling deflated. Sarah's suggestion that Maureen might be his mother was really bothering him.

'Ah look, never mind that, I shouldn't have said anything . . . I'm sorry this trip hasn't been as successful as you'd hoped,' Sarah said. 'But you still have time.'

'Hey, it's hardly your fault—I just hope I get to the bottom of it soon. I'm already over halfway through.'

'I think the answers are here somewhere, Greg, don't lose hope yet.'

As Greg walked Sarah home that night, the moonlight had turned the sea shimmering silver as they walked along the cliff path back to the village.

When they reached her cottage, they stood chatting on her doorstep, listening to the waves lashing against the base of the cliff beneath them in the background.

Suddenly he reached out and touched his fingertips with hers. 'Thank you for a wonderful evening, Sarah,' he said. 'I don't think I'll ever forget it—you, this place—it's all been wonderful.'

'Goodnight, Greg,' she said before pulling her hand away from his. She turned away from him and began walking up the path.

'Goodnight, Sarah,' he whispered as he watched her slip inside her cottage.

*

Sarah put her key in the lock and let herself into her cottage. The evening spent with Greg in Tadgh's restaurant had been wonderful. Although she had been there many times over the years, she knew that she would never forget that night. She had hardly dared to breathe as he had touched his fingers to hers while they had been saying goodbye. She had felt a jolt of electricity flood through her veins. As she had allowed her fingers to meet his, she couldn't help but wonder what did this mean? Was it just a friendly gesture, or did it mean something more? Did he have feelings for her, or did he just want a casual fling, a holiday romance to pass the time in Inishbeg Cove? Reluctantly, she had let her hand fall away from his. It was all well and good for him, going back to his old life in America, but she would be the one left behind to pick up the pieces of her broken heart. She knew that's what would happen because she had been there before. It had taken her a long time to build herself back up again after Conor had stopped writing to her when she realised that their relationship was over and that he had found a new love in Australia. What was she thinking opening herself up again? It was crazy allowing herself to fall for Greg.

She climbed into bed, and her mind whirred unhappily in the darkness as she waited for sleep to come. Thoughts swam about in her head. Why did he have to be from America? She had been happy before he had arrived and turned her life upside down. What did the future hold for her? All those nights she had sat on her own, longing to share her life with someone to chase the loneliness away. Now she had a chance of that, but he was leaving before it could even begin, and she felt cheated. Her mother had had a saying, *'What's for you, won't pass you.'* It obviously just wasn't meant to be.

Chapter 27

Greg walked home thinking about the evening he had spent with Sarah. It had been magical. Every part of it—from the most romantic setting, to the delicious food, and then the walk home under the cool night sky beneath the light of a million stars—it had all been perfect.

Sarah was everything he had ever wanted in a woman, someone kind and caring, a beautiful person inside and out. She had turned on its head everything he had previously thought were the ideal qualities in a partner. He now realised he clearly didn't know himself well at all.

It was typical that he had found her on the other side of the Atlantic. He felt that familiar anti-climactic slump that he always felt lately whenever he thought about going home. In the interests of self-preservation, he needed to stop this now before he fell any deeper. He knew his fragile heart couldn't withstand much more battering. He couldn't risk giving himself to another again because he would never survive more heartache. He would be fine once he returned to North Carolina, he told himself. Once he was back on US soil, he would feel differently and he would forget all about this crazy trip. But no matter how much he tried to convince himself, something inside him told him that Sarah would be on his mind for a lot longer than he realised.

As Greg entered the guesthouse that night and walked into the lobby, he saw a blade of light coming from underneath the door into Maureen's living room. He stopped outside it and listened for a moment. He could hear the noise of laughter from something she was watching on the television. Finding her in his room was still really bothering him.

He couldn't shake it off, no matter how much she denied that anything untoward had happened.

That night he lay in bed looking at the ceiling as the hours changed. It had started to rain outside, and he listened to it pitter-patter off the roof. His head chased between his fruitless search for his birth parents, to thoughts of leaving Sarah when he returned home, and back again to Maureen's strange behaviour. In the stark clarity that night-time ramblings always brought, he had to admit that it had been a crazy idea anyway travelling halfway across the world to a place he had never even heard of. He still hadn't managed to uncover who his parents were, and it was starting to look as though his whole trip to Ireland had been a gigantic waste of time. What had he expected? Had he really believed that people would open up their doors to him, confess their long-held secrets, and invite him into their families? He had been naïve in coming here.

He still couldn't shake his doubts about Maureen. He was sure she knew something; in fact, he was certain of it. There was something about her behaviour that kept niggling at him. He was completely frustrated by his lack of progress. He was going home soon, and he needed to get some answers. He had tried treading gently but it had proved fruitless. Maybe he should just have it out with Maureen for once and for and all. He couldn't go back to North Carolina with any loose ends. Once he was back in the US, it would be impossible to get to the truth. It would be game over then. Maybe it was the wine, but he suddenly found himself pulling back the duvet and planting his two feet on the floor.

The room was chilly in the cool night air. He threw on his robe and treaded softly down the stairs. The guesthouse was quiet, save for the sound of creaking pipes in the attic; it would be several hours yet before the noise of the breakfast rush would ring between its walls.

When he reached the lobby, he lifted the bell off the reception desk, but then something stopped him. What was he supposed to say to her? How could he word it? She would think he was completely deluded. Then another voice within him said, *to hell with it,* and before he could change his mind, he had lifted the bell again and rung it.

It took a few moments, but after a while a bleary-eyed Maureen appeared. 'Greg, what's the matter?' she said, rubbing her eyes.

'Well, something has been bothering me—'

She looked at the clock on the wall behind the desk. 'At three fifty-one a.m.? Unless it's the location of the fire extinguisher, you'd better go back to bed.'

He shook his head. He was here now—in for a dime, in for a dollar—he needed to ask the questions which had been sitting heavily on his mind.

'I can't wait any longer.' He took a deep breath. 'I need to ask you if you know who my birth parents were?'

Chapter 28

Maureen's mouth hung open as her expression changed to aghast. Greg felt as though he was waiting an eternity for her to speak. Then she did something he wasn't expecting—she laughed.

'What's so funny?' he asked.

'I most certainly do not, Greg.'

'Well then, why have you been acting so bloody odd?' he said, losing his cool with her.

'I am not!' she said indignantly. 'Who's the one waking me up in the middle of the night? That's odd!' She pulled the cord of her dressing gown tighter around her waist.

'Yes, you are! First, you were trying to warn me off. Then, I find you snooping through my things—'

'I only told you to be careful. I just didn't want you upsetting people in our village, we're a community, we look after one another, that's all it was. Honest, to God, you Americans love a bit of drama!' She shook her head, clearly exasperated by him.

'It still doesn't explain why you were going through my stuff.'

'Oh, for heaven's sake!' she threw her hands up in despair. 'I thought we've been over this, I told you I was cleaning!'

Greg grew frustrated. She wasn't backing down, and although he still didn't quite believe her, he didn't see what else he could do.

'So you don't know anything that might help me?'

'No, Greg.' She sighed heavily. 'No, I don't. Now if you don't mind, I'd like to get some sleep. Some of us have an early start in the morning.'

*

When Greg finally fell asleep that night, he dreamed strange and disturbing dreams. He woke in a sweat after one particularly awful nightmare where Sarah and Maureen were trapped in a room together. The room was filling with water, and they were both screaming for him to let them out. There was a big padlock on the door, but he couldn't find the key to free them. They were banging frantically, begging for him to open it but no matter how hard he searched, he couldn't find the key. Suddenly his mom and dad had appeared and chastised him for not being able to help them. Then Maureen and Sarah had started to drown. Their panicked voices were still ringing in his head as he bolted upright in the bed. Beads of sweat dotted his brow, and he felt a flood of relief when he realised it was just a dream. He breathed in deeply, waiting for his heart rate to calm down.

Greg fell back asleep sometime later, and it was after ten when he finally woke up. As he ran soap over his body in the shower, he had an uneasy feeling in his stomach. He decided to skip breakfast; if he was honest, he was feeling more than a little embarrassed by his 3 a.m. visit to Maureen. It had seemed so urgent at the time, but in the cold light of day, he realised just how ridiculous he must have seemed waking her up like that in the dead of the night. She must think him insane. He still thought she knew more than she was admitting, but what more could he do? He had no choice but to take her word for it.

He headed out for his daily run around the village to help clear his head. In the distance, lingering morning mist hung suspended over the navy blue mountain tops, and droplets of dew clung to the golden yellow furze. Greg loved the colours up there; they were vibrant and rich and so full of drama. He drove his body on against the bracing wind, even though his calves ached and his hamstrings burned as his feet pounded the headlands. It felt like a penance of sorts for his night-time antics. As he wrapped back around by the cove, the wind spread through the grassy dunes like a silver wave.

After his run, he called in to see Sarah. His morning visits to her had become one of the highlights of his day. It was crazy to think how he had only known her for a few weeks, and yet in that time she had become a huge part of his life. It was yet another thing he would miss when he returned home.

'I really enjoyed last night,' he said. 'That restaurant is something special. I've never been anywhere like it.'

'I'm glad you liked it. I couldn't let you leave Inishbeg Cove without going there.'

'So have you heard anything back from Irish Post?' he asked.

She shook her head. 'Not yet.'

'No news is good news,' he said with forced optimism.

'Well, hopefully . . .' she said, trying her best to sound upbeat in response.

'I had a chat with Maureen last night,' Greg continued.

'Really? And?' She put down the envelopes and stood up off her chair, resting her two elbows on the counter, giving him her full attention.

'She denied it all.'

'Well, that's good, isn't it? At least you can rule her out now,' Sarah said.

Greg shook his head. 'I don't know what it is. I still have my suspicions about her.'

'Look, Greg,' she said, 'if she is hiding something, the truth will come out eventually, it always does in the end.'

He nodded. 'I hope you're right. Short of waterboarding her, I don't see what else I can do.'

Sarah threw back her head and laughed. God, how he adored her laugh. It was sweet and carefree, like eating ice cream on a summer's day.

'I wouldn't recommend that to start with—maybe try something a bit gentler first like making her listen to Britney Spears music on repeat?'

He loved her sense of humour, the way she was on his wavelength. She just got him. Their eyes met, and she suddenly stopped laughing. She looked away from him quickly and picked up the pile of envelopes once more and began shuffling through them.

The bell tinkled then, and Mrs Manning entered. She was

still using the stick to get around and made her way slowly up to the counter. 'I . . . eh . . . should probably go and let you get back to work,' Greg said.

'Every time I'm in here, you seem to be here too,' Mrs Manning remarked to Greg as he passed her on the way out. 'You must have an awful lot of postcards to be sending back to America!' A wry smile was playing on her lips.

Greg felt heat creep up his face. He knew the old woman was teasing him, but were his feelings for Sarah that obvious? He quickly mumbled something resembling goodbye and hurried out the door, eager to escape the post office.

'Did I say something wrong?' Mrs Manning said to Sarah with faux innocence after he had left. The old lady was clearly enjoying herself. 'So how are you today, Sarah love?'

'I'm great, Mrs Manning. And yourself?'

'Fabulous! Every day you wake up at my age is a bonus!' she said with her deep, throaty laugh. The sides of her eyes crinkled with mischief. She had purple eye shadow on her lids and fire-red lipstick. Even at the age of ninety-two, she was so glamorous. She had once been an actress in Dublin and had been quite famous apparently. Sarah didn't know the full story, but from the bits she had heard, Mrs Manning had had her heart broken and escaped to Inishbeg Cove to get away from it all and ended up never leaving.

'You and the Yank seem to be getting on well?' she continued.

Sarah could feel herself beginning to blush. She felt embarrassed that Mrs Manning had picked up on it; she always was useless at hiding her feelings. She was like a lovesick teenager whenever Greg was near, and she hated it. She hated how out of control she felt. In a little over a week he would be leaving this place, and they would both be going back to their real lives. She was annoyed with herself. She should be concentrating on doing all she could to save her post office instead of letting her head get carried away by Greg.

'Anyway, how's everything?' Sarah asked, keen to change the subject.

'Well, my news is that John—that's my son in Australia—

he doesn't like me living alone since I had that fall. He wants to put me in a home, but I won't hear of it.'

'I'm sure he just worries about you,' Sarah said.

'But I've always been independent. He knows I would never survive in a home. Whatever about living here on my own—it'd definitely be the final nail in my coffin if I went into one of those places!' she said theatrically. 'They're full of old people.'

Sarah had to hide her smile; the woman was in her nineties but didn't classify herself as old. Sarah hoped that she would have half of her spirit when she was that age.

'Any word yet from Irish Post?' Mrs Manning asked.

'Nothing yet, Mrs Manning,' Sarah said with a heavy sigh akin to air leaving a punctured tyre. Everyone that came through the door seemed to be asking the same question. It was all anyone in the village seemed to be talking about.

'Well, fingers crossed. This isn't the last they've heard from us, we won't take it lying down, we'll put up a good fight.'

Sarah smiled sadly. Her village was the best in the word, she knew they all had her back, but she couldn't help but feel like a failure. There was such pressure sitting heavily on her shoulders to save the post office, and she didn't know what to do. She was sure she was going to let them all down.

'Of course, we will,' Sarah said, forcing optimism into her voice even though she felt anything but.

Chapter 29

The smell of Maureen's cooking wafted up the stairs as Greg came down for breakfast the following morning. He had decided that he was going to have to face her eventually; he couldn't hide from her forever.

He entered the dining room and greeted the other guests —a couple from Northern Ireland and a woman from Dublin —before sitting down at his usual spot by the window. There was no sign of Maureen. He noticed there was an envelope waiting for him on his place setting on the table. It was simply addressed to: *The American*. Curiosity overtook him, and he quickly ripped along its gummed seal. He took out a folded sheet of paper, opened it up, and read. His heart felt as though it had stopped, and his hands felt clammy. It simply said: *'Go home.'* He looked around the room, suddenly feeling as though he was being watched, but the other guests were all chatting and eating as normal.

Maureen came out then with a tray and placed his usual breakfast down in front of him. 'Good morning, Greg,' she sang. 'I must say I prefer seeing you at this time instead of in the middle of the night.'

'This letter, where did it come from?' he asked quickly, ignoring her barbed remark.

'I found it in the postbox this morning, and since you're the only American staying here, I presumed it was for you. Why, is something wrong?'

He shook his head. 'Oh, it's nothing—'

'Will you have tea or coffee?' she continued.

'Coffee, please,' he said, folding the letter and sticking it into his pocket to show to Sarah later. After Maureen's recent behaviour, his first instinct was that it was from her, but she was acting very normally and didn't seem to be the least bit anxious around him. Surely she wasn't that good an actress?

After breakfast he decided to skip his run. He went straight to see Sarah. He hurried through the door and saw the reclusive Ida and Timmy O'Malley were waiting in the queue while Sarah was serving someone he didn't know. The first customer left, and then it was Ida's turn.

'Ah, Greg, how are you getting on?' Timmy said, swinging around to him as Ida moved up to the counter. 'Did you have any luck finding your parents yet?'

Greg shook his head. 'Not yet, I'm afraid. I keep coming up against dead ends.'

'It was a different era back then,' Timmy said sadly.

Suddenly a voice spoke, catching Greg unawares. He looked up to see Ida was talking to him. 'You should leave the past in the past,' she said. Her voice was measured but forceful. 'No good comes from raking over old ground.'

Greg had never heard her speak before, and judging from Sarah's and Timmy's open-mouthed reactions, they weren't used to hearing her voice either. He felt his heart start to hammer and pinpricks of sweat broke out on the back of his neck. First Maureen had told him off, then the letter had arrived this morning, and now Ida was cautioning him too. It felt like he was getting warnings everywhere he went.

'Ida,' he said curtly. 'How are you today?'

The woman grunted a reply before turning and leaving the shop without finishing what she had come to do. Greg couldn't help but feel uneasy. There was something about Ida that always made him feel this way. Something about her made him fearful. It was as if the woman had a sixth sense; a warning from her was a warning that should be heeded.

Sarah looked at Timmy and back to Greg again. 'What was that about?' she asked, clearly dumbfounded by Ida's behaviour.

'Aragh, never mind her,' Timmy said, looking over at the door.

'Maybe she's right,' Greg said with worry lacing his voice. His arrival in the village had unsettled someone; the question was who? 'Maybe whoever it is doesn't want to be found . . .'

'Take anything that that one says with a pinch of salt, you know what she is like,' Timmy said, looking at Sarah for backup.

Sarah nodded and forced a smile on her face, but Greg knew she was only doing it to reassure him.

'She wasn't always like that you know,' Timmy continued.

'Oh really?' Sarah said, her interest piqued.

Timmy nodded. 'She's a strange fish all right, but she used to be like all the young ones running round here when she was younger. Her parents couldn't keep a hold on her. She was pure wild; she was courting a fella from over the road. Then her father Leamy died. A quare fella was Leamy. He had been the herbalist in the village, as had his father before him. Well when he died, Ida took over for him for a while, but she just stopped one day and wouldn't help anyone. She turned everyone away from the door no matter what you called to her with. She didn't go out anymore with the young ones, she kept herself to herself, and she's been that way ever since.'

Greg was finding it hard to marry this image that Timmy was portraying of Ida. It was hard to imagine her having ever being fun-loving and carefree, but then again, grief did strange things to people. He, of all people, knew that.

After Timmy had left and they were alone, he took out the letter that had landed on his table earlier to show to Sarah. 'This arrived at the guesthouse this morning,' he said, handing it to her.

Sarah gasped as she read it. 'There's no postmark or address or anything, so it looks as though it was hand delivered.'

'Do you think it could be from Maureen?' he asked.

Sarah paused thoughtfully. 'Well, maybe . . . but after what has just happened here this morning, I think perhaps Ida knows more than she's willing to share too . . . Why else was she warning you off unless she has something to hide herself?' she said. 'I know she's strange, but I've never seen her get involved in anything before. Why is she suddenly so vehement about this?'

Greg shrugged.

Sarah continued. 'I think we're on the right track, Greg.

I can feel it. Either Maureen or Ida know something, we just need to figure out what ...'

Chapter 30

September 1976

Despite my exhaustion, I began to cradle the infant. My arms felt stiff at first, unaccustomed to holding a baby, but gradually I felt my muscles start to relax as I eased into it. As I looked down at my newly born son, I couldn't believe how small he was; I had never seen a baby so tiny. He suddenly started mewling and balling his little fists angrily. My arms were jaded as I tried to jiggle him up and down, but his little mouth opened in a large, angry o-shape, and he just cried harder and more furiously. I didn't know what to do; I felt like such a failure because I couldn't soothe him. He was only minutes old and already I was letting him down. The weight of responsibility of what we had done was crushing. How had we been so naïve to think that we could deliver a baby and take care of it on our own? We had been selfish, thinking of our-selves and our own desires first and not the infant who was put-ting their trust in us to take care of it. Now my dreams seemed foolish. I didn't know the first thing about caring for a baby. At a loss what to do, I started to sing to him the lullaby 'is ceol mo chroí, thú' that my mother once sang to me, and suddenly he began to calm. I looked down upon his downy face, and he stared back up at me. His eyes were deep pools of navy blue as he took me in. It was as if we both shared a deep familiarity, a sense of know-ing one another well already. I knew then that his needs would always come first, and I made a promise to do whatever it took to keep him safe.

Chapter 31

Greg didn't fancy spending the evening sitting in his bedroom in the guesthouse alone with his thoughts, so he decided go next door to *The Anchor* for a drink. The fire was glowing in the grate, and the air smelled strongly of wood smoke. Skipper lazily opened half an eye as he entered but closed it back down again, satisfied that all was well in the pub.

Greg was the only person in the place, and Jim was standing watching the weather forecast on the TV. It was so different to the night of the céilí when it had been thronged full of people dancing to the lively music. Greg perched himself up on a stool at the bar and ordered a pint. The creamy taste of Guinness had grown on him over the last couple of weeks.

'What will you have, Greg?'

'A pint please, Jim.' He had learnt in his short time in Ireland that you didn't order a 'pint of Guinness'. Guinness was just referred to as 'a pint'.

Jim set about pulling the dark stout into the glass. He left the pint to settle for a minute before adding the creamy head on it.

'So how're things?' Jim asked as he placed the glass down in front of Greg.

'Truthfully? They've been better,' he answered with a heavy sigh. He decided against telling Jim about the poison pen letter. He couldn't shake his suspicions that Maureen was involved somehow.

'No luck tracking down your parents then?'

Greg shook his head. 'I just keep hitting dead ends. I don't think they want to be found ...'

'You still have some time left, don't lose heart ,' Jim counselled before leaving him alone to nurse his pint.

Greg was enjoying the soothing feeling as the alcohol took effect and began to numb him from his painful reality. Time wasn't on his side, his end of the egg timer was rapidly running out of sand, and he knew that if he went back home without any answers, then his search would be over. If he didn't uncover the truth now while he was in the village, he never would.

When it was finished, he ordered another one.

'So where's Sarah tonight?' Jim asked as he placed the second pint down in front of him. 'You two seem to be getting along like two peas in a pod lately . . .' There was a playful smile dancing on the corners of his lips.

'She's become a good friend to me, that's all.' Greg knew he was blushing, and the more he became aware of it, the more he felt the heat colour his face.

'I never suggested otherwise,' Jim said, grinning at him.

'Well, anyway . . .' Greg began to fluster. 'I'm going home next week, so nothing is going to happen—'

'So let me get this straight,' Jim said, leaning in towards Greg. 'You *do* have feelings for Sarah?'

'It's complicated,' Greg said, allowing his elbows to slump down onto the bar.

'It doesn't need to be,' Jim said matter-of-factly. 'Does she know how you feel?'

'No—'

'Well, why don't you tell her?'

'Because it'll just make everything harder in the long run . . . and besides'—Greg sighed—'I don't know if she's even that into me . . .'

'Look, Greg, I've known Sarah all her life. I mean it, I remember her as a baby. Trust me, I haven't seen a sparkle like that in her eyes in such a long time.'

'Really?' A tiny flame of hope began to fill Greg's heart.

'Yes, really—Sarah doesn't open her heart up too easily.'

'Do you really think she likes me?'

Jim nodded. 'I do.'

'I've never met anyone else like her,' he whispered, finally daring to admit out loud what had been in his heart for the last while.

'Why spend your last few days fighting against it when you could have something special before you leave? You have one shot, use it wisely, Greg.'

Jim busied himself in the bar leaving Greg to think over his words. As he sat in the pub by himself, he couldn't help but miss her company. Was Jim right? Should he risk telling Sarah how he felt? Even if the feelings were unrequited? If there was a chance that Sarah felt the same way about him, shouldn't he at least try? Surely a few days together was better than nothing at all, but then the rational side of his brain would kick in and tell him that he was crazy. Selena had stripped his bare heart out of his chest and torn it to shreds. How could he ever allow himself be vulnerable to someone else?

He had to keep on reminding himself that it wasn't real. It was just a holiday romance where everything felt more intense because the time he had with her was so short. He was on the rebound; he had been cast adrift after losing his mother and then Selena too, and he was desperately searching for a branch to cling to. His feelings were just heightened by the change of scenery; it would be different once he was back home. But yet something within him told him it was stronger than that, they shared a deeper connection, and he was sure he'd never felt that with anyone else before.

As he sat brooding over it all, his phone beeped on the bar in front of him with a message. He picked it up and saw it was from Sarah. It simply said, 'Can you come over?'

His heart fell. It wasn't like her to text him like that. Something must be wrong.

He pushed the stool back and stood up to leave. He picked up his jacket from where it was hanging over the stool and slid his arms down into the sleeves.

'Where are you off to? You haven't finished your pint,' Jim asked.

'It's Sarah, she asked me to call over,' Greg said quickly.

'Good man, Greg,' Jim said with a wink. 'That's the spirit.'

Chapter 32

Greg hurried out of the pub and headed straight for Sarah's house. When he reached her cottage, smoke streamed out of the two little chimneys sitting on each gable end of the roof, hitting the cool night air in small cumulous clouds.

He pushed open the gate and walked up the little path. He knocked gently on the timber door and waited.

'Greg—' she said when she opened the door for him to come in. 'Thanks for coming.' He followed her into the cottage where the stove was lighting, giving the place a cosy feel. He studied her face for clues as he wondered why she had called him. Greg noticed she looked pale and drawn.

'Is everything okay?' he asked as he removed his hat and gloves, basking in the warmth of the cottage.

'I'm sorry for texting you so late, but I didn't know who else to ask—' Worry lines creased a V between her eyes.

'What's happened?'

'A letter arrived from Irish Post this afternoon. It's about the post office. I'm sorry, Greg, but I didn't know who else to call.'

'Well, what does it say?'

'That's the thing . . . I can't bring myself to read it—when I opened the letter and saw whom it was from, I put it back in again, and I've been staring at the envelope ever since. I'm terrified it'll be bad news, Greg.'

'It might not be,' he said. 'The petition from the villagers might have worked.'

She shook her head doubtfully. 'Oh, I don't know . . .'

'Do you want me to read it for you?' he offered.

'Would you mind?'

'Not at all.'

She took the letter from where it was sitting on her kitchen table and handed it to him. He noticed her hands were trembling. He removed the paper from the envelope, unfolded it, and read down through it. He felt himself sink further with every line he read.

'Well, go on—what does it say?' she asked before he had finished.

'I'm sorry—' he said.

'What is it?' Her eyes were begging him for good news, and his heart broke that he wasn't going to be able to do that.

'Well . . . they have received the petition and have noted the villagers' concerns . . .' he began, '. . . but the closure will still go ahead as planned. I'm so sorry, Sarah.' He walked over and put his arms around her. She crumpled in against him, defeated and broken. A few weeks ago he had never met Sarah, he didn't even know of her existence, and now here she was in his arms, leaning on him for comfort. They had both been living lives at opposite sides of the world unbeknownst to either of them that their paths were set to cross. You never knew what life had in store for you. In just a few weeks she had become such a big part of his life.

'I've let everyone down,' she whispered.

'No, you haven't, you've tried your best.'

'But it wasn't enough.'

He hated seeing her like this and not being able to do something to fix it. She didn't deserve it; she was a good person and worked so hard for the village and everyone in it.

As she stood in his arms, he breathed in the scent of her lemony shampoo. She was so close to him that her breath was warm on his skin. He thought about what Jim had said to him. There was no way he could tell her how he felt. It wasn't fair. She didn't need any more complications or drama in her life.

*

Greg had left Sarah's cottage that night feeling completely deflated. He wanted to help her, but what could he do? He could hardly fund the post office himself.

He had returned to *Cove View* and crept up the stairs to his room without being heard. His heart was flooded with sadness as he thought of Sarah when he went to sleep that night.

Not wanting to face Maureen, Greg decided to take his breakfast in the pub the next morning. Skipper wandered over lazily to greet him, and Greg rubbed his silky ears before sitting down at a table by the window.

'The head on you!' Jim remarked as he placed his plate down on the table in front of him.

'Cheers, Jim,' Greg mumbled.

'You look like you didn't sleep a wink,' Jim continued. 'Did you see Sarah after?'

'It wasn't like that,' Greg said quickly in case Jim was getting the wrong end of the stick. 'Sarah got some more bad news actually—'

Jim's smile deflated like a three-day-old balloon. 'Is everything okay?'

'Well it's the post office, it looks as though this closure is definitely going ahead.'

Jim shook his head dolefully. 'Nobody stops capitalism.'

'But surely the local politicians can see what is happening? I just wish there was something I could do to help her. I feel so useless,' Greg said.

'They're all living in big cities and towns—they've no idea what life is like for people living in isolated communities in rural Ireland,' Jim said. 'The only thing that those people listen to is votes!'

'That's it,' Greg cried as suddenly a thought started to take seed in his brain. 'You're right!' The idea was still vague, but it was enough to give him something to cling to. 'That's what I need to do! Just you wait and see. Inishbeg Cove might be a small village, but those hotshots in Dublin have seen nothing yet!'

Chapter 33

Greg hurried up the stairs after he had eaten his breakfast. He went into his room, shut the door, and took his laptop out from his suitcase where he had stored it in the wardrobe. When he had been packing to come to Ireland, he had had a vague notion of keeping on top of work emails while he was away, but in reality, he hadn't taken it out once since he had arrived in the village.

Jim's words were still spinning around inside his head. He was right; the only way to save the post office was to put pressure on the local politicians. They needed to get the word out about what was going on in Inishbeg Cove. The politicians wouldn't want bad publicity in their area. It was then that the idea came to him about organising a protest march in the village. They could tell the media about it to raise awareness of what was happening. Maybe some of the local papers would even turn up to cover it! If they could just get a little bit of publicity, then surely that would help to highlight the village's concerns and put a bit of pressure back on the government.

Greg opened up a blank document on his laptop and began drafting a poster calling the villagers to come and march to save the post office. He knew time wasn't on his side; he was going home the following week, so although it didn't leave much time to organise it, he decided to arrange the march for the next Saturday. He would ask the shops and businesses to put the poster up in their windows.

When he had finished working on the poster, he began typing up a sort of press release to send out to the newspaper editors. Although he had never written one in his life before, he figured any attempt was better than nothing.

Except for short breaks for food, Greg stayed in his room the whole day working on the plan. He had spent a lot of time using Google to find the names of local media contacts and political figures. The Internet in Inishbeg Cove was patchy at the best of times, and it was even worse in the guesthouse. It took a long time, but eventually he managed to gather the information together. He knew he would need a bit more help, but at least he had made a start. He could always ask Sarah or some of the villagers for more information. When he finally closed down his laptop that evening and switched off the light for sleep, he felt happy that he was doing *something* to help—even if his plan didn't work, at least he would have tried.

Greg rose early the next morning, keen to start the day. Dawn had broken through the dark, and the salmon pink sky was slowly transmuted into white spring light as the sun rose over the cove. Seagulls squawked, arcing gracefully over the trawlers returning to shore to unload their catch.

After he had dressed and ate breakfast, he went to the shop and bought a packet of envelopes. Then he headed into the café. He ordered a coffee and scone from Ruairí and took a seat. There were already a few villagers in the place. The sea-swimmers had taken the seats by the fire, and the café was full with the sound of contented chatter. He took out his laptop once again to finish off his plan.

'You're looking busy this morning,' Ruairí remarked as he placed the coffee and scone down on the table beside him.

Greg pushed his laptop to the side to make way for the plate. 'What do you know about press releases?' he asked, looking up from the screen.

'Not a lot, why?'

Greg explained what he was doing to Ruairí.

'Has Sarah given you a job to do? I thought you were supposed to be here on holiday, eh?'

Greg began to blush at Ruairí's teasing. 'She doesn't know a thing about it actually,' he said quietly. 'I just want to help her . . . I hate seeing how worried she is. Will you have a read of what I've written so far?'

'Sure.' Ruairí crouched down beside him and began reading.

'It looks good to me,' he said when he'd finished. 'It certainly highlights the village's concerns. Fair play to you, Greg.' Ruairí clapped him on the back and went back to serve his other customers while Greg continued to work away, tweaking it word by word until he finally felt it was coming together.

With the media ticked off his list, the next thing he needed to do was to try and get the politicians on board, but Greg soon realised that this was going to be more difficult than he thought because he couldn't understand the Irish political system. He had spent a lot of time the night before trying to research the local political representatives but had got nowhere. At home they had Members of Congress, but the system was different in Ireland, and he was getting confused. To make matters worse, some of their titles were in Gaelic and he wasn't sure what the terms stood for.

He looked around the café and saw that the morning rush had quietened down a bit, and Ruairí was cleaning off a table beside him.

'Perhaps you could help me again for a minute, Ruairí?' he called, beckoning him over.

'Fire away—'

'Well, I've been trying to find out online who the local government representatives are but I feel like I'm going around in circles—I keep seeing these *Teach-ta Dallies* but I don't really get it.'

Ruairí laughed at his weak pronunciation of the Gaelic words.

'It's pronounced *Chochta Daw-la*. *Teachta Dála* is the Irish term for member of the parliament, which we call *Dáil Éireann*. We refer to them as TDs for short, and Inishbeg Cove is represented by three TDs in the Dáil. We also have the local counsellors representing various political parties who haven't been elected as TDs but are always hungry to get into power, so it would be worth getting them involved too —they're all going head to head for the election later this year, so they'll want to be seen lending support to your campaign. They'll welcome any opportunity to shout about the damaging policies of the current government. Make sure you tell them about the march; they won't miss a chance to have their faces shown, especially if there's a photo opportunity involved,' Ruairí said wryly.

'This so helpful, thank you, Ruairí,' Greg said, busily writing down the names of the politicians as he called them out to him.

'No worries, I can print those press releases off for you too when you're finished,' he offered.

'That would be great, thank you!'

Thirty minutes later while the printer spewed out the posters and press releases, Greg made a few calls to find out the names of editors for the newspapers. Then, when he had the press releases put into envelopes, he began addressing each one by hand.

'Thank you so much, you've been a great help,' he called to Ruairí a short time later when he was leaving the café with an arm full of envelopes.

He walked down the path and headed straight to the post office.

'That's a lot of envelopes, Greg,' Sarah said as he came through the door.

'They're press releases.'

'For what?' she asked in bewilderment.

'To save the post office. Here's a poster to stick in your window,' he said, taking one from the top of the pile and handing it to her.

Sarah was speechless as she took the poster from him and read it aloud:

> *'Save our Post Office*
> *Please come along and march this Saturday*
> *Meeting 12 p.m. sharp at the shipwreck'*

'You've organised a march?'

'Uh-huh,' he nodded.

Tears clouded her eyes as he told her then about his plans. 'I can't believe you've done all of this for me.'

Greg was embarrassed by her gratitude. 'I want to help you,' he mumbled.

Her shoulders slumped downwards. 'I really don't think they're going to change their minds that easily, but I appreciate what you're trying to do,' she said kindly.

'Well, we have to at least try,' he said.

She smiled. 'Sorry I'm being so negative. I guess I just feel like I'm fighting against the tide. Thank you, Greg—for everything. Thank you for not giving up. I'm so glad you came here, you know? You've been a breath of fresh air since the day you arrived.'

He felt heat creeping into his cheeks. 'Are you going to stamp these envelopes or not?' he said, trying to change the subject.

'All right, Mr Bossy!' She took the envelopes from him and began stamping them.

Her mouth fell open as she worked through the pile. 'You're sending these to the national newspapers?'

'Sure! Why not?'

'Well . . . it's just I don't think they'd be interested in something this small.'

'We'll let them be the judge of that. Meanwhile, they're getting it,' Greg said.

The door opened and Mrs Manning came in. 'Hello, Sarah. Oh hello, Greg.'

'Hello Mrs Manning, how are you today?'

'I'm keeping well, thank you. You two look like you're up to no good.' The lines at the side of her mouth creased upwards as a grin spread across her face. Her lively eyes always had a look of devilment in them.

'Greg's been busy—he's organised a march to save the post office.'

'Oh, well, isn't that marvellous! What a great idea! Well done, Greg. You're a treasure! It's hard to believe you're only here a wet week, it feels as though you've lived here all your life!'

Greg felt a warmth radiate inside him at the surprise compliment. 'It's on this Saturday—we're meeting at midday at the shipwreck. Will you come, Mrs Manning?' he asked.

'Of course, I will!' the old woman said, tapping the counter with her stick to emphasise her words. 'It's good to see someone doing something useful. Anyway, I just wanted to drop you in a few eggs, Sarah, my ladies have been working flat out!'

'Thanks, Mrs Manning,' Sarah said, taking the box from her. 'That's so kind of you.'

'Right, I'll be off now, the dinner won't cook itself!' she said cheerily as she shuffled back towards the door.

'Don't you want something?' Sarah called after her.

Mrs Manning shook her head. 'No, love, I was just calling to see how you are.'

'She's a character,' Sarah said, shaking her head after she was gone.

'People really depend on this place. It's almost like a drop-in centre!'

'I just wish the government could see that,' Sarah said with a heavy sadness.

'I've a few more things I need your help with, maybe we could meet for a drink this evening to go through it all if you're free?'

'You're on. Say around seven?'

He left Sarah get back to work, and he headed home to *Cove View*. He sat up on the bed with his back resting against the headboard and the laptop on his knees. He began to Google the contact details for the politicians that Ruairí had given him. Then, he set about calling the politicians one by one. As Ruairí had said, he was met with an overwhelmingly positive response. They were all eager to get behind the cause in an election year and promised that they would be at the march.

*

That evening Greg was both ravenous and exhausted by the time he was due to meet Sarah. He had been so engrossed in organising the march that he realised he had eaten nothing since the café that morning. He changed out of his earlier clothes, deliberating between a shirt and a sweater and eventually settling on the sweater. Then he headed downstairs to the bar.

As he looked around, he saw she hadn't arrived yet. He ordered a pint for himself and took the liberty of ordering a white wine for her.

'Well, how's yourself?' Jim asked.

'I'm good thank you.'

'Are you meeting Sarah is it?' Jim said, nodding to the white wine.

Greg nodded.

'And how's everything going there? Did you ever have that chat with her?'

Greg shook his head. 'No, not really.'

'And what's stopping you now?'

'Well, she's enough going on with the post office, and besides, I'm heading home next week.'

'Hmmh,' Jim said clearly unimpressed with his efforts. 'Faint heart never won fair lady,' he mumbled as he began pulling the pint.

Greg gave Jim one of the posters to deflect attention away from his love life. 'Would you mind sticking this up?'

'What's is it?' he asked, taking it from him and reading it while the pint was settling.

'I've organised a protest march to save the post office. Will you come along? We need all the support we can get.'

'I'll definitely be there. Well done, Greg.'

Mr Murphy was sitting up at the end of the bar. 'Did you hear Greg has organised a march to save the post office?' Jim called up to him.

'By God, you're some man!' he said to Greg. 'And you a blow in and all!'

Greg laughed. 'Well, will you come, Mr Murphy?'

'Count me in,' he said. 'And what's more, I'll bring Rita and a few more with me too. You can't beat a bit of people power.'

'Great!' Greg said, buoyed up by their enthusiasm.

Sarah came in the door a few minutes later. 'Hi, Greg,' she said.

He handed her the white wine.

'I should be the one buying you a drink for all you've done!' she chided.

They sat down in a booth beside the window. A candle flickered lazily on the table, and the lights across the bay twinkled in the darkness beyond.

'Jim's going to put a poster in the window,' Greg said, feeling pumped. It had only been a few hours, but already his campaign was gaining momentum. The power of community was an amazing thing. 'And tomorrow I'm going to call to all the shops and businesses to spread the word around the village and to ask them to put up posters.'

'I feel bad for you doing all this,' Sarah said, taking a sip from her drink. 'You come to the village in search of your parents and you get dragged into all of this!'

'Don't apologise, I like being involved. In fact, I'm enjoying it. I haven't felt this useful in a long time.' It was true; although he wished the circumstances were different, helping Sarah to save her post office had given him a renewed sense of purpose. He felt needed here, and he liked how that felt.

'But you're doing all of this to help me, and I still haven't been able to help you to find your parents.'

'That's hardly your fault,' Greg said, suddenly being brought back to the reality of the reason he was in the village in the first place. It was all well and good throwing himself into organising protest marches, but he would be going home without any answers if he didn't uncover any details about his birth soon. He had been here for almost three weeks now, and he still was no closer to finding out the truth. He had hit dead end after dead end. He had to admit that in his darker moments, he was starting to wonder whether his mother might have got some of the details wrong? Had her mind been confused in old age? He had seen from his time in Ireland that there were lots of villages with similar names, only yesterday he had a seen a place called Inishmór on the TV. What if his mom had got the place name mixed up and he was here in this village on a wild goose chase? But then he would remember her description of the cottage on the headland and would feel guilty for doubting her. Surely it couldn't just be a coincidence?

'Did you get any more letters since?' Sarah asked as her elegant fingers closed around the stem of her wine glass.

'No, only a death threat today—'

'What?' Sarah gasped, almost dropping the glass from her hand.

'I'm joking,' Greg laughed.

Sarah visibly relaxed. 'Don't do that to me!'

He lifted his pint and took a sip from the creamy head. 'I'm starting to think that they don't want to be found,' he said wistfully. 'Maybe they just didn't want me—'

'We're so close; I can feel it. Don't lose heart now. We just need to keep digging.'

'I'm running out of time—I've only a week and a half left.'

'So are you looking forward to heading back home?' Sarah asked. She was tracing her finger up along the condensation on the outside of her glass.

He sat back in the chair. He knew they couldn't avoid the topic of his imminent departure for any longer. It felt bittersweet to be talking about his return to America. It was as though he was being woken from a fantastic dream whenever he thought about his life back home.

'Honestly? Not really. My life in North Carolina is a world away from this—it's hectic, it's pressurised. I work crazy hours. I've to sort out all of Mom's stuff too and decide what to do with the house . . . It's funny, I know I've only been here for a few weeks, but I feel as though it's been years. Being in Inishbeg Cove has allowed me the space just to breathe, and I've forgotten what that felt like.'

'The village has a funny way of creeping under your skin all right,' Sarah said, smiling.

'I've never been anywhere like it.'

'Well then you'll just have to come back again to visit,' she said, changing her tone back to its usual breeziness. Was he imagining it, or did he see a hint of sadness in her eyes?

*

Darkness had descended like a cloak, and the yellow lights of the village guided them as Greg walked Sarah home. The night's sky was dotted with stars as bright as quartz, and a full white moon blanched the path before them. A dog barked in the distance. Their sense of hearing was sharpened by the darkness, and they could hear the rustling of animals and the crackling of dry twigs in the hedges.

When they reached her cottage, they stood outside talking, both keen for the evening not to end. The sea pounded the rocks beside them, and Greg could taste tiny salt crystals on his lips. She was so close that he could feel her breath on his face, and his heart began to beat just a little bit faster.

'I'll miss you, Sarah,' he said suddenly.

Her eyes met his. 'I'll miss you too, Greg.'

Emboldened by the alcohol, he found himself reaching across for Sarah's hand and taking it inside his own. Before he had time to think about it anymore, he leant across, closing the distance between them so they were just inches apart, and started kissing her. His lips, warm and full, met hers. He had wanted to do this ever since he had got to know Sarah, and it was every bit as magical as he had dreamed about. It felt so good, so, so good. His hands held her face, her hair brushing through his fingers. He felt himself grow hard as his skin tingled underneath her fingertips. Suddenly their kisses begun to get more urgent, and they fell back against the timber door as their mouths searched soulfully for one another under the moonlight. It felt as though this kiss wasn't enough; he needed more. They needed more.

She pulled back and their eyes locked together, full of urgency. 'Do you want to come in?' she whispered.

His face suddenly clouded over. As the meaning of her words hit him, it was as though he had crash-landed back to Earth. What was he doing? His impending departure was looming. He knew he was getting in too deep. He had a plane to catch next week, and his brain was telling him to stop it now before he got hurt. If they spent the night together, there would be no going back. *Be sensible here, Greg, don't get in any deeper.*

'Actually, I think I should probably head on . . .' he said.

She looked crestfallen, and his heart ached. How could he tell her that he wanted to stay with every fibre of his being and hold her in his arms until the sun came up? He wanted to hold her in his arms and never let her go.

She nodded, but there was an unmistakable sting of rejection in her eyes.

'Sure,' she said.

Greg knew she was probably confused; hell, he was confused! He was giving her mixed messages; one minute he was kissing her full of passion and desire and the next he was pushing her away. When his heart was in charge, he couldn't help himself, but then his brain would kick in, and he knew he needed to put the brakes on. It was better for both of them this way. But boy was it hard. How was he meant to say goodbye to Sarah?

.

Chapter 34

Sarah felt stupid; pure and utter stupid. She was mortified. She wanted to climb out of her own skin and run away, never to be seen again. Why had she let herself get carried away by it all? She had known Greg was only here for a month—the man had never told her anything else—but yet she had allowed herself to fall for him. And my goodness had she fallen. She tingled just thinking of his lips on hers. At first when he had leaned over to kiss her, she had been stunned. She had frozen, it was new territory for them—there was no going back—but she had pushed out the doubts from her head and allowed herself to melt into his embrace. As she fell into his kiss, her body had responded as every synapse came alive and began to buzz with little charges of electricity. She could still feel the trace of his stubble against her cheek; his smell, so deep and manly, was still in her nostrils. When they had kissed, his top had risen up slightly, and she had felt the skin on his broad back, sending tiny pulses coursing through her veins. She felt safe and secure in his arms. When he held her, she felt like she was the most important person in the world. She had never kissed anyone else like the way she had kissed Greg this evening. It had felt as though their hearts were singing together, but as soon as she had invited him in, it was as though the spell had been broken.

How had she got it so wrong? She hadn't done that lightly; it had been long time since she had opened her heart to anyone. She had wanted it so much, and she thought he had too. It seemed she was nothing more than a holiday romance to him. It had hurt when he had pulled away from her. Although he was still holding her in his arms, something had changed between them, and Sarah wasn't sure what. Had she misread the signals? Had she been too forward? Too easy, maybe? Was she so out of touch with the dating scene that she had made a huge faux pas? She had been single for a long time, and maybe things had changed. Had she broken some golden rule?

She turned the key in the door to her little cottage and let herself in. Sarah O'Shea, you are an idiot to be opening your heart up to men, she chastised herself, why do you never learn?

Chapter 35

As Greg walked home that night, he couldn't get that kiss out of his head. It felt as though his heart was swelling inside his chest every time he thought of Sarah. It had been perfect until he had gone and ruined it all. She meant too much to him to be messing her around like that.

How could he explain to Sarah that he hadn't wanted to leave? That he had wanted to stay with her like he had never wanted to stay with anyone ever before? He had wanted to hold her in his arms all night long and to wake up to her sweet smile in the morning, but reluctantly he had let her out of his arms, said goodbye, and headed home to *Cove View*.

He replayed their magical kiss in his mind once again. The taste of her lips still lingered on his. The feeling of their softness against his had been tentative at first, before she got braver and it had fired up into breathless kisses as their bodies yearned for one another. He could feel his skin breaking out in goosebumps just thinking about it. But Greg knew that if they had spent the night together, he would be setting himself up for heartache and he would never withstand it. In order to protect his heart, this was the way it had to be. He was saving them both from being hurt. He felt he had made a difficult but ultimately sensible decision, so then why did his heart feel so heavy?

*

When Greg woke the next morning, his first thought was of Sarah. He felt sick to the pit of his stomach whenever he thought about how he had left things with her. He had taken advantage of her friendship. He couldn't get the image of her hurt face out of his head. Had he really kissed her and then walked away? But what else could he do? She had looked so confused by his sudden coolness when he had declined her offer to come in. The unmistakable sting of rejection had been written all over her features. He didn't want to start something only to run out on her a week later; surely walking away from her had been the lesser of two evils? He couldn't risk hurting her for the sake of a short fling. She had become a good friend to him, and he didn't want to jeopardise that or worse still for her to think he was taking advantage of her. And it had only dawned on him during one of his many periods of broken sleep during the night that maybe she had just wanted a nightcap and he had read too much into it.

He hid his face in the pillow and groaned aloud. Why, oh why, was he so bad with women? He would need to go see her in the post office first thing to apologise.

After he had showered and dressed, he headed downstairs and stepped out into a glorious Inishbeg Cove morning. The low spring sun cast shades of pink and orange around the village. He breathed the briny air deeply into his lungs to help clear his fuzzy head. He looked out over the cove, the tide was out, and the fishing boats lay lopsided, beached up on the washed sand. The sea-swimmers were towelling themselves off after their swim and drinking from thermos flasks.

'Good morning, Greg!' Mrs O'Herlihy greeted him from inside her shop as he passed the door.

'Good morning!' he called back to her. It felt as though he had been in the village for years instead of just a few weeks. That was one of the things he would miss most about the place. It was such a simple thing, but whenever someone greeted him by name, it gave him a sense of belonging. Even though he had only been there for a few weeks, the people of Inishbeg Cove were starting to feel like family to him. For the most part they had welcomed him so completely that he felt like a different man than the one that had first arrived in the village a few short weeks ago. He knew that no matter what happened in the search for his parents, at least he would be going home with fond memories of Inishbeg Cove and its people—well, most of them anyway.

When he reached the post office, he took a deep breath

before pushing the door open. He was glad to see it was empty.

'Hi, Sarah,' he said sheepishly as he approached the counter.

'Greg, good morning.' She busied herself stamping a bundle of mail and wouldn't meet his eyes. He felt like a complete jerk. Why had he kissed her and ruined a perfectly lovely friendship?

'I need to talk to you.'

'Oh?' She was looking back down at her bundle of mail.

He took a deep breath and thrust his hands into his coat pockets. 'Well, I think I owe you an apology—'

'For what?'

He cringed. How was he going to find the words without embarrassing both of them? 'Well, you know ... last night ... I never meant to lead you on like that ...'

'It's okay ... you don't need to apologise,' she cut across him quickly.

'Well, I wanted to come in, I really did, but I thought it best if I didn't ... you know, with me heading home next week and everything?'

'You're right, Greg. In the cold light of day, I can see that. It was just the wine. I'm glad one of us was sensible.' She looked up at him and smiled, but it didn't quite stretch up to her eyes.

He felt his shoulders sink downwards. It was his turn to feel disappointed now, even though it was totally hypocritical. Although she was agreeing with him and saying everything that he knew was right and sensible, he couldn't help but feel a weight of regret flagging him down. Maybe things had become too complicated for her and she would be glad to see the back of him when the time came for him to leave. She couldn't have felt too strongly about him if she was able to turn off her feelings as easily as you would turn off a faucet. It seemed she was quite happy to stop things developing any further between them too. Then he chastised himself, what did he want? Did he want her to be hurt? Did he really want to leave Sarah wounded and heartbroken at his return home? No, it was better like this; at least he knew she would be okay when he went back to North Carolina. He on the other hand . . . well, he wasn't so sure he'd be able to say the same thing about himself.

'So no hard feelings?' he asked, plastering a smile on his face.

'Of course not,' she said, smiling brightly back at him. 'You've only a few more days left, let's just forget about all that other stuff and get back to the real reason you're here. We need to try to get you some answers before you return home.'

She continued shuffling through her mail as awkwardness charged the air. He hated it. He hated how last night had changed everything between them, and he didn't know what to do to make things right again or even if he could.

Chapter 36

On the morning of the march, Greg heard the rain before he had even opened the curtains. He listened for a moment as it pelted fiercely against the windows. He got out of bed, and when he pulled back the curtains, he saw a mosaic of raindrops clouding the glass before running down along the windowpane in rivulets. His heart sank; this was bad news. He was worried that a lot of people, particularly the elderly, in Inishbeg Cove wouldn't want to come outdoors in this sort of weather, and who could blame them?

They had put so much work into organising the march; everyone had played a part. All the businesses in the village had put up the posters he had designed in their windows. He and Sarah had spent the day before making placards to bring along. He really hoped the weather wasn't going to cause it all to fall flat on its face at the final hurdle.

Once again, Greg decided to take his breakfast in the bar that morning. He still hadn't returned to the dining room since the letter had arrived.

'So today's the day, eh?' Jim said as he put his usual fried breakfast down on the table in front of him.

'Yeah, fingers crossed the rain doesn't put everyone off,' Greg said, feeling gloomy as he looked outside at the rain dancing off the puddles beyond the window.

'Aragh, they won't melt! A little bit of rain never hurt anyone.'

After Greg had eaten, he made a few phone calls to double-check that the journalists were still coming along to cover the story. Then when he had finished, he headed up to Sarah's cottage.

They had both been so consumed with organising the march over the last few days that to Greg's relief they hadn't had time to dwell on the fateful night of their kiss. Although, there was no denying that something had definitely shifted between them. By kissing her, everything had changed and now awkwardness sat in the creases where once there was a lovely friendship.

'Are you ready?' he asked, stepping into her living room.

'As ready as I'll ever be,' she said, biting down nervously on her lip. 'What if nobody turns up, Greg?'

'They will; we can't let a bit of rain dampen our spirits!' he said with a confidence that he didn't really feel.

They grabbed the placards they had made. Greg's said, 'Inishbeg needs its Post Office' and Sarah's read, 'Save our Post Office, Save our Community'.

As they stepped outside, they were both glad to see that the rain was beginning to ease off. The thick charcoal clouds had dispersed, and a hint of blue sky had begun to emerge. 'You see! Even the weather is on our side,' he said, winking at Sarah as they headed down towards the shipwreck.

They turned the corner on to the main street, and Greg couldn't believe his eyes when he saw a large crowd carrying banners and posters had already started to assemble in front of the shipwreck. They both stopped walking, moment-arily gobsmacked. Sarah looked over at the gathering with her mouth hanging open. Then, she looked at Greg and mouthed, 'Wow.'

'And we still have thirty minutes before we're due to start!' he said, grinning at her.

They continued to walk over, and as they got closer, he read a banner that said, 'Enough is Enough - Inishbeg says No!' and another read, 'We're Not Third Class Citizens'. Another poster depicted a coffin with the words 'R.I.P. Inishbeg Cove' written inside it.

Greg scanned the faces in the crowd and saw Jim and Maureen had come and Mrs O'Herlihy from the supermarket had already arrived. Tadgh and Senan from the restaurant were there too. Even frail old Mrs O'Sullivan had turned up with her walking frame. He spotted Mrs Manning and Mr and

Mrs Murphy and Timmy O'Malley, but there were many more he didn't recognise.

'Do you know all of these people?' Greg asked Sarah.

She shook her head. 'I don't recognise half of them,' she whispered. 'There are far more people here than live in Inishbeg Cove.'

It was only then that they both realised just how much support she had. Somehow what was happening to Inishbeg Cove had managed to capture the public's sympathy.

'Good morning, Sarah,' Mrs Manning said with a wink when they had reached the gathering. 'I told you we wouldn't let you down!'

Greg saw tears well in Sarah's eyes. He felt a burst of pride in his heart. He was so happy for Sarah that the village had got behind her, but once again he felt that familiar bittersweet twinge. It was as though a mirror had been held up to reflect everything that he was sorely lacking in his own life. He longed to feel that same sense of belonging that Sarah had here. And although it now seemed likely that he would be returning home without discovering who his parents were, his time in the village had been good for him; the place, the people had helped repair his wounded soul and allowed him escape from the realities of his life back home. During his short time in Inishbeg Cove, this community had taken him in and given him a sense of purpose again, but pretty soon he would be leaving it all behind him, and his heart sank at the thought of going home to his old life and the vast emptiness of it all. He lived in one of the busiest cities in the United States—he didn't even know his neighbours' names, and he doubted they knew his. He was essentially anonymous. And now that his mom had died and Selena had broken up with him, it was even going to feel even more so. If he had learnt anything from his time in the village, it was just how much he craved that sensation of being included. He wanted to belong somewhere. He longed for the feeling of knowing that the community had your back and the reassurance that no matter what happened in your life, you'd be okay because the village and its people would always be the safety net ready to catch you.

'Greg, look,' Sarah cried. His eyes followed to where she was pointing where a large bus full of people was making its way down the main street.

'Surely they're not all here for the march?' Sarah asked, looking at him in bewilderment.

'We'll soon find out!' Greg said.

They waited for the coach to park up, and then a rotund woman with soft features came down the steps. Greg guessed she was about fifty.

'I'm looking for Sarah O'Shea?' she asked the crowd.

'She's over there.' Someone pointed in Sarah's direction. The woman came up to Sarah and pumped her hand warmly.

'It's lovely to meet you, Sarah. I'm the postmistress of Ballyboyle Post Office. Our village isn't much bigger than yours. Our Garda Station closed last year, and they've taken the A&E from our regional hospital. We haven't been threatened with closure *yet,* but if things keep going the way they are, it's only a matter of time. So when we heard about what was happening to the post office in Inishbeg Cove, we knew we had to take a stand. That's why myself and few others'— she gestured to the people climbing down from the bus behind her—'wanted to come here today as a mark of solidarity. We need to send a message to the government that this stops now!'

The corners of Sarah's eyes crinkled as her face broke into a wide smile. 'Well, thank you, I really appreciate your support.' She looked around and surveyed the gathered crowd who had all turned up to help her cause and felt a surge of hope that maybe, just maybe, all was not lost yet.

Just then a large white van with a huge satellite dish on the rear pulled up alongside them. The RTÉ logo was emblazoned on the side. Greg dared not hope. He knew from his research that RTÉ was Ireland's national TV and radio channel, but he hadn't sent them the press release, he just assumed this would be too small a story for them to cover. Somehow they must have heard about the march and decided themselves that it was newsworthy enough to cover.

'Oh my God, Greg, it's RTÉ News!' Sarah squealed.

The van door opened, and a glamorous woman in a red

tailored suit stepped down. Her face was familiar to him from the snippets of news that he had watched since he had come to the village. Sarah looked at him in panic. 'That's Tríona Quinn—what the hell is she doing here?'

Tríona began making her way towards the crowd. Her blonde blow-dried hair bounced over her shoulders as she walked.

'I'm looking for Sarah O'Shea?' she said to Tadgh.

Tadgh pointed in Sarah's direction.

'Well go on, go over to her!' Greg encouraged, gently nudging Sarah forward.

'But what am I supposed to say to her?' she said, looking flustered as Tríona Quinn was getting closer.

'Are you Sarah O'Shea?' Tríona asked when she reached them.

'Yes,' Sarah said in a small voice.

'I'm Tríona Quinn from RTÉ News.' She held out her hand to shake Sarah's. 'We heard about the march taking place here today and how this small village is taking a stand against the spate of closures of rural post offices. I was wondering if I could do a short interview with you about it?'

'I—I—' Sarah began to stutter.

'She'd love to,' Greg said, cutting across Sarah.

Sarah shot him a look. 'What are you thinking! I can't go on national television, Greg!' she hissed at him.

'Of course, you can, if you want to save your post office, this is your best shot to get the message out there.'

While the cameraman set up, Tríona flipped open a make-up compact and began touching up her face in its mirror. Then when the cameraman was ready, Tríona pushed a microphone in Sarah's face. 'And three, two, one . . .' she counted down for Sarah before turning towards the camera. 'I'm here in the small village of Inishbeg Cove in the West of Ireland. Inishbeg Cove is typical of many small villages along the Wild Atlantic Way. Located on the edge of the sea, it faces a daily battle for its very survival. But the threat of rural isolation is a real fear for the villagers here as they fight to save their post office. Sarah O'Shea is the postmistress here in Inishbeg Cove. Sarah, tell us about the purpose of today's march?'

Sarah looked over at Greg, begging him to do the interview for her, but he knew it was her story to tell. The words had to come from her mouth. He gave her a reassuring smile, urging her on.

'Well . . .' Sarah began nervously as she turned back towards the camera. 'We're a rural village fifteen miles from anywhere, so for the people in Inishbeg Cove, the post office isn't just somewhere they go to post a letter, it's the place they go to pay their bills, do their banking, or sometimes they come in just for a chat. The post office is the heartbeat of our village. If we lose our post office, our village will die.'

'Sarah, if you could give the government one message here today, what would it be?' Tríona asked, thrusting the microphone back into Sarah's face.

'Well, I suppose I would ask them not to just look at the numbers on paper but to *really* look at our village—our village is just one of many dotted around the country fighting for survival—this isn't just about Inishbeg Cove, this is about all the small villages in rural Ireland trying to stem the tide of urbanisation. I think the numbers who have turned out here today is testament to that. A lot of our villagers are elderly, they don't drive, there is no bus service either, so what will they do if they lose their post office? How are they going look after their basic communication needs? Don't these people deserve the same services as the people living in the towns and cities in Ireland? The government need to ask themselves, if it was their village, how would they feel at the threat of being cut off?'

'Well, I think Inishbeg Cove is certainly sending out that message loud and clear. Thank you, Sarah,' Tríona said, terminating the interview before turning back to the camera. 'This is Tríona Quinn for RTÉ News.'

'Oh God,' Sarah said as soon as the camera had stopped filming. 'I can't remember what I said! It was a blur . . .'

'Trust me,' Greg said, grabbing her on either side of her arms. 'You were amazing! You really got the word out there.'

'Do you think so?' she asked sceptically.

'Stop doubting yourself.' He looked down at his watch,

'It's twelve o'clock. Are you ready?' he asked.

She gulped. 'Let's go.'

Sarah and Greg led the crowd and began marching down the main street. Ruairí had managed to get his hands on a megaphone, and he began chanting, 'Save our post office—Inishbeg Cove says No!' The crowd echoed it as they walked. The news crew filmed as they filed past. Greg turned around and looked back at the hundreds of people walking behind them. People of all ages had turned out to support Sarah. There were babies in pushchairs, young children on scooters, and even Mrs Manning with her walking stick, and Mrs O'Sullivan crouching over her Zimmer-frame shuffled along at the rear. They moved through the village in a slow wave. It was amazing to see the power of community in this small village. All these people had turned up today in solidarity with Sarah, and he felt so proud of her. This was testament to the good person that she was. When he looked at her now, her face so passionate and alive, surrounded by people who loved and respected her, as she battled to save her post office, he didn't think she had ever looked more beautiful. How was he ever going to say goodbye to her? How he wished he didn't have to leave. Who knew, if they had had more time together, perhaps something wonderful could have started to blossom, but he'd never know. He forced himself to push all those thoughts from his head—what mattered now was Sarah, and Greg was going to do all he could to help save her post office. He knew once he returned to North Carolina she'd be okay. She would be held in the palm of the village's hand.

When they reached the church at the end of the main street, they turned and walked back towards the shipwreck once again. Ruairí had arranged for a few of the local teenagers to help serve teas and coffees and some of his famous sticky lemon curd buns. Everyone lowered their placards and banners and began to tuck in to his delicious treats.

With their coverage filmed, Tríona Quinn made her way back to the van and the news crew started to pack up, already talking about the location for their next broadcast.

While people stood around chatting and drinking their teas and coffees,

Sarah asked Ruairí for the megaphone. It made a squeal as she took it from him, but eventually a hush broke out amongst the crowd and Sarah began talking.

'Before everyone leaves,' she said nervously, 'I just wanted to thank you all from the bottom of my heart. Thank you to each and every one of you for coming to support the post office today and for making Inishbeg Cove the best place in the world.' Tears glistened in her eyes. 'Even if we don't succeed, you've done the village proud.'

A cheer rang out amongst the crowd.

After people had begun dispersing, Sarah and Greg headed back towards the cottage carrying their placards.

'Well done,' Greg said as they walked. 'I think you've done everything you can possibly do. It's in the hands of the government now.'

'That's what I'm afraid of,' Sarah whispered.

As they neared her cottage, they saw a cloaked figured coming towards them on the path up ahead.

'Isn't that Ida?' he said. He had noticed that she was one of the few villagers who hadn't been at the march.

Sarah nodded. 'It is.'

'Hello, Ida,' Sarah greeted as they reached her on the path.

She merely grimaced, narrowing her eyes at them. They were as hard as stones, and anger burned deeply within them. A shiver snaked its way down Greg's back.

'I don't get what her problem is?' he said after they had passed her and were out of earshot.

Sarah shook her head. 'I don't know, Greg . . . she's behaving really strangely. She has always been reclusive, but she isn't normally like this . . .'

'What do you mean?' he said, feeling a tightening in his chest.

'There's definitely something that she isn't telling us . . .' Sarah turned around, and her eyes followed Ida's back as she walked towards the village.

'Well, she's certainly not leading the Inishbeg Cove welcoming committee, that's for sure!'

Sarah giggled. 'Think about it, Greg, that's twice now that

you've seen her up in the old cottage—don't you think it's more than a coincidence that it's the same place where you were born? Then she tries to warn you off! I wouldn't be surprised if the letter was from her too . . . I think your arrival in the village has rattled her somehow.'

'But why?'

'Perhaps she knew your mother . . . She's the right age profile; she would have been young enough when you were born . . . Maybe we should call to see her,' Sarah said.

'But what are we going to say to her?'

'She has always been odd, but I've never seen her acting like this. She knows something. I'm sure of it. I think we need to ask her straight out what is going on.'

'I don't know . . .' Greg said with huge uncertainty weighing him down. The idea of confronting Ida terrified him. 'I don't think she'll react well to something like that.'

'Are you afraid of her, Greg?' Sarah asked, her lips turned up at the sides in amusement.

'Well, she might put a spell on me or something,' he said feebly.

Sarah laughed. 'Come on, scaredy cat,' she said, linking her arm through his. 'I think it's time we found out what she knows.'

Chapter 37

September 1976

It seemed like I was waiting forever for him to return. The daylight began to fade, and the autumn twilight began to push in. I was shivering and scared. I was petrified he was going to bring my parents to me; I would be in so much trouble if he did that. I felt beyond helpless as I looked down at the tiny baby in my arms who was relying on me to protect him.

When the early evening dusk was replaced by a cloak of darkness, I started to worry that he had run out on me. And who could blame him? We were in over our heads. Our plan had been conceived from teenage romance, but now I saw it for what it really was, nothing more than a childish fantasy.

A while later I saw a torchlight in the distance, and when I heard his voice outside the cottage, I felt a flood of relief. I chastised myself for doubting him. Deep down I knew he would never have done that to me, he loved me. I needed to put my trust in him; he was going to help us.

He came through the door, but I startled when I realised that he wasn't alone. There was a man with him. An older man who I didn't recognise. Instinctively I tried to hide the baby and the evidence of the birth.

'It's okay,' he said, rushing forward. 'This is Samuel - he's going to help us.'

'Are you okay?' the other man asked, bending down to me on his hunkers. 'Do you need medical attention?'

His accent wasn't from around here; he was American. He was very well dressed, wearing the kind of clothes you only saw on TV or magazines. Who was he? And why was he here? My mind was trying to keep up with what was going on, but it seemed as though shocks were being assailed at me from every angle.

'Please, no,' I said, shaking my head. 'I'm starting to feel a little better.' I tried to sit up a straighter. Although I still felt weak, the bleeding seemed to have eased, and I was starting to feel a bit stronger.

'Don't worry, I'm going to try and help you,' Samuel said quickly. 'Is the baby still attached?'

I nodded.

Samuel took out a penknife and helped to cut through the sinewy cord.

'Samuel and his wife are desperate to have a baby-' he said shortly afterwards.

I looked up at him in confusion, trying to understand what was being said. My mind was slow. I was still reeling from the shock of it all, and I was finding it hard to keep up with everything. I was looking at the infant in my arms in astonishment as if remembering afresh that I had created this child. That this child was mine.

'We'd give it a good life, I promise you,' Samuel interrupted. His eyes locked on mine, and in them I could see a deep yearning. There was a sadness reflected in them that told me that there was more to this man's story.

'You want to take my baby?' I said looking at Samuel and then back at him as what they were saying began to hit me.

'It's for the best,' he said to me with desperation pooling in his eyes. 'What hope does he have with us?' I noticed his shoulders had slumped down, and I knew that it was over. Our plan was gone. My heart sunk, but even under the crushing disappointment of his words, I knew that he was right. We didn't have a hope. I felt I had aged a decade in the last few hours. Yesterday's me seemed like someone I barely knew.

'I don't want to force you to do anything,' Samuel was saying. 'But if you need a home for your baby, can I just say that my wife and I have so much love to give, and I promise you that we would give your baby the best life.' I noticed tears brimming at the corners of his eyes.

They were both looking at me, waiting for my decision.

'Come on, you know it's for the best,' he urged.

I knew the odds were against me. What life could I possibly

give this baby? His life was a blank canvas ahead of him; I knew that Samuel and his wife could paint a much prettier picture than we ever could. Where a life with us would probably be all greys and blacks, Samuel could give him money and security—all the things I couldn't give to him. I looked down at my infant son who was sleeping calmly in my arms as if he knew that this stranger was going to help us. I remembered the promise that I had made to him, and I knew I needed to put his future before my own. Giving him to Samuel was for the best. I lifted my son up close to my face and breathed his newborn smell deep into my nostrils. I rubbed my finger over his tiny features and traced the whorl of his hair. I begged my memory never to forget his scent or how his hair felt under my fingertips. I bent my head and kissed him delicately on his velvety forehead for the last time. I told him that I loved him and that I hoped I would see him again one day. Then I stretched my hands outwards and gently placed my infant son into a stranger's arms.

Chapter 38

Greg's heart was pounding as they pushed open the creaking gate and walked up the narrow path leading towards Ida's whitewashed cottage. It was small with a low thatched roof and a wooden half door painted fire engine red. A small square window sat on either side of the door where colourful flowerpots cluttered the sills. Tufts of wild garlic scented the air. Two sheep were grazing in the garden. They stopped eating the grass to look at Greg and Sarah with curiosity before bending back down and continuing on.

'Here we go,' Sarah said, giving a gentle knock on the door. Greg took a deep breath. His heart was hammering.

A moment later the top half of the door was opened, and Ida looked startled to see they'd followed her home.

'What do you two want?'

'Sorry to disturb you, Ida,' Sarah said, 'can we come in for a moment?'

She narrowed her eyes at them but without saying a word opened the bottom half of the door to let them in. Greg noticed she was carrying a baby lamb in her arms. It was strange seeing her without her big cloak, although her fox-like face was lined with age, she was younger than Greg had first thought. He guessed she was probably in her late sixties or early seventies, but there was a sparkle in her blue eyes that showed a young spirit.

They followed her into a small kitchen, sparsely furnished with just a simple table and two chairs. A rocking chair stood in the corner. Shelves ran around the walls where myriad brown glass bottles sat. Pots bubbled on the Aga and bunches of herbs, tied up with string, hung down from the rafters to dry. The place had a strange smell; it was rich and earthy and somehow calming to the senses. Ida sat down into the rocking chair, cradling the lamb on her lap. She picked up a bottle of milk and began to feed it, and it gulped the milk greedily. Greg felt as though he had stepped back in time. He pretty sure he was standing there with his mouth hanging open.

'Well, don't just stand there like a gombeen,' Ida barked. 'Sit down!'

Greg and Sarah came to their senses and took a seat at the table.

'What brings you both here?' she said eventually.

Sarah cleared her throat to speak, 'Well, Ida,' she began, 'as you know, Greg is trying to trace his birth parents. He was born in this village in September of 1976, and he was wondering if you knew anything that might help him.'

The woman's face clouded over. 'Didn't I tell the pair of ye already to leave the past in the past!'

'Ida, please,' Sarah begged. 'He hasn't got long left before he has to return home. If you know something, won't you help him? He has travelled all this way for answers; he just wants to know where he came from. Can't you see that?'

Anger flamed in her eyes. 'No good comes from raking over old ground, why can't *you* see that!' she retorted.

'Ida, I have to ask, did you know Greg's mother?'

It felt like Sarah had rolled a grenade into the middle of the room. The older woman remained quiet for what felt like the longest time. Greg could see many expressions fleeting across the woman's face; there was shock and anger, even deep sadness. Had Sarah's words unsettled her? Neither of them dared to speak. Ida looked at Greg's face and studied it hard; he locked his eyes on hers, begging her to be honest with him. Whatever Ida said next was going to determine whether she would help him or not. Suddenly the lamb bleated breaking the tense silence. Sarah and Greg jumped in fright.

'Please, Ida,' Sarah encouraged gently. 'If you know anything, anything at all, no matter how small it is, it might be the key Greg needs to solve the mystery surrounding his birth.'

'But there are people—people still alive who won't want this—' Ida was shaking her head, clearly struggling with some inner turmoil about what to do.

'Greg has been through a lot over the last few weeks; he's just lost his mother back in North Carolina, and then he learns that his parents weren't his birth parents. I think he deserves some answers. Come on, Ida, please help him,' Sarah pressed. 'Don't let his trip here be in vain.'

'I can't.' She shook her head stubbornly.

'Look, Ida, I hope I don't cause offence, but it's just your behaviour has been very strange since Greg arrived in the village.' Sarah paused to take a deep breath. 'I need to ask you—are *you* Greg's mother?'

They watched as Ida's body crumpled in the chair before their eyes. The heavy beat of a clock counted down the silence. Eventually Ida turned to Greg and opened her mouth to speak. He held his breath as he waited for what she was about to say, knowing deep within that this was to be a watershed moment in the search for his birth parents.

'I'm not your mother, Greg.' She paused. 'But I think I know who is . . .'

Chapter 39

September 1976

Rain coursed down as we walked along the road back towards home. It ran from my hair, dripping down along my face but I didn't have the energy to wipe the droplets away. My legs were weak and jellyish, and my stomach felt as though it was on fire. Neither of us spoke, it was as if we were both too stunned by the afternoon's events and were locked inside our own thoughts. How quickly twenty-four hours had changed everything. I knew I had to go home and try to act as though nothing had happened, but how was I supposed to do that? How was I supposed to get on with my life again? I knew I would never be the same person anymore.

The moon cut a white path along the road as we walked past my father's fields on either side of the road. Land that was passed down from eldest son to eldest son through the generations. My oldest brother would inherit it when my father passed on. Being a landowner was important in Ireland, and as a farmer with over five hundred acres of prime pastureland, Daddy was well respected in our community. It also meant that we had a certain social standing to adhere to, and I knew that me arriving home with a baby conceived outside of wedlock would not be tolerated. Mammy would parade the five of us into mass every Sunday morning like ducks in a row. She was the Minister of the Eucharist, and my older sisters sang in the choir. She and Daddy were pillars of the community; they never could have imagined how much I had let them down.

It was already dark by the time we reached my gate, and I knew I would be in trouble. I walked down the avenue cloaked in darkness by the majestic stature of two-hundred-year-old oak trees. I noticed that the old gatekeeper's cottage at the end of the avenue where Dermot the farmhand slept was in darkness as I passed by.

'Are you sure you're okay?' he asked.

I nodded, not trusting myself to speak for if I did, I was sure I would fall apart.

We said goodbye, and I felt so heavy as walked down the long avenue. It was as if I was physically weighed down by grief.

Soon the yellow lights of the farmhouse came into view like a beacon in the distance. When I reached the house, I took a deep breath before gently pushing open the kitchen door. Mammy jumped up from the table.

'Where were you?' she shouted at me. 'Have you any idea how concerned we were? We were out of our minds with worry! Your dad and Dermot are out searching the fields for you!'

She suddenly noticed my damp clothing. 'Look at the state of you. You'll catch your death—you're soaked through!' She rushed over and began pulling me out of my wet coat.

'Sorry, Mammy,' was all I could manage.

'Did you miss the bus or what?' she continued.

I nodded. 'I'm not feeling well—' I was so tired. I needed to sleep.

She looked like she was ready to explode, but something about my face must have told her to keep a lid on it.

'Go down to your room and get out of those wet clothes immediately,' she ordered.

I did as I was told and went down to my bedroom. I began undressing, peeling the sodden clothes off my body, but the effort exhausted me, and I found myself lying down on the bed. I just wanted to go to sleep and never wake up.

'Della?' Mammy called, sticking her head around the door a few minutes later. 'I've heated up some of the stew I made earlier for you.'

'I'm not hungry.'

She shook her head. 'That's what happens when you go around in wet clothes! You've probably caught a chill, I'll run you a bath.'

I was too tired to protest and dragged myself up.

The warm soapy water was heavenly to my weary body. I lay

back against the enamel tub and closed my eyes. When I opened them again, I got a fright to see blood from my body mixing in with the bath water, turning it a coral pink colour.

Mammy knocked on the door. 'Can I come in?' she called.

'No!' I said in panic. 'Just give me a second—'

'For goodness' sake, it's nothing I haven't seen before, Della!' she said, clearly exasperated. 'We're all women! I'll leave your nightdress warming up in the hot press for you.'

'Thanks, Mammy.' I felt tears spring into my eyes. I wanted to slide under the water and never come up again. 'I'm exhausted, I think I'll go straight to bed when I'm finished here,' I said.

'You go get an early night, and we'll talk about this in the morning,' she called back to me through the door.

Tucked up in bed that night, I fell into the deepest sleep of my life, but I soon woke up in a nightmare. Samuel was hitting the baby. I was screaming at him to stop, but he wouldn't listen to me. Droplets of sweat laced my forehead. In another one, I dreamed my baby was with me, and when I woke, I began searching for him beside me, desperate to hold him once more, but there was no baby there. I hoped we had done the right thing and that Samuel was taking care of our baby. I said a prayer to Our Lady. The nuns always said Our Lady listened to our worries. Although I knew she would never forgive me for what I had done, I asked for her forgiveness for our baby. I prayed that our baby wouldn't pay for the sins of its parents.

I fell back asleep again and slept fitfully until I woke the next morning. I noticed my pillow was wet underneath my face, and I ached all over. Not just aches from all the walking we had done, but every part of me seemed to hurt. Even my skin was sore to the touch. My breasts were full and tender, but I had no baby to feed. I looked at the calendar hanging beside my bed. Today's date had a heart around it. I had been looking forward to this day for weeks, but now it had arrived, and I had never felt so low. All my hopes and dreams had come crashing down around me.

The bedroom door opened, and Mammy stuck her head around it like she did every morning.

'Time for school, Della,' she called.

She went back down to the kitchen, and I dragged myself out of bed. I was startled to see that my bed sheets were badly stained. I quickly changed the sheets, stuffing them into my schoolbag. I would hide them in a bin in the town. Then I dressed for school and made my way down to the kitchen.

Mammy had grey porridge waiting on the table for me, and I felt my stomach heave at the sight of it.

'Are you not going to eat breakfast?' she asked, looking at me.

I shook my head. 'I'm not hungry.'

'You're looking a bit pale; I hope you haven't caught a cold now.' She was concerned.

I assured Mammy that I was okay, put on my coat, and left the house.

My legs were as wobbly as a newly born calf's as I walked down the avenue towards the top of the road. Even the weight of my school bag, which I usually wouldn't notice, now felt cruelly heavy. A pain so severe that it caught my breath gripped my abdomen. I was getting a lot of these pains. They would come in waves. I had to stop to bend double from the ferocity of some of them. Was this the pain of grief? I had heard people say that when you lost someone you loved, that the pain was almost physical. Was this what they meant?

I was late by the time I arrived at the bus stop. None of the other schoolgirls were there, so I knew I had missed the bus. It was just as well anyway because there was no way I could go to school in this state. But I couldn't go home either. I decided to call to his house. I needed to see him; I wanted his reassurance that we had done the right thing. I needed him to tell me that we would be okay. It seemed we had built up so much for the last few months, and now that our baby was gone, I wasn't even sure what was left between us anymore. No matter what else happened, I knew for certain that our relationship would never be the same again. What had taken place yesterday had fundamentally changed me as a person. I couldn't see how I would ever smile or laugh again; something had died inside me when I said goodbye to my baby boy.

I walked along the road in the direction of the village. I kept my head down in case one of the neighbours might be passing and ask me if I wanted a lift to school. We were only a mile from *the village, but the walk had never taken me as long. My steps seemed to be getting slower as I walked, and my lungs burned. I had to stop and catch my breath and let my legs recover every few minutes.*

When I finally reached his house, I was feeling worse than ever. I banged the knocker against the door. I waited, but no one came to answer. I tried again, but there was no one home. I guessed he had gone to work.

I felt so lonely and deflated as I turned and walked away from his house. It seemed as though for everyone else this was a normal day in Inishbeg Cove, people went to work or school or they went to the village for their groceries, but my world had come to a standstill.

I was feeling queasy and needed to lie down. The pain in my stomach was getting worse. Was this normal after having a baby? I really wished I could ask someone, but whom could I turn to? I could hardly ask Mammy or the girls in school.

It was then that I thought of Ida. Sinéad Ward had told us all in school the week before that she had gone to see her because she always got such bad pains during her time of the month. She had been too embarrassed to go to Dr Fitzmaurice, so she had gone to Ida instead and she had cured her.

Ida wasn't too much older than me. I didn't know her well; she was odd and unconventional. I knew her parents were both dead, but she kept to herself. After Leamy, her father, died, Ida had stepped into his shoes to help look after the village's needs. Dr Fitzmaurice had always been sceptical about Old Leamy's curative powers and never missed an opportunity to make a sarcastic remark about his work as a herbalist, but I had once heard Mammy say to Daddy that Old Leamy was a miracle worker, that he had 'the gift'. I don't know why, but there was something about Ida that told me I would be able to trust her. There was a kindness in her eyes.

I tried to walk faster as I passed through the village towards her cottage, but the pains in my abdomen kept bringing me to a halt. It was as though my whole body was seized in a vice grip. Each one took my breath away; they were so sharp.

I kept my head down as I passed the grocers with its usual Friday queue out the door. I desperately hoped I wouldn't meet

Mammy or Daddy or else I would have a lot of explaining to do.

As I reached Ida's thatched whitewashed cottage, I noticed the red paint was flaking on the small windows. Hydrangea and delphiniums and a lot of other flowers I didn't recognise bloomed with fecundity in the garden. A herb patch with names written on tiny wooden stakes grew beside the door. Suddenly the pains seemed to ratchet up another level. I was caught by a particularly fierce one and had to stop to hold on to the gatepost. I really hoped Ida could fix me. She was the only hope I had.

Chapter 40

Ida

In 1976 I was young, we were carefree, and the days always seemed endlessly sunny but when my father died that summer, everything changed. My own mother had died a few years before, and I had no family left. My father had been the herbalist in the village ever since I could remember. People would come from far and wide with their ailments. There would often be a queue outside the door; children with rashes, colicky babies, or older people with arthritis would all flock to see my father, and he would cure them all. I had spent my childhood helping him, so when he died, it was the natural order that I would study his recipe books and become a herbalist too. I knew the herbs to pick and the right tincture for a cough that wouldn't shift or what to rub on an aching back, but when Della Forde called to my door that day, I was out of my depth. She was weak and breathless, and her eyes were pools of desperation. I wasn't that much older than her myself, but I had the sense to see that something was seriously wrong with her.

I knew Della to see from around the village. She had always been a pretty girl, always well turned out too. You'd see her in mass in the finest of wool coats. Her dresses were made from the most expensive fabrics in Duane's drapery. She wore silks and satins in rich colours that were expertly cut by hand and would drape elegantly over her slim body. You'd know just from looking at her that she came from money, but I can tell you she looked a pitiful mess sitting in my cottage before me that day. I invited her in, and she sat shivering by the Aga even though it was a warm September day.

'I need something, Ida,' she said to me.

'What is it? What's wrong?' I had asked her. She looked wretched.

'I need something for stomach pains,' she said.

'What kind of pains?' I had enquired.

Suddenly her whole face blanched and grimaced as she clutched her abdomen. I knew that nothing in my father's recipe books was going to fix this.

'I think you need to go to Doctor Fitzmaurice, Della,' I advised. It didn't happen too often, but I remember there were a handful of times when Daddy would have sent patients to Doctor Fitzmaurice if he felt it was something too serious for him to deal with or if the symptoms required more investigations. He had always said there was an equal place for both herbs and medicine but that sometimes you needed to err on the side of caution. He was never one to take chances on someone's health, and I heard that warning ringing in my ears.

But Della had shaken her head quickly. 'No, I can't. Please, Ida. You're the only person I can turn to.'

'I want to help you, of course I do, but I don't think I can,' I said.

'Please, I can't go to Dr Fitzmaurice—can't you give me something to take away the pain?' Her eyes were begging me to help.

It didn't sit well with me, but she was desperate and clearly in a lot of pain and distress. 'Well, when did the pains start?' I enquired.

'Yesterday,' she said.

'It could be trapped wind,' I suggested. 'Maybe it's dandelion root you need.' I began rooting in the cupboard for the glass jar where I stored the dried roots.

'No, it's not that -' she said quickly.

'Well, what is it then?' I said, turning back around to her. I noticed she wasn't meeting my eyes. 'I can't say.'

'Della, I can't help you unless you tell me exactly what the problem is.'

Then her shoulders had slumped down, heavy with defeat. 'Ida, you have to promise me that you will never, ever breathe a word of this to anyone. Mammy and Daddy would kill me if they knew.' Tears filled those large green eyes of hers, and I felt desperately sorry for her. I just wanted to help fix whatever was wrong.

I sat down onto a chair. 'You have my word, Della.'

'I gave birth to a baby yesterday,' she said, suddenly giving way to tears.

'Well, where is it?' I had asked, jumping up, panicked that there was a tiny infant abandoned somewhere.

Della had shaken her head. 'We gave it to a couple from America. They're on holidays here. They wanted a baby, so we gave it to the man . . . we were going to run away together and have the baby, but he came early, and we didn't know what to do . . . he said he'd have no life with us, and he's right. They could give him so much more than we ever could.' Her whole body convulsed with tears.

'It's okay,' I soothed, draping a blanket over her shoulders.

'He was beautiful, Ida, you should have seen him. He had a scrunched-up face like a little old man's, and he had the deepest navy eyes that made you think he'd seen it all before. I didn't want to let him go—' She shook her head sadly and whispered, 'he'll never know how much I love him.'

Fat tears descended down her face, and I passed her a handkerchief.

'Sometimes our hardest choices are our most selfless acts,' I had said.

'I need to ask you about the pains, Ida—is it normal?' she said, dabbing at her eyes. 'They won't stop, and there's no one else I can ask.'

She was asking me for advice, but what did I know about childbirth and its aftermath? Suddenly I felt I was in over my head. I desperately wished my father had still been alive to offer his counsel. 'I really think you need to see Doctor Fitz-maurice,' I repeated.

'Ida, I can't -' She was panicked, and I knew that she was starting to question her decision to trust in me.

'I'm sorry, I don't know how to help you,' I said. 'Perhaps if my father was alive, he would know what to do.'

I felt useless. Never had I seen a patient in such distress, and I was failing her. I couldn't recall anyone presenting to my dad with these symptoms in all the years I had been helping him.

'You have to give me something, it's unbearable,' she cried.

I reached up to the shelf and took down Dad's *Materia Medica*, the leather-bound book which contained all his herbal recipes. It was his bible. I had watched him carefully write his recipes onto its pages with his fountain pen, his neat writing almost calligraphy-like. He always took his time, taking care never to make a mistake. He had sketched colourful pictures of the flower part and leaves of the different herbs he used for each recipe. I had been studying it but so far hadn't come across any symptoms like Della had. I leafed through the book and tried to read the indications. I knew dandelion root was good for stomach upsets, but this was different. I hurried through the pages, looking for something—anything at all—that would tell me what to give this girl. Daddy had a section for stomach upsets, coughs, and colds. Finally, I saw a section called *Women's Health*. I saw that he had indexed several subheadings, and there was a large section for *Pregnancy*. Eventually, I found a page with the heading *Post-Natal*. I quickly scanned through the pages. There were remedies for exhaustion and the baby blues, but I found something that I thought might help Della. It was a recipe for a tea made from nettles and motherwort. It said motherwort could be good for toning the uterus and help to soothe after pains and nettles can help stop the bleeding. I quickly began to prepare it, and after it had brewed, poured some into a mug for Della to drink.

'I think this will help you,' I said, handing her the warm mug.

'It's disgusting,' she said, shaking her head as she took a sip.

'It's either this or you take yourself off to Doctor Fitzmaurice,' I quipped.

She drank the rest of it without complaint. I put the remainder of the brew into a glass bottle for her to take home.

'If your condition worsens, you need to see Doctor Fitzmaurice,' I warned as she was leaving my cottage soon after.

I never heard from her again, so I assumed the tea had worked but three days later I was in the shop when I heard Mrs O'Herlihy saying to a customer that it was terribly sad what had happened to Della Forde. To this day I can still remember the chill that went through me when I heard those words. I walked up to the counter and asked Mrs O'Herlihy what had happened to Della, and she told me that she had died during the night. I thought I had misheard her, so I asked her again, and she said in a voice I'll never forget that Della Forde was dead.

Chapter 41

September 1976

As I left Ida's cottage with my bottle of tea, I felt a surge of hope that maybe I would be okay. I was sure I would now recover without anyone ever discovering what had happened. Although I was feeling so unwell, at least I had medicine now, and I was certain Ida had set me on the right path to feeling better again.

'What are you doing home here at this time?' Mammy asked when I returned home.

Daddy and some of the farm labourers were sitting at the table eating their dinner. Mammy was busying around them and pouring tea into their mugs.

'I'm not feeling well—'

'Did you walk all the way? Why didn't the nuns ring me? I would have gone in and collected you!'

'I needed the fresh air,' I lied.

She cocked her head suspiciously at me holding the teapot aloft. Her eyes bored into mine, and I found myself looking down at the lino covering the floor.

'You must have caught a chill from your wet clothes yesterday,' she said eventually. I knew she didn't want to make a scene in front of the workers. 'Go down to bed and I'll bring you in a hot water bottle.'

I climbed in between the cool sheets and lay there shivering. Mammy came in a few minutes later with the hot water bottle. She walked over to my bed. 'You don't look too good, you're very pale,' she said, sitting down on the side of the bed. She placed her hand on my forehead. It felt cool against my skin. 'Hmmh,' she said. 'You're a bit hot all right. I'll get you some paracetamol.'

I had to do my best to keep the tears back. I longed to spill

*everything out of me and ask her for help. I wished I were four
years old again when she could take all my worries away with a
hug. All I wanted was for her to take me in her arms, stroke my
hair like I was little girl, and whisper that it was all going to be
okay.*

*I flitted in and out of sleep for the rest of the day. I would
grieve for my baby in my dreams and grieve afresh when I woke.
I tried to drink some more of the tea even though its acrid taste
made me want to vomit. I was willing it to start working, but I
just seemed to be feeling worse with every passing hour.*

I woke to Mammy placing a damp cloth on my brow.

*'You were rambling,' she said softly. 'You were talking
about a baby. You've got a bad fever, love.'*

*I noticed the curtains were drawn, and it was dark outside.
She began trying to feed me soup, but I turned my face away and
fell back asleep once more.*

*When I woke again, I could hear voices in the room, but I
didn't have the strength to open my eyes to see who they were.
I lost all sense of time. How long had I been here? Was it hours,
days, or maybe even weeks? I was disorientated and couldn't tell
if it was daytime or night. I recognised the booming voice of Dr
Fitzmaurice.*

'She got drenched the other day,' Mammy was saying.

'A bad flu,' he said.

*Then it all went into dreamlike state where I wasn't sure
if I was sleeping or awake anymore. I was haunted by horrible
dreams where the baby was crying and I couldn't help him. I tried
to reach out to him, but someone was always holding me back.
Sometimes I would hear strange voices and sounds. One time I
could hear Mammy crying beside me; it was a frightening, almost
wailing banshee type of cry. She was squeezing my hand so hard
that it hurt.*

*Another time it was Daddy's voice calling me. 'Della, love,
can you hear me? Wake up, Della, please.' His voice didn't sound
like it normally did. It was softer somehow, its rough edges
smoothed out. He was normally a man of few words, he would
grunt good morning at the kitchen table, and that might be all
you would hear from him for the whole day. I couldn't remember him ever speaking to me with such tenderness. I tried but*

couldn't form the words to reply to him.

The last time I woke was to the nasal voice of Father Byrne leading a rosary. I heard my sisters' voices praying beside me. Their frantic Hail Marys getting faster and more urgent with every decade.

But how were they to know that their prayers were futile? Our Lady wouldn't help me now.

Chapter 42

Greg felt as though he was being buried under rubble as the weight of Ida's words hit him. He felt crumpled and defeated. Sarah reached across, took his hand in hers, and gave it a squeeze.

'So my mother is dead?' he asked eventually.

'I'm so sorry, Greg,' Ida said softly.

'Did you ever find out what happened to her?' Sarah asked, clearly in as much shock as Greg was at this sorry tale.

'Mrs O'Herlihy told me that Della was being treated for a bad flu. That she had caught her death on her way home from school one day and took ill. Doctor Fitzmaurice had been up to her a few times apparently, but they couldn't get the infection under control. Mrs O'Herlihy had sighed and tutted at the tragedy of it all. Then she asked me if I was feeling okay, she said I looked like I'd seen a ghost, but I couldn't get the words out to reply to her,' Ida recalled. 'I turned and ran out of the shop. I cried the whole way home. I was in total disbelief at what had taken place. I blamed myself; I should have made her go to Doctor Fitzmaurice sooner. I should have made her tell her parents; they could have helped her. I could have saved her. In the days after Della's death, I gleaned bits of information from whispered conversations. Everywhere you went in the village, people were talking about it saying things like *"God love her, such a shocking thing to happen to a beautiful young girl like that"* or *"She went swiftly in the end, Lord rest her soul".*'

'Didn't anyone know she had had a baby?' Greg asked aghast.

Ida shook her head. 'Nobody seemed to know. That broke

my heart even more. The young girl had obviously died from complications after childbirth and nobody knew. The poor, desperate soul, I was the only person who could have helped her, but I let her down. The thought of her being so close to dying and still being too afraid to tell people what was actually wrong with her was devastating. I was tormented by what ifs. If she had presented to Doctor Fitzmaurice sooner, if she had told him the story that she had told me, could they have saved her? I couldn't help but feel that I had made a bad situation worse by letting her think I had a cure. She was drinking tea thinking it would help her. If I had known it was so serious, I never would have given it to her, and she would have been forced to get medical help. I had been naïve in my treatment; my father would have been horrified at my judgement call. I had only been looking after people for a few months and already someone had died. I wasn't a herbalist with a gift of helping people, I was a danger!'

'It wasn't your fault, Ida,' Sarah said softly. 'It sounds like the perfect storm of events.'

'I stopped helping people that day; I couldn't be trusted. I never made another tincture again except for what I've needed myself over the years.'

'How was her family afterwards?' Greg asked, feeling the words catch in his throat. Della's family were *his* family, and he felt such sadness for these people and the loss they had had to bear.

'The funeral was awful. I've never seen the church so full. Nobody could believe that a young girl in the prime of her life had died from the flu. Her parents were broken people. Her father never got over it; he died a couple of years afterwards. Everyone said he died of a broken heart.'

'Did you ever think of telling them what you knew?' Sarah asked.

Ida shook her head. 'To be honest, I thought about it a lot, especially in the months after her death. I was torn for years afterwards. But Della had been so adamant that they shouldn't know, and I wanted to respect her confidentiality. I hadn't been able to help her; the least I could do was honour her wishes in her death. Besides, I didn't want to cause the family any more grief. They had been through enough without me tarnishing the memories they had left of her. And anyway, what good would it have done? It wouldn't bring her back.'

Greg nodded. 'I'd probably do the same.'

The little lamb bleated, and Ida placed it down gently onto the floor. She turned to Greg then, looking him directly in the eyes. 'I'm sorry, Greg, for not being very welcoming to you when you first arrived in the village, but you have to understand that I was afraid. I didn't want you to taint Della's memory. I couldn't bear the thought, but I can see now you won't do that. That girl went through enough before she died, she deserves to be left in peace.' Ida paused. 'She loved you, Greg—you have to know that—I know she didn't get long with you, but her whole face lit up when she described to me how beautiful you were. Don't judge her too harshly. She did what she thought was best for her infant son—giving you up was the ultimate sacrifice. I know for a fact that she would have been so proud of the man you have grown into.'

'What about my father, Ida, did Della ever tell you who he was?'

She shook her head. 'I definitely think she was in a relationship of some sort. She had used the word "we" several times when she came to see me that day, but I never did find out who the baby's father was. I often thought about him though. Had he known that she was gravely ill? Had he tried, like me, to get her to see the doctor? Was he sitting in his house somewhere in the village full of regret wondering if he could have done more to save her?'

Greg felt another wave of disappointment floor him. If Della had kept her pregnancy a secret, it was doubtful that anyone knew about her relationship.

'What about Della's family?' Sarah asked hopefully. 'Are any of them alive? Although I don't know of any Fordes in the village—'

'Mrs Forde passed on a few years ago, Lord rest her. Most of Della's siblings left the village for work or when they got married.'

Greg nodded, resigned to the fact that the search for his

family in Inishbeg Cove was at an end.

'But there is one person in your family still here in the village,' Ida continued.

He felt a tiny seed of hope begin to germinate inside him. 'Who is it?' he asked quickly.

'Maureen Hegarty was Della Forde's sister,' Ida said.

'Maureen from *Cove View*?' Greg was shocked.

'Maureen is your aunt, Greg.'

Chapter 43

Greg's head was reeling as they left Ida's cottage. Over the course of a few hours, he had learnt so much about his past and had so many emotions to process. It had been hard to hear that his mother was dead and harder still to learn that her death hadn't been an easy one. His heart broke at Ida's description of a desperate, teenage girl too afraid to seek the medical attention she needed. He couldn't help but wonder at what kind of a society struck such fear into young women where they would rather risk death than ask for help? He felt a mixture of heavy sadness and blinding anger that she had died in this way.

His father still remained a mystery. It reminded him of the colouring books he had spent so long poring over as a child —it was like he had coloured in part of a picture, but yet his father's silhouette remained white. Greg really didn't want to think badly of him, but it was hard not to wonder if he could have done more for her. Did he do all he could to help his birth mother in the aftermath of his birth, or was she left ill and alone in her dying days? It was almost too unbearable to think about. It seemed as though everyone had let her down.

'I'm sorry, Greg,' Sarah said, placing her hand on his arm and stroking it tenderly as they walked back towards the village.

'I'm going straight over there to see her,' he said.

'Who?' Sarah asked, looking at him. Worry creased two vertical lines between her brows. 'Maureen?'

'Uh-huh.' Anger powered his steps along the pavement.

'Do you think that's a good idea?' she cautioned. 'At least sleep on it first. This isn't the kind of thing to go in with all guns blazing—it's a delicate matter—'

Greg shook his head. 'No way! I told her why I was in the village. She had figured it out, she knows who I am, and yet she *still* wouldn't help me. I knew she was hiding something! Well, I've had enough of being lied to—first Mom and Dad and now Maureen—I can't take any more lies!' he blazed as they walked towards *Cove View*. 'I'm her nephew! How can she be so cold? We share the same blood for God's sake!' Even he was surprised by the anger in his tone.

'Okay, Greg,' Sarah said. 'If that's what you want, then I'm coming with you.'

*

Greg put his key in door of the guesthouse and marched inside to the lobby. He walked up to the reception desk and pressed the bell.

'Greg, did you have a nice day?' Maureen asked a few moments later when she appeared from her living quarters. 'Oh, hello, Sarah—I wasn't expecting to see you,' she added. She was smiling sweetly. Greg recognised it as the smile she used for all her guests. He wanted to reach across the desk and wipe it off her face.

'Maureen, I need to talk to you—' Greg started.

'Is everything okay with your room, Greg? If the thermostat is too low, I can higher it up a bit for you? It's a bit nipp—'

'The room is fine,' he said, cutting across her. 'Can we go in here?' He walked behind the desk and led the way into her living area.

'Well . . . okay,' she said, coming after him. 'What's the matter, Greg, you look like you've swallowed a—'

'I know who my mother is—' he blurted.

Greg and Sarah watched as Maureen's composure faded. Silence sat heavily between them for what felt like an eternity. The grandfather clock in the hall kept an even tick with every second that passed.

'So you found her then, that's good news,' she said eventually with forced brightness sugaring her words. 'Will you be returning to North Carolina soon?'

Greg noticed that she wasn't meeting his eyes. He couldn't believe his ears, and he shook his head in disbelief.

'Maureen, I know you are my aunt.'

Her eyebrows arched up into her forehead. 'I don't know what you're talking about!' she spat, her eyes ablaze. She walked over and shut the door behind them.

'Please, Maureen,' Sarah implored. 'Greg will be returning home soon, doesn't he deserve to know the truth?'

'I think Greg has done enough digging.' There was a wave of emotion in her voice.

Greg was incensed. How dare she treat him like this! 'Enough is enough! I've had enough of being lied to! My parents did it for my whole life, and now you're doing it too! I can't take anymore!'

'You should be more careful before going around making false accusations!' She was like a dying wasp, in denial that the game was up and determined to stick to her story until the bitter end.

'I only want the truth—nothing more than that. I know that Della Forde was my mother and you were her sister!'

Suddenly at the mention of Della's name the woman began to slump downward. Sarah rushed forward to guide her onto a chair.

'I'm sorry, Maureen,' Greg said. 'I know this is painful for you, but I only want the truth. Please—I'm begging you! Please tell me what you know.'

Her eyes met his, and eventually she opened her mouth to speak, 'Della was my sister—'

'Please go on,' Greg urged.

Her face seemed suddenly etched in pain. She took a deep breath. 'She was a true beauty. The rest of us had bellies and hips, but not Della, she was as thin as a rake. But with that beauty came a price.' Her voice was barely audible, and Greg and Sarah strained to catch every word. 'She had men eyeing her up from a young age. I had heard she'd been seeing a young fella from the town, although I never saw them together myself, but there were rumours, you know? She began putting on weight, which was obvious on a tiny frame like hers. She was able to hide it by wearing big, old jumpers. I was away in college during the week, but we shared a bedroom when I would come home for the weekends, and I would see her getting into bed in her cotton nightgown. The weight was all in her stomach like she had put a football in there. She never told me she was pregnant, although I had my suspicions. I hoped I was wrong. I would say prayers for her. I would have helped her if she had asked me to, but she never did.' She shook her head, and tears filled her eyes.

'I was in college when Mammy rang to say that she had taken ill with a bad flu. I didn't think much of it, sure everyone got the flu, but when she rang the next day in tears to say it wasn't looking good and that I should come home immediately, I knew it was serious. I got straight on the bus home, but it was too late, she died that afternoon. I never got to say goodbye to her.'

'But why didn't you tell your parents if you suspected she might have been pregnant?' Greg couldn't understand these people and their ostrich-like attitudes of sticking their heads in the sand.

'Sure, I never really knew for sure that she was! It was just a suspicion—she had never said anything to me, and I never said it to her, it was just the way we were. When she died, I felt so guilty. If I hadn't been away at college, I would have seen she was sick, and I could have told them what I thought might be wrong with her. I was angry with myself for not asking her if she needed my help or not telling Mammy and Daddy that I suspected she was pregnant sooner. But I knew she wouldn't have wanted that or else she would have told them herself.

'After she died, I decided not to say anything. It wasn't fair on anyone—not on Della's memory or Mammy and Daddy who had lost their child; they didn't need any more bad news. My family was grieving—did they really need to hear that bombshell when I wasn't even sure that I was right? I wanted them to remember Della in the best possible way, not tainted with the shame of a fallen woman. I couldn't bear to do that to her. I don't know if Mammy and Daddy ever figured it out or if they ever did a post-mortem. If they did, it was never spoken about. It was one of those things confined to the family's cabinet of secrets. Time has put a lacquer over the pain, I know it's there—I can still see it—but it's been buried inside me until now. Your visit has reopened that old wound, and it still stings like a fiery burn, Greg.'

'Have you ever told anyone this before, Maureen?' Sarah asked gently.

She shook her head. 'Never. Until this moment. Not even Jim. Please don't think ill of Della, it would break my heart if you did. She was so young.'

'Of course, I don't think bad of her—my heart breaks for everything she went through,' Greg said.

Maureen nodded. A tear wound its way down her cheek. 'Even after all these years, I still go to her grave every day to talk to her.'

'Where is she buried?' Greg asked.

'She's in the family plot in the graveyard. She's with Mammy and Daddy now, Lord rest her soul.'

As much pity as Greg had for Maureen, he found it hard to understand why she had been so unforthcoming with the truth. 'I can't understand, why didn't you tell me this before?' he asked. 'I asked you outright the other day, and you denied it! You've seen me here for the last few weeks, you've known the reason for my visit, why didn't you tell me any of this?'

'Sure, how could I be sure it was you? You have to remember that I didn't even know for sure that Della was pregnant; it was just a hunch. And even if she was, I never knew if she had had the baby or what happened to it.' She paused. 'The first day you checked into the guesthouse I felt as though I had seen you before, and I spent the whole day trying to work out where I knew you from until it finally clicked that you were the living image of Della. It was only when you told me your story that it triggered wild thoughts in my head, and I found myself wondering if you could have been Della's baby. But I dismissed them straight away and told myself I was being ridiculous. I wouldn't be the first grieving person to imagine seeing the face of their loved one after they had passed away.'

When she explained it like that, Greg could understand things from her perspective. He of all people knew that grief made you do funny things. Certainly after his mother had died he had thought he saw her everywhere. He would see an older lady in the street with the same shape and neat, white bobbed hair like hers and his heart would soar until they turned around and he would realise with sinking despair that it wasn't his mom and just a cruel mind trick. He reckoned it was the body's way of protecting you from the awful finality of death, as if we still need to see our loved one's face in our daily lives because we can never let them go completely.

Maureen continued, 'But I couldn't shake the doubts, and when you found me in your room that night, I was checking your passport to see if I could discover your date of birth. I saw you were born three days before Della died, and I began to wonder then if it was more than just a coincidence. I have to say your resemblance to Della is striking. It is like looking into a mirror.'

'Really?' Greg's heart swelled. He realised then just how much he needed to hear this, to hear he belonged to someone. To feel a connection. He felt tears spring into his eyes.

Maureen nodded. 'She had full lips just like yours, and your eyes are the identical greyish-green colour—it's the same shade as the sea before a storm hits. To be honest, it's strange looking at you here, it's like a part of her has come back to life.

'And what about the letter that somehow landed onto my breakfast table—did you write that too?' His tone wasn't angry, just hurt.

She looked sheepish. 'I did. I'm sorry, Greg, I shouldn't have done that, but I panicked ... I was afraid—'

'How did you find out all of this anyway? I didn't think anyone ever knew about her pregnancy?' Maureen asked.

'It seems that Della had gone to Ida for help in the days before her death,' Sarah said.

'Ida the herbalist?' Maureen's face read shocked.

Greg nodded. 'Della had begged Ida to give her something to help with pain. She told Ida she had had a baby. Ida urged her to go to the doctor, but she wouldn't hear of it. The next thing Ida heard was that she had died.'

'Oh my poor, Della,' Maureen cried out as if wounded. She bent forward and cradled her head in her hands. 'What must she have gone through?'

Greg spoke softly, 'I know; it's difficult to think about.'

Maureen looked up again from Greg to Sarah. 'To this day, I still wondered if the doctors were right and that a bad flu had taken her from us, but from what you're saying, it sounds like it definitely was complications following childbirth. Oh Lord Bless her soul. She must have been so scared and alone,' Maureen whispered. 'If only she had told me . . .' Maureen shook her head sadly, 'I would have helped her.'

'She was so young,' Sarah said kindly. 'She probably didn't realise how serious it was. We all think we're invincible as teenagers.'

Maureen nodded in agreement. 'She was only child.' She turned to Greg. 'I'm sorry, Greg,' she said. 'I really wasn't trying to deceive you. I was just frightened. I didn't know what you were going to uncover. This is extremely difficult for me. I hope now that I have explained a little more that you might understand where I was coming from.'

The emotional toll was written all over poor Maureen's face, and Greg actually found himself pitying her. He nodded. 'I know this must be so hard for you, Maureen, but I really appreciate your honesty.'

'I must say I wasn't expecting this when I saw you this evening. This has been quite the day. I've so much new information to get my head around. I hope you don't mind, but I think I'm going to retire for the evening. I'm exhausted.'

Greg was feeling the same himself. 'Before you go, Maureen, can I ask if you know who my father was?' He desperately hoped Maureen could fill in the final piece of the puzzle for him.

Maureen looked over at the window where yellow lights twinkled across the bay. 'I've often wondered myself over the years who he was too. No, Greg, I'm sorry. I've told you everything I know.'

Chapter 44

Wind was singing through the dunes, and it whispered over the tiny sand grains as Greg and Sarah walked along the beach. The gulls fought and screeched over the small shellfish left behind by the outgoing tide. The sky above the cove was ablaze in shades of salmon and crimson as the sun set on yet another day. It gave the light an ethereal quality like they were looking at the world through a sepia filter.

Sarah had suggested they go for a walk to get some fresh air after Maureen had retired to her room, and Greg had gladly agreed. He knew it wouldn't do him any good to go and sit alone, marauding over the day's events.

'Are you okay?' Sarah asked eventually.

He nodded. 'I'm just trying to get my head around it all.'

'It's a lot to take in all right,' Sarah said in agreement.

'I can't help but feel guilty for what happened to her,' Greg said.

Sarah stopped walking and turned to face him. 'But how can you blame yourself? You were only an infant, just hours old!'

'I know, but the harsh truth is that if she hadn't been pregnant with me, she would probably still be alive today.'

A gull swooped down and cawed hoarsely overhead. They both fell silent and continued on walking.

'It was a combination of things—a perfect storm of bad luck. It wasn't your fault or your father's. It wasn't Maureen's fault or even Della's parents' either. Who knows, maybe even if she had sought medical help, they still might not have been able to be save her? We'll never know. Times were different back then. There was such stigma around unmarried mothers, it's difficult for you and me to understand it, but Ireland was a dark place for women in the seventies. It was society that really let her down.'

'I just wish I had been able to get to know her, to find out what she was really like, y'know?' he said sadly. It had been nice listening to Maureen describe his birth mother earlier. It was like she had started to sketch in the outline, and Della had been brought to life by her words. Greg knew she must have been an extremely courageous and determined young woman to endure all that she went through.

They reached the end of the cove where the cliffs climbed up to the headland overhead. They made their way across the beach and climbed the worn path that wound its way through the rocks and up over the dunes that led them back to the village.

'Do you want to go to the graveyard and see if we can find where she is buried?' Sarah suggested.

Greg had seen the graveyard on his runs around the village, but he had noticed it in the same way as he had seen the church or the GAA pitch—it hadn't really impacted on him. For some reason, as he had embarked on his journey to Inishbeg Cove, he had never envisaged himself visiting a grave. He realised, with crushing disappointment, that he had hoped for warm arms around him rather than staring down at a cold marble headstone. But he knew he couldn't leave the village without paying his respects to Della Forde. He owed her that much at least. He exhaled heavily. 'Let's do it.'

They walked up the main street in the direction of the church to where the graveyard was situated behind a crumbling stone wall at the back. Greg climbed over the worn steps in the wall. He reached up and helped Sarah down after him.

As he looked around him, it was like stepping into another world. Greg had never seen a cemetery so old. At a glance he saw headstones with inscriptions covered in lichen and moss that were at least several hundred years old. At home the cemeteries were laid out in an orderly fashion and the tombstones ran in neat lines, but here the tombstones were higgledy-piggledy, almost chaotically arranged. The ground was hilly and undulating with older tombstones leaning heavily as if worn down by their age.

Sarah led the way towards the back of the graveyard to where the newer burial plots were. Brightly coloured flowers wrapped in cellophane decorated some graves of the recently deceased. They wandered around reading the head-stones for Della's name as a brisk wind tossed leaves around on the path before them. The graveyard took on a shadowy feeling in the half-light as they searched for Della's final rest-ing place. Suddenly Greg felt the air being sucked out of his lungs when his eyes landed on her name etched on the head-stone before him, and he fell to his knees. A simple bunch of daffodils lay on the grave tied with a delicate yellow ribbon. He noticed it was neatly tended, and the grass around the edges was recently trimmed. Little eruptions poked through the stones where someone, Maureen he guessed, had picked out weeds. He felt a flood of emotion as weeks of hurt and pain spilled out of him. Sarah leant forward to grip his shoul-der and squeezed it tightly. 'I'll give you a few minutes by yourself,' she said softly.

'Thanks,' Greg mumbled.

As Sarah retreated back towards the church, Greg stared at the cold grave in front of him. He traced his finger over Della's name and date of birth etched in the cool marble. His head was spinning. A few weeks ago he had lost his mother —the woman who had raised him—the woman who he had thought was the only mother he would ever have, but then he had learnt he had another mother, and after the shock had subsided, he guessed somewhere at the back of his mind he had harboured some stupid, childish fantasy about building a new relationship with her. He knew he would never replace the relationship he had had with his mom—how could he, she had been a wonderful mother to him—but he had hoped that they could have some kind of maternal closeness that he was desperately missing since his mom's death. It was like Eve's apple; it was a tantalising balm, luring him with the hope of a fresh chance of security and love, and he knew his sore heart was desperately crying out for that, but now that dream was thwarted too. He had lost two mothers in the space of several weeks, and his head was finding it difficult to process all these conflicting emotions. He had never known Della, but yet he was grieving for her. Grieving for what might have been, grieving for all that she lost. He knew that his search ended here, and it was time for him to stop running and deal with everything he had learnt over the last few weeks. Greg knew the time had come for him to go home.

'I'm sorry, Della, for how life treated you,' he whispered. 'I wish I could have known you, but because of you, I had a wonderful life, thank you for giving me a chance.'

Eventually the pink dusk gave way to darkness, and Greg picked himself up again to leave. He saw Sarah's silhouette in the distance as he made his way back towards the church. The temperature had dropped, and the evening air was chilly.

'I'm so sorry, Greg,' she said, linking her arm through his when he came back over the wall. 'I know that was difficult for you. Will you come back to mine for a cuppa to warm up?' Sarah cajoled. 'We might catch some of the march on the news, what do you say?'

It was hard to believe that the march had only taken places just hours earlier; Greg felt so much had happened since then. He had lost so much.

He nodded wordlessly, feeling too broken to speak.

They went back to Sarah's cottage where she lit the fire. Soon the room was filled with the peaty smell of turf, and they both rubbed their hands in front of the crackling flames to warm up. Then Greg sat down on the armchair while Sarah made a pot of tea. After it had drawn, she poured it from the pot in an amber arc to fill two large mugs. She handed one to him and sat down on the sofa opposite with her own.

'Get that into you,' she said.

'Thanks,' he said, clasping the mug in his hands, savouring its warmth.

'I'm sorry things didn't turn out as you'd hoped in your search for your birth parents, but I'm glad you finally got the truth today.'

Greg nodded. 'I'm glad I know what happened, even if things didn't turn out like I had hoped, at least I finally have some closure.'

She picked up the remote and flicked on the TV, and they both fell quiet as they watched the RTÉ News. They held their breath as they saw the village appear on the screen. Sarah watched from behind her fingers when she saw herself being interviewed as she told the nation about the plight of her village. Then they saw the long procession make its way down the main street. Seeing it on the television, they saw that the turnout was much bigger than either of them had realised.

'I'm so proud of everyone,' Sarah said as Tríona Quinn signed off her report.

'If this doesn't stop them, nothing will,' Greg said.

'Well, either way, I've done everything I can now.' She turned to him. 'Thank you, Greg, for everything. I couldn't have done it without you. You've been a rock for me over the last few weeks.'

Greg knew it was time to tell her what had been on his mind. He took a deep breath. 'I've been doing some thinking,' he announced.

'Oh yeah?' Sarah stilled and lowered her mug.

'I think it's time I headed back to North Carolina. I've got what I came here for, there's nothing more left for me in the village. I've decided I'm going to change my flight and go home a bit earlier,' he said.

'Ah, Greg, I know you're disappointed but don't make a rash decision to leave. You still have a week left. Take your time. All isn't lost yet—we still can trace your father; he might be alive.'

Greg shook his head. He had already made up his mind on this. He wasn't able for it. He just felt too broken by what he had learnt. He had let his walls down and paid a big price emotionally. 'I don't have the heart for it. I don't think I'd cope with any more lies or rejection.' He needed to go home now with all his newfound knowledge and start the healing process. He needed to repair himself again and get back to the old Greg.

'I get that,' Sarah said.

'It's time I got back to reality anyway. I can't run away forever.'

Sarah nodded. 'You have to take care of yourself.'

Greg desperately wanted to tell her that it wasn't easy for him to go, that he would be leaving Inishbeg Cove with a heavy heart. He wanted her to know how he felt; he needed her to know just how important a person she had become in his life. How grateful he felt to have met her. He went to speak, but the words seemed to stick in his throat.

'What?' Sarah said, looking at him expectantly.

'It's nothing—' He had only known her for a few short weeks, yet he was dreading saying goodbye to her. He knew they would always stay in touch; even when he returned to North Carolina; he would make sure to stay in contact with Sarah. He had made a true friend in Inishbeg Cove, and when you found someone like that in your life, you held on to them.

'It's just that I'm really grateful for your friendship,' he continued. He was mortified by his choice of words. They felt stiff, like words you would say to a colleague at a retirement party. They didn't convey just how important a person she had become in his life. 'I know I didn't exactly get what I came to the village for, but I'm so glad I met you, Sarah.'

Her cheeks pinked. 'Me too, Greg. I've loved having you in Inishbeg Cove; I'm going to miss you . . . life has been'—she paused—'a bit brighter with you here.' She looked down and began tracing a finger up and down the side of the mug.

'Maybe you might even come to North Carolina to visit sometime?' he ventured.

'Maybe . . .' Sarah said. 'I guess when the post office closes, I'll have a lot of free time on my hands!' She cracked a half-smile.

Suddenly he felt insensitive to her worries. He had been stuck inside his own head, dealing with his own emotions, and he had forgotten she had her own battles. 'Hey, it might not happen, don't lose hope yet. I'm sorry for running out on you when you're going through your own problems.'

'Don't be daft. I'm not on my own—I've the whole village behind me.'

'You do,' he said agreeing, feeling that familiar ache in his heart once more. She belonged to them, and they would circle around and protect her.

Chapter 45

Sarah closed the door behind Greg that night with a sinking feeling in the pit of her stomach. The day she had always known was coming ever since he had arrived in the village was somehow here. Whenever thoughts of Greg's return to North Carolina had entered her head, she had always pushed them out quickly again before they could take seed. Back then his return to America had seemed like a faraway event, a blurry outline somewhere in the distance. Now that he had announced his departure, she couldn't help but feel a sense of disappointment, and she couldn't understand why she would feel like this. Greg had never given her any reason to think he wouldn't be returning home. She guessed that even when the head warned against something, the heart could still get carried away regardless.

Sarah didn't sleep that night as she thought about Greg's impending departure. She had considered telling him how she felt but in the end had decided against it. What good would it do? He still had to return to North Carolina, he had a job and a whole other life over there. He couldn't stay even if he wanted to. And besides, he might not even feel the same way about her. After all, he was the one who had put coolers on things after they had kissed. No, she had decided that telling him how she felt was just going to make it all the harder to say goodbye when the time came, and she couldn't allow her heart to be exposed like that.

She rose before her alarm had even sounded the next morning. She was exhausted having spent the entire night lying awake with her thoughts. She got up and wrapped her dressing gown tightly around her. She made her way into the bathroom and flicked on the light. She caught one look at her bleary eyes in the mirror and switched the light back off again. She went downstairs and busied about her cottage. She cleaned out the ashes from the grate and put out a bowl of food for the stray cat that was creeping up along the glass with its front paws, asking to be fed. When she was finished, she cut herself a thick slice of Ruairí's brown bread and slathered it with butter and marmalade as an extra treat for herself. She needed a bit of cheering up this morning. She took a bite, but it felt like cardboard in her mouth as she chewed. She pushed the plate away from her; things must be bad if she had lost her appetite, she thought wryly to herself.

'You're in luck this morning, cat," she said through the window, gesturing at the plate.

The little tabby cat cocked his head to the side as if listening closely to her. She couldn't help but smile despite her mood.

After she had showered and dressed, she stepped outside her cottage to go to work. The weather seemed to mirror her feelings; a slate grey sky hung above an eerily calm sea. She went back inside and swapped her woollen coat for her rain jacket. She had heard on the radio that there was a storm forecast to make landfall later. She wrapped her scarf double around her neck and then headed on for the post office.

She opened up and was kept going with the usual business of people sending letters, collecting pensions, and paying bills. When she caught a glimpse of Greg walking up to the counter a while later, her breath caught a little in her chest and her heart somersaulted. She looked at him wearing running tights and a pale-blue Lycra T-shirt that clung to the damp skin of his chest, hinting at his toned physique underneath. Tiny beads of sweat dotted his brow, and his dark hair glistened with raindrops. She felt an urge to run her fingers through it and brush them all away. She realised then just how much she looked forward to his morning visits after his run around the village. It was all these little routines that she was going to miss so much. He stood to the side and waited until her customers had finished before making his way up to the counter.

'Good morning,' she said, forcing a smile on her face, but she knew it didn't quite stretch up to her eyes. 'How are you doing today?'

'I'm good, slowly trying to get my head around it all, but I'm glad I finally learnt the truth about what happened back then even if some of it was painful to hear.'

Sarah nodded. 'I'm glad you got some answers too; at least your trip here wasn't in vain. Have you seen Maureen since?'

He shook his head. 'No, she wasn't at breakfast this morning, so who knows, maybe she's avoiding me.' He shrugged his shoulders but was clearly hurt.

'Give her time, Greg, what she learnt yesterday must have been very difficult for her.'

'Yeah, you're right.' He sighed. 'You're always able to see the good in everyone.' His face broke into a smile, and she felt herself begin to blush. They both fell silent, and he picked up the pen Sarah left on the counter for customers to use and began twirling it between his fingers. 'Anyway, I just wanted to tell you that I've booked my flight—'

Her heart thudded to the floor. She couldn't look at him. She didn't want him to sense her disappointment. 'That's great, Greg, I bet you're excited to be going home now.'

'Yeah, I'm looking forward to it, it's time I got back to normal.' She noticed that despite his words, he didn't look too excited. His whole body seemed to belie him. His shoulders were slumped downwards, and his face had taken on a look of resignation. 'I can't stay here forever,' he added.

If only, she thought but didn't say it out loud. 'So when do you leave?'

'Tomorrow morning.'

'Right.' She tried not to act stunned, but she hadn't expected it to be so soon. She thought she would have a few more days with him, but tomorrow?

'Will you meet me for a drink tonight?' he asked.

'Of course! We have to give you a good send-off, Inishbeg style!' She tried to sound upbeat, but it was in direct contrast to how she was feeling inside.

After he had left and she was alone in her post office,

she felt tears push forward and fill her eyes. *Stop it, Sarah*, she chastised. *You are being ridiculous,* she told herself as she brushed them away, but still they kept falling. It was one of the things she hated most about herself was how close her emotions always were to the surface. She had only known him for a few weeks, and a part of her felt she was being melodramatic, but she was just starting to realise that she had fallen for him hook, line, and sinker.

The bell tinkled, and Mrs Manning came in the door. She took one look at Sarah and knew instantly that something was up. 'What's the matter with you? It's not more bad news about this place, is it?'

Sarah quickly wiped her eyes with the back of her hand. 'Oh, no, sorry, it's nothing like that—'

Mrs Manning cocked her head in concern. 'Well, what is it then? Come on now, Sarah, I'm long enough in the tooth to know when something's up. Spit it out.'

'Oh, Mrs Manning—' She dissolved, and suddenly the tears spilled out uncontrollably. 'Greg is going home tomorrow," she sobbed, 'and I'm—I'm afraid I'm after falling for him'—she stopped to wipe her nose—'badly,' she added.

'I see,' the older lady said thoughtfully, leaning onto the counter for support. "Open up that door and come out here to me."

Sarah did as she was told, and when she appeared, the old lady threw her arms around her.

'I tried not to, but I couldn't help myself,' Sarah sobbed.

She took Sarah's hand in her own, which was mottled with age spots, and ran her fingers along the back of it in a maternal fashion.

'Oh, Sarah, love, the head doesn't rule the heart, dear, it's always the other way around,' she said kindly. 'Does he know how you feel about him?'

Sarah pulled back. 'Of course not,' she said quickly. 'His whole life is over there. It could never work between us, but still I couldn't help falling for him.' She shook her head at the stupidity of it all. She was angry with herself for allowing her heart to be exposed and vulnerable like this. 'I haven't felt like this about someone in a long time,' she whispered.

'Since Conor Keogh, you mean?'

The whole village remembered her relationship with Conor, probably because it was her only relationship. They all knew that Sarah had been left broken-hearted when he moved to Australia and eventually stopped calling her.

'Well, yeah—'

'And what about a long-distance relationship, aren't all the young ones doing that these days? Sure going to America is like going to England nowadays! It's not like in my day when you went on a boat for a week to get there. They can do wonderful things with technology nowadays. Would you not try that?'

'He lives in America, it's not like we could just hop on a plane and spend weekends together. The distance is too far; it just wouldn't work. Besides, I don't even know if Greg feels the same way about me.'

Mrs Manning started to laugh then, a deep cackling that disrupted the atmosphere in the room.

'What is it?' Sarah asked.

'Oh, he likes you all right, there's no doubt about that!'

'Do you think?' Sarah asked, blowing her nose into a tissue.

'Sure, you'd have to be blind not to notice! Why don't you tell him how you're feeling?'

Sarah shook her head quickly. 'No way, I can't, Mrs Manning—'

'I don't know'—Mrs Manning shook her head in despair —'you young ones make it all so complicated! In my day when you liked someone, you told them! Sometimes you have to be brave. You have to take a risk and open up your heart, or how else can you let love in?'

'Well anyway, it's too late now,' Sarah said stubbornly. 'He's leaving in the morning.'

Mrs Manning shook her head. 'Take it from someone who has been on this Earth for a while—when you love somebody, let them know. You might not get another chance.'

Chapter 46

Sarah and Greg fought against a strong gust of wind as they opened the door of the pub. They hurried inside, glad to see that Jim had the fire lighting, making the place warm and inviting. There were a few regulars sitting up at the bar, but otherwise it was largely empty. Skipper was sprawled across the floor in his usual spot, snoring gently. Jim was watching the weather forecast on TV while polishing a glass with a dishcloth.

'Sarah, Greg,' he greeted, turning away from the TV. 'How're ye doing? Looks like there's a storm due in off the Atlantic. It's true what they say: March comes in like a lion . . .'

The normally chatty barman fell quiet then as he served their drinks. Greg wondered if Maureen had told him about yesterday's events? It occurred to him as Jim pulled his pint that they were actually related now albeit through marriage. In all the times Greg had sat in this pub chatting to him, he never would have guessed that Jim was his uncle. It felt as though once again the world had spun around on its axis and threw up some more bombshells for him.

'It's Greg's send-off,' Sarah said, elbowing him jokily to make conversation with Jim.

'Are you leaving already?' Jim asked in genuine surprise as he put Greg's pint down on the bar.

'I can't stay on vacation here forever, as much as I'd love to,' he said.

Jim lowered his voice and leaned in across the bar to him. 'Maureen told me everything. I'm glad you got what you came here for, Greg,' Jim said. 'It's been a big shock to her—well, to both of us actually—but I think it's been a good thing, you know? I can't believe she carried the weight of a secret like that around for all these years . . .' He shook his head sadly. 'If there's one thing I know, it's that these things are better out in the open.'

Greg nodded. 'They are,' he agreed. He felt relieved that Maureen had opened up to Jim about the past. She had carried a burden on her shoulders for a long time, and it was time for her to ease the load. Greg was glad Jim would be able to support her.

'You'll be missed,' Jim said. 'I know you've only been here a few weeks, but already you're like one of the locals.'

Greg laughed. 'Well thank you, Jim.' He felt pride swell in his heart at the compliment.

They took their drinks and sat down in their usual spot.

Mrs Manning came in a while later with a delivery of eggs for breakfast in the morning. She spotted Sarah and Greg and winked across at them. Sarah started to blush.

'What is it?' Greg asked.

'Oh nothing,' she said with a wave of her hand. 'She's up to no good again,'

They spent the night talking and laughing. That was the thing with Sarah; she was so easy to talk to. Hours flew by like in minutes in her company. When he had been with Selena, there would often be awkward silences when they were together. He had just thought it was normal. He desperately wished that he could freeze time and they could stay like this forever. He was keenly aware that every hour which went past, was an hour closer to leaving her.

They stayed chatting until Jim called last orders, and slowly they both put on their coats, resigned to the fact that it was almost time for them to say their goodbyes. They said goodnight to Jim and headed outside where they were assailed by a squall of wind. Rain spilled from the sky, and a wild gale raged. The waves were rough and choppy in the cove, and the boats were tossed around as if a child was playing with them in the bath. They quickly realised that while they had been cocooned inside the pub, wrapped up in conversation, the storm had been brewing. They started to run, hurrying through the village, trying to dodge the puddles as they went.

A swirling wind sucked up leaves on the path and spat them out again further down the street.

'Do you want to come in for a while until the rain stops?' Sarah asked breathlessly as soon as they reached her cottage. Greg gladly agreed, eager to delay their goodbye for as long as he could.

She put her key in the lock, and they both hurried inside. A gust of wind followed them into the cottage, and Sarah struggled to shut the door behind them with the force of the wind. Greg threw his shoulder against it, sealing them inside the sanctuary of her home.

'It's a rotten one,' Sarah said as she hung up their wet coats to dry. Raindrops dotted her hair like crystals and ran down along her face. Greg longed to reach out and wipe them all away.

'Will you share a bottle of wine with me?' she asked, lifting down a bottle of Rioja from the wine rack.

'I won't say no,' Greg said, shaking the rain from his hair.

She opened the bottle of red and poured them both a glass. Then she lit the fire, and soon the place was warm and cosy as the heady aroma of blackberries and spice mingled with the smell of the turf. They could hear the waves swell and crash in foamy bursts outside. The rain beating off the roof was like a ticking clock, reminding them that time running out. When a particularly violent wave crashed against the rocks beyond the window, the lights started to flicker.

'Uh-oh, it looks like there's a power cut on the way.' Sarah jumped up, rooted in the drawers for a box of matches, and then hurried around the cottage lighting candles. She tossed Greg a handful of tea lights, and he began doing the same.

Suddenly another huge gust swirled around the cottage, and sure enough, the lights went out so that the living room was lit solely by the soft glow of candlelight.

'Just in the nick of time!' Sarah said, laughing as she clinked her wine glass against Greg's.

The little cottage was battered by the elements as they stayed up late into the night talking. They finished the first bottle and then opened another.

'It doesn't seem to be easing up,' Sarah said after a while.

Greg knew he probably should head back to *Cove View*, he had an early start in the morning, but he would have done anything to delay the inevitable farewell that was looming ahead of them.

Sarah filled both their glasses once more before flopping down onto the sofa beside him again. 'I hope the storm doesn't affect your flight,' Sarah said as the wind continued to rage beyond the windows.

'I could think of worse places to be stranded,' Greg said, his voice laced with regret.

'I'm really going to miss you,' she said in a sad voice.

'You've become a very special person to me, Sarah,' he blurted. The wine had made him braver, his feelings looser. The lines had been blurred between friendship and romance. They were both trying hard to stay on the side of friendship, but some invisible force kept pulling them across the line until he wasn't sure what side they were on anymore. 'I mean it; please keep in touch.' Now that he had found her, he really wanted to keep Sarah in his life. He *needed* her in his life. Everything was easy with her; there were no games or agendas. She was honest with her feelings, and somehow it made it easier for him to be honest with his too. He just wished there wasn't an ocean between them.

Feeling braver from the wine, he leant across towards her, and his mouth searched for hers. Her lips were soft and full against his own, but suddenly the warmth of her mouth was gone, replaced by cold air, and he realised with a sting that Sarah was sitting back against the sofa in shock.

'I'm sorry, I shouldn't have done that,' he said, pulling away. 'I'm so sorry.' He was giving her mixed messages. He kicked himself. He was a jerk. He stood up to leave.

'It's okay, I just wasn't expecting it,' she said, looking down at the honey-coloured floorboards as awkwardness charged the air between them. 'We've both had a lot to drink.' Her face looked so doleful lit by the candlelight, and his heart twisted. How could he have been so stupid to ruin their last few hours together by doing something as crass as trying to kiss her? What must she think of him?

Then before he realised what was happening, she was standing up too and was walking closer towards him, closing the distance between them. She reached out and cupped his jaw in her two hands. Her soft lips brushed against his. It was so unexpected that for a second or two he just stood in shock, afraid to move in case she stopped doing it. When he realised that she wanted this too, he pulled her closer to him and breathed in her musky perfume that he loved so much. Their lips met, and all the passion that had been building during the weeks leading up to this moment was unleashed.

'Will you stay?' she whispered. 'I know we've only got one night together but let's make it special.'

'Are you sure you want this?' Greg said, leaning in to kiss her once more, letting his fingers entwine with her hair that smelled of citrus shampoo.

'I've never been more certain of anything in my life,' she said. 'I couldn't stop myself now even if I wanted to.'

Greg had to switch off the part of his brain that told him that this was a mistake, he turned off the voice that reminded him that he was going home in the morning, and it was going to be even harder to get on that plane once they crossed this line. He would worry about the consequences tomorrow. Something amazing was happening between them, and he didn't know whether to be excited or terrified by it. He wrapped his arms around her, and butterflies danced in his stomach. They kissed the whole way up the stairs.

'You are so beautiful,' Greg whispered as they fell back onto her bed. 'You don't know how much I've longed for this moment.'

He pulled off her top and unbuttoned her jeans. Her body was as stunning as he had always imagined. He traced delicate kisses along the pale skin of her collarbone. Her hands were trembling as she pulled his sweater off over his head, and his skin came alive as her hands ran over his bare torso. Suddenly their kisses became more urgent. They both wanted more.

*

Greg woke up with Sarah's hair fanned out across his chest; its shades of honey and caramel highlighted by the dawn light that was creeping around the sides of the window. He could hear the sea crashing gently outside, normal weather restored once more. He felt his heart sink. This was the day it all had to end.

He took a second to savour the moment. He wanted to cherish it and remember every detail of Sarah before the time came for him to return to his old life. He kissed her lips, and her eyes flickered open as she started to wake. He smiled down at her. Instead of this being the beginning of something special, he couldn't help but feel like it was the end. Like he was on his last walk to the execution chamber. *Stop it, Greg*, he chastised himself. He had to remind himself that he had once been happy before he had ever known about Inishbeg Cove. His life had once been enough for him. He knew he couldn't let a month away cloud everything, but since he had come here, it was like a door had opened into a whole new vibrant world filled with glorious colours and sounds. He had tasted a new way of life, and now it was hard to close that door and go back to his reality when he knew what else was out there. His time in the village had cast a spotlight over his entire existence, but now he needed to turn that light off and get on with things.

'Good morning, beautiful,' he whispered.

Sarah sat up against the pillows and yawned.

'What time is it?' Her voice was still peppered with sleep, and he wished he could wake up to that voice every morning.

'Almost six, I need to get going to the airport.' He sighed.

She nodded, but there was an unmistakable sadness in her eyes.

'I'm going to miss you so much,' he said.

'Me too,' she said, lying back against his chest. He loved the feeling of her slotted under his arm like she just belonged there.

'We'll keep in touch, Sarah—I'm going to try and book another trip maybe in a few months' time.'

'Sure,' she said. Greg knew that she didn't believe him. She thought he would go back to his old life and forget all about her, but how could he? He could never forget Sarah.

They kissed goodbye for the last time, then Greg stole out into the Inishbeg dawn and made his way back to the guesthouse.

*

As Greg walked along the main street back towards *Cove View*, the village looked as peaceful as a summer's day. The sky was washed a shade of clean cerulean blue as a new day dawned. Birds twittered their early morning song oblivious to the pain in Greg's heart.

It had been awful leaving Sarah like that, knowing that things were now over between them. The night they had spent together had been one of the most perfect moments of his life. It felt as though he had left a huge part of himself behind. Greg knew he would never forget her.

The guesthouse was still sleeping as he gently turned his key in the door. It would be several hours before it would come to life with people traipsing up and down the stairs and Maureen running around with the breakfast trays. He climbed the steps taking care not to make any noise. He opened his room door and took his case out of the wardrobe where he had stowed it only a few weeks earlier. He moved around placing his clothes into it.

It didn't take him long to gather up his stuff. He took a final look around the room that had become a sort of home for him during the last few weeks, then he pulled the door behind him and headed downstairs.

When he reached the bottom, he saw Maureen was standing in the lobby waiting for him. They had managed to avoid each other since her confession the other evening, and Greg wasn't sure what they had left to say.

'Greg—wait—I wanted to talk to you,' she said.

He stopped and placed his cases down on either side of his feet.

'Jim said you were leaving,' she continued, eying up his luggage. 'You don't need to hurry off. You've paid up until the end of the month.'

'It's time I got back to work,' Greg said.

Maureen nodded. 'I'm sorry things didn't turn out as you'd hoped ...'

'It was always going to be a long shot, but at least I have some closure now.' He lifted his cases again, ready to head outside to his hire car.

'Would you mind if I wrote to you?' she asked with a nervous tinge to her voice.

Greg knew they had had a rocky start and probably would never have a conventional aunt/nephew relationship, but at the end of the day, they shared the same blood.

'I'd like that,' he said, nodding.

Maureen was his family, and if he had learnt one thing over the last few weeks, it was that you had to treasure the bonds you had with people, no matter how weak they were. Who knew, maybe through letters they could build bridges.

Chapter 47

A slow, silent tear snaked its way down Sarah's face as she read through an email that had landed in her inbox. She brushed it away, but there was another one to replace it. No matter how many she wiped away, they kept on coming. She tried to read the email again, but the screen was blurry through her water-filled eyes.

Greg had left for the airport that morning, and as she said goodbye to him in the cool morning air of her cottage, she felt like he was taking her heart away with him.

He had only been gone for a few hours, and she was already missing him so much. She had known him for a matter of weeks, but it was only now in his absence that she realised just how attached she had become to him. In the short space of time they had spent together, she had developed a connection with him that she had never felt with anyone else before. Even when she had been with Conor, she had never had that same sense of ease that she felt in Greg's company. She loved the way he would always usher her through a door first, the way he listened—really listened—when she told him about her day. The way he cared for her, like they were characters in an old-fashioned black-and-white movie. She knew he had been crushed by what he had learnt in Inishbeg Cove, but she hadn't expected him to leave so abruptly. She tried not to think about her future without him. She tried not to think of what could have been. If only she could stop thinking altogether.

She had taken Mrs Manning's advice about opening up her heart to him, she had been brave and let him into her heart, but it was all for nothing. She wished now that she had kept it shut because she knew she wouldn't be feeling so low now. A part of her felt stupid, she had always known he was going home to North Carolina, he had never let her think otherwise, and now that it had become a reality, she was left feeling bereft. Their night with one another just reinforced all that she would miss. It had been so long since she had been intimate with someone, and she had been terrified that she had forgotten what to do or, worse, that he would laugh at her inexperience, but he couldn't have made her more relaxed, and it all seemed to come back naturally. He had made her feel beautiful, and it had been a long time since a man had made her feel that way. As he had stroked her skin, his fingers made butterflies come alive in her body. He had taken his time, kissing her décolletage, his lips trailing sensually along her body. Her heart had been thumping so loudly she was sure he must have been able to hear it. She had gasped as his hand had connected with the bare skin of her thighs. The night they spent together had been perfect in every way, and even if it was all they could ever have, she knew she would never, ever forget it.

The hardest part of all was the knowledge that if their circumstances or timing had been different, they could have had something great together. She knew she would never meet anyone like him ever again. He had said he would stay in touch with her, he had even asked her to come visit him, but people said these things loosely without really meaning it. He would probably go back to his life in North Carolina, settle straight back in, and forget all about her and her village.

She stared at the email once more and reread it but couldn't take in the words. *Come on, Sarah, get it together*, she chastised herself.

She heard the bell go, and she looked up to see Timmy O'Malley coming through the door.

'Good morning, Timmy,' she said, quickly composing herself and forcing a smile on her face as he made his way slowly up to the counter.

'Hi, Sarah, it's a cold one out there but at least that wind has died down. There's a lot of damage to the boats in the cove, and there is debris scattered around the place. The village really took a hammering!' He removed his sheepskin gloves and rubbed his hands together to warm them up.

The mention of the previous night's storm brought Sarah back to lying in Greg's arms as it lashed the cottage walls.

'How's the Yank getting on?' he continued.

At the mention of Greg, Sarah had to squeeze her eyelids tightly together to keep any watery signs of her broken heart in check. 'He left this morning actually.' She glanced at the clock on the wall, mentally calculating that he would probably be there now at the airport waiting to board his flight. On a normal day, he would have called into her in the post office around this time to say hello when he was coming back from his run. It was all those little things that she would miss. Everything now seemed duller without him.

'Oh? I didn't realise he was going back so soon. Did he get anywhere in his search in the end?'

Sarah paused, wondering if she should say anything, but what did it matter now? The secrets were out in the open; there was no reason to keep them covered any longer. It was time. She nodded. 'He did actually'—she paused—'Timmy, do you remember a girl called Della Forde?'

Timmy thought for a moment. 'Maureen's younger sister? I do, of course, it was very sad what happened to her.'

'You remember it?' Sarah was surprised to get a straight answer. In their search for Greg's parents, they had hit wall after wall, but Della was obviously well known in the village.

'Well, sure, the whole village was in shock. Only seventeen years old and she caught a bad flu on her way home from school and the poor crathur died a few days later. You don't forget that too easily!'

'Well, it seems that Della was Greg's mother—'

The creases and crevices lining his skin were deeply engrained as he frowned.

'Are you sure, Sarah? She was only a young girl . . .'

'It appears she had a baby unbeknownst to anyone and gave it to an American couple who were on holiday in the village, to raise. She died a few days later, and it looks as though it was probably from complications post-childbirth. She never told anyone that she was pregnant, let alone that she had had a baby, and when she fell ill, the doctor was treating her for a flu.' Sarah shook her head at the tragedy of it all. Every time she thought of Della's plight, her heart ached. 'It seems nobody ever knew she had had a baby.'

Timmy removed his flat cap, exposing a shiny bald patch surrounded by white wispy hair and brought it close to his chest. 'Lord, rest her soul,' he whispered.

Suddenly Sarah thought of something; if he remembered Della, then maybe he would remember who her boyfriend had been. 'Timmy,' she began slowly, 'do you remember who Della was going out with before she died?'

The old man paused, his head full of thought. 'Della had no shortage of admirers that's for sure—'

'But can you remember if there was anyone in particular?' Sarah pushed.

He scratched his head in thought, and eventually he spoke. 'Now, there was someone . . . I don't know for sure if it was anything really . . . but it is only now that it has occurred to me—'

'What is it?' There was a hint of impatience in her voice, but she needed to know.

'Well, like I said, I don't know if there was anything between them but . . . there was one fella in particular that she seemed to be taken with . . . I was a few years older than him, but we used to pal around together sometimes. His father drove the school bus to the convent, and he used to help him out. I would notice him at mass, his eyes would scan around the church, and then when he saw Della, they would smile across the aisle at one another as if they had a secret that was only understood by them. But it was at her funeral that I realised that maybe they had shared something more because he sobbed and sobbed his whole way through the mass. I remember another one of the lads commenting that it was strange carry-on. I mean, we were all upset, but he seemed to be devastated. I just thought that funerals did funny things to people, but looking back, I recognise it as grief—we were all upset at such a tragedy, but he was more broken than the rest of us were.'

'What was his name?' Sarah asked, holding her breath

and crossing her fingers below the counter, silently praying that she would finally get the answer to the mystery that they had spent so much time desperately searching for. *Come on, Timmy*, Sarah urged internally.

'Albie. Albie Walsh,' he said.

The name didn't ring a bell with her. 'Do you know where he is now?' she said, opening the hatch door and rushing out from behind the counter and placing her two hands on both of sides of Timmy's arms to emphasise the urgency.

'Aragh, I'd see him on and off, but I gather he isn't too well, the last I heard he was in Grovetown.'

Grovetown was a small hospital not far from Inishbeg Cove where they looked after patients with long-term care needs.

'Thank you so much,' Sarah said, leaning in to plant a kiss on his lined cheek before running towards the door.

'Wait,' Timmy called after her. 'Where are you off to?'

'I need to see Greg before he gets on that plane.'

Chapter 48

Greg was sitting in the airport lounge, full of travel-weary business people with bored faces who looked as though they saw the inside of too many airports. They were clicking on laptops and willing the time to move forward as quickly as possible. It felt like the day after Christmas Day. It had that same depressing, anti-climactic void that was always felt after you've spent so long looking forward to something, and then suddenly it's all over. He had hooked his phone up to the Wi-Fi, and an avalanche of emails from work and other life stuff instantly began to download. It was like he had switched off his life in North Carolina while he had been in Inishbeg Cove, and now he was being dragged from the haven that the village was, back into reality.

It only seemed like yesterday that he was stepping aboard the flight to Shannon full of hope and excitement about what lay in wait for him in the village, and now, here he was heading back again and facing into the deep fathoms of his grief. Once he was back in North Carolina, he wouldn't be able to avoid it anymore. He knew he hadn't really given himself time to grieve his mother properly; he had thrown himself headfirst into his journey to Inishbeg Cove. The tiny village dotted on the rugged shore of Ireland had been a Band-Aid to salve the wound. It had been a distraction for a few weeks, but now the bandage had been ripped clean off and the wound cut deeper than before. Right now he was in the shallow waters watching the waves coming towards him, but he could see the full extent of his loss up ahead in the distance like a tidal wave waiting to hit him, and he was scared it might wash him away without a trace when it did.

There was so much he would miss about Inishbeg Cove. Simple things like his morning runs along the sand washed clean by the tide or watching how the weather changed the light over the village. He would miss the warmth of the people and the simplicity of their lifestyles and how they didn't get caught up in the things that dragged him down at home. Being in the village had made him realise that it wasn't your zip code or your career progression that were important, but instead, it was the richness of the relationships that you had with the people in it, that mattered most. They had figured out what truly was important. His time in Ireland had made him realise just how much he was missing from his own life.

Most of all, though, he would miss Sarah. He couldn't get her face out of his head as he had left her cottage that morning. He was tormented by what ifs. What if they didn't live in different countries? What if they had met at a different stage in life? But it was futile hanging on to what ifs because the reality was that they did live on opposite sides of the world and that wasn't going to change. He didn't know how he was going to try and get on with things without her in it. She had come to mean so much to him. He didn't have anyone else like that in his life, someone with whom he could confide his hopes and fears, without any worry of judgement. Sarah understood things, often without him having to even voice them—she just got it. Even when he had been with Selena, he could honestly say that in their three years together he had never talked to her to the same depth as he had with Sarah during the last few weeks. Sure, he had acquaintances and work colleagues, but he realised with a heavy sadness that he didn't have anyone in his life with whom you could just pick up the phone and they would listen. His friendship with Sarah had opened his eyes up to what he really needed in a relationship, someone kind and gentle. There were no sharp edges with her, no hidden motives, just a softness, almost bordering on purity, which was refreshing having only ever dated people that were cynical and looked after their own needs first.

When you were with Sarah, it was easy. She made you

want to be a better person because she was a better person. He hoped she would keep in touch with him because now that he had found her, he didn't want to lose her. Perhaps he might even be able to wrangle a few more vacation days in the summer and go back to visit her. He felt awful for leaving abruptly when she was so worried about the future of her post office, but he knew he wasn't leaving her on her own, she had the power of the whole community behind her. Even if her worst fears were confirmed and the closure went ahead, Greg knew the village would take care of her. You were never on your own in a place like Inishbeg Cove. She would survive. She was far stronger than she gave herself credit for.

He continued scanning through the emails with a half-hearted appetite until he heard a voice announce boarding for flight EI111 to JFK, the first leg of his journey. He sighed wearily, then stood up and gathered up his belongings to go on his way.

He left the relative calm of the lounge and stepped into the full-blown chaos of the airport. The unmistakable buzz of excitement of people eagerly setting off on an adventure was in direct contrast to his own feelings. He joined the long line at the security check when he suddenly heard a voice call from behind.

'Greg!'

He looked around him, but all he could see was a sea of people, each one getting on with their own journey. He turned back around, thinking he had misheard, and continued waiting in line.

'Greg, wait!' the voice called again.

He swung around once more, and it was then that he saw her. Sarah was running towards him. He dropped his hand luggage on the floor and ran to meet her. Her hair fell down around her face, and she was rosy-cheeked—exactly like she had been on the night of the céilí. His heart sang at the sight of her. The crowds melted away, and it felt as though they were the only people in the airport.

'Sarah?' Greg said in amazement, holding her close to him because if he didn't, he was afraid she might disappear from his life again. 'What are you doing here?' he asked, studying her familiar face once more. It felt so good to have her in his arms again.

'I think I know who your father is,' she said breathlessly.

'You do?' he said, pulling back from her.

She nodded. 'His name is Albie Walsh, and he's in Grovetown Hospital.' She filled him in on the rest of the story and how it all led to this man. 'I can't be one hundred per cent sure, but I have a hunch. I thought you should know before you board your flight.'

Greg felt as though he was sitting on a spinning top watching the world around him whizz past in a blur of melted colours. On the one hand, he could be within a hair's breadth of getting answers about whom his father might be, but the more cautious part of him couldn't help but wonder, what if Sarah was wrong? Or worse still, what if she was right, but Albie Walsh didn't want to see him? He wasn't sure his fragile heart could take any more rejection.

He heard the final boarding call for his flight being announced over the tannoy, and he knew he had a decision to make. Maybe he was a glutton for punishment, but if Sarah was right—and he had a feeling that she was—then he couldn't get on that plane. If there was a chance, no matter how small, that Albie Walsh was his father, then he needed to see him before he left. A woman glared at them and shook her head impatiently as she made her way around where they were standing, blocking her path in the middle of the floor.

'Come on,' Greg said, reaching for her hand and enjoying the feeling of how it slotted so naturally into his own once again. 'Let's go.'

Chapter 49

It took a while, but eventually Greg managed to get his luggage off the plane, and then he and Sarah hurried out of the airport in the direction of the car park.

'Nice parking,' he remarked at how her car was parked at a jaunty angle to the rest of the cars.

'Hey,' she said, elbowing him playfully. 'I was in a hurry, okay?'

He laughed and put his case in the trunk. Then he hopped in, and Sarah drove them back along the same roads he had driven on when he had first arrived in Ireland.

Soon the suburbs melted away, replaced with acres of rolling pastureland where sheep and cattle grazed happily, and motorways turned into winding boreens as they drove deep into the Irish countryside. Now that he wasn't in the driving seat, he was able to truly admire the scenery in all its breathtaking beauty. The vibrant colours of spring contrasted sharply against the pigeon grey sky. As the road climbed high above the coastline, he marvelled at how the blanket of grassy hillocks dropped down to meet the silvery ocean. He could just about make out the sandy peninsula where Inishbeg Cove sat far off in the distance. As he stared out the window, transfixed by Ireland's raw and rugged beauty, he wondered if his parents had experienced a similar sense of awe as they had stared out onto the same scenery.

His heart was hammering as he thought about what awaited him in Grovetown Hospital. Could Sarah have finally cracked the mystery? He was afraid to get his hopes up just in case it would lead to another disappointment, but he really hoped she had got this right and they weren't on another wild goose chase.

He couldn't help but wonder why Albie was in a care home? Timmy had told Sarah that Albie and Della had been the same age, which meant he would be roughly around sixty now. Surely, he was too young to be in a nursing home?

'We're nearly there now,' Sarah said after a while. 'Grovetown is only a few miles from here.'

They continued down a road where pretty wild flowers dotted the hedgerows, and eventually they saw a sign saying 'Grovetown Hospital'.

They turned off the main road and followed a tree-lined avenue, broken with intermittent speed ramps. The drive snaked along until eventually a low-roofed building with buttermilk yellow roof tiles came into view. Two elderly ladies were sitting on a bench on the lawn with clusters of bright yellow daffodils growing near their feet.

They parked the car and went inside to a light-filled atrium. A smiling middle-aged woman greeted them at the reception desk. She wore fuchsia-coloured lipstick with a matching silk scarf tied around her neck.

'Welcome to Grovetown, how may I help you?'

'We're looking to speak to a gentleman called Albie—' Greg suddenly realised that he didn't know his last name, and he looked across at Sarah for help.

'Albie Walsh,' Sarah interjected.

'We believe he is a patient here,' he continued.

The woman looked taken aback. 'Is he expecting you?' she asked cautiously.

Greg shook his head. 'Well, no—'

Her eyes narrowed. 'Albie doesn't usually have visitors.'

'Well, it's a long story—'

'Well, perhaps you can fill me in? I'm sure you can appreciate that I can't let strangers walk in off the street to see our patients.'

'No, of course not,' he said quickly. He knew that if he had any hope of being allowed to visit Albie, then he would need to be honest with this woman. 'You see I've reason to believe that he might be my father.'

Between them, he and Sarah filled her in on the rest of

the story, and she listened dumbstruck. Something obviously tugged at her heartstrings because when they had finished, she said, 'Let me check with his care assistant to see if he is up to visitors.'

They watched through a glass partition as she headed off down the corridor and began speaking with another lady. *Please,* he begged silently, *I'm so close—don't cut me off now.*

After a few minutes, the two women walked back to the reception desk together.

'Hi, I'm Fiona. I'm Albie's care assistant,' the other woman said, offering Greg a slender hand. 'I don't know if you're aware, but Albie is a multiple sclerosis patient here. Unfortunately, his disease is quite progressive. His range of movement is limited, although his speech is good, and his mind is perfect.'

Greg felt himself sink. Multiple sclerosis could be a cruel illness. His father had had a friend with the same condition, and his bouts of relapse had been heartbreaking to watch.

'He tends to tire easily,' Fiona continued, 'but given the circumstances and because I think it would do Albie good to have some visitors, I'll allow you in for a few minutes. Now if he's not up to it or doesn't want to see you, then you'll have to leave straight away, okay?'

'Absolutely,' Greg agreed, relieved to at least be getting a chance to speak to Albie.

'Follow me.'

Fiona led them through a lounge area where a group of elderly patients were sitting watching a chat show on the TV. They passed an open door where more residents were gathered around a table painting.

'It's arts and crafts day today,' Fiona remarked as they walked by.

They followed her down a corridor towards Albie's bedroom. 'Now then, here we are.' She knocked softly before entering. 'Albie,' she said gently. 'You have some visitors.'

Greg felt his heart beat faster. They entered the room and saw a man sitting in a wheelchair with his back facing them. He used a joystick to turn it towards the door. He was much younger than the other residents they had seen, and immediately Greg could see a resemblance. Albie had Greg's almond-shaped eyes and his dark colouring, even Albie's hands were the same broad shape as his were. Sarah noticed it too; she looked over at Greg and smiled.

'Visitors for me? Are you sure about that, Fiona?' Albie said, moving closer to study them.

'This is Greg from America, and this is Sarah the postmistress of Inishbeg Cove,' Fiona said, introducing them.

Albie looked at them in confusion as he tried to work out why they were there. 'I don't mean to be rude, but I don't know them from Adam! Why are they visiting me?' he asked Fiona in bewilderment.

'I'll let them tell you that.' Fiona nodded at Greg encouragingly, urging him to tell his story.

Greg took a deep breath before beginning. 'Albie, my name is Greg Klein, and I'm visiting here from North Carolina. My mother recently passed away, and in her will she left me a letter telling me that I had been adopted from Inishbeg Cove. This was the first I had ever known about being adopted, so you can imagine what a shock it has been for me. Anyway, I decided to travel to Ireland to see what I could find out about the circumstances of my birth, and with Sarah's help, I've managed to discover that my mother was a girl called Della Forde. Does that name mean anything to you?'

The man's face suddenly froze; pain was etched in its lines. Something had registered with him, Greg was sure of it. It felt like forever while they waited for him to speak.

'I haven't heard her name in years,' he said eventually. 'You are Della's child?' His eyes were wide. Greg tried to read his expression, which looked to be a mixture of hope and disbelief.

'I believe am,' Greg said. 'Obviously I can't do a DNA test, but yes, I'm pretty certain that she was my mother.'

'Is it really you?' he gasped. He reached out his hand to touch Greg's, but his movements were restricted, so Greg moved closer to him. Albie's grasp was weak as he tried to clasp Greg's hand. 'You don't know how long I've dreamed about this moment,' he said. Tears filled his eyes. 'I never thought you would come. I thought I would die without getting to see you again.'

Greg saw Sarah dabbing her eyes with a tissue, and he felt a tear slide down his own face.

'I'll leave you alone for a few minutes, if you need anything, push the call button,' Fiona said, quietly excusing herself.

'Della was the love of my life, but we were so young,' he said as he thought back to a time long ago. 'We were only seventeen, and we thought we knew it all, but on that September day we realised just how out of our depth we were. When Della discovered she was pregnant, we knew if we stayed in Inishbeg Cove, she'd be put into a Mother and Baby home and our child would be put up for adoption. So we had a plan, you see. I had saved up some money, and we were going to run away together and get married before the baby was born, but as the saying goes, "make plans and God laughs". The baby came early, and we were both unprepared. We didn't know anything about delivering babies. The only place we could think of where we could go without anyone finding us was a cottage up on the headland. Della was so brave as she gave birth, but afterwards she was bleeding a lot. We didn't even have anything to cut the cord with. I was in a right state wondering what I should do, but any time I mentioned getting a doctor, she'd lose her mind. Eventually as she grew weaker, I knew we couldn't put off getting help any longer, and even though she begged me not to leave her, I had no choice but to run and get help. As I was making my way down to the village, I saw a man I didn't recognise walking on the headland. I called to him, and he came with me. When he reached the cottage, he obviously saw how young and out of our depth we were, but he helped cut the cord and to clean up Della without any judgement. I think it was only then that the shock of what had happened hit home with me. The responsibility to care for this tiny baby was sitting heavily on our young shoulders. What kind of a life could an infant have with us? We couldn't turn to our families for help, the baby would have been placed in an orphanage, and neither of us wanted that life for our child ... It felt surreal at the time, and I can't even remember how we discussed it, but it was as though the man could read our minds. He said he knew a couple that wanted a baby desperately and that they would give it a loving home where he would never want for anything. Della and I placed our trust in him. We both knew that we needed to put our infant son's needs before our own. It was right thing to do, and although it broke both our hearts, we kissed our son goodbye and then handed our baby over to him.'

'Can you remember the man's name?' Greg asked, hardly daring to breathe.

'Samuel—Samuel was his name. I never even got his surname,' Albie said sadly.

Greg felt his shoulders sink with relief. The last piece of the jigsaw puzzle had been slotted into place. Finally, he had proof that Albie was his father. He had found the man who had given him up all those years ago at last.

'Samuel was my father,' Greg said quietly. 'He and his wife, Alice, raised me.'

'Did they look after you?'

'They did; they were great parents. They couldn't have cared for me any better.'

Albie sighed heavily. 'Thank God, I've spent all these years wondering how things had turned out for you. In darker times, I questioned my decision to give you away and wanted to track him down to make sure you were okay, but I only knew his first name; I didn't know anything else about him. I was so naïve, I thought we'd just give the baby to this couple and, although we were heartbroken at the time, that eventually everything would carry on as normal, but how wrong I was . . .' He shook his head mournfully. 'I tried to catch Della after school for a few days, but she never came, and I had no way of finding out how she was doing. Her family never knew about our relationship—they never would have approved—so I couldn't call to her house. It was a horrible thing, needing to see her but not being able to. I'll never forget the day I heard the news that she had died. It was a bolt from the blue. The whole village was talking about it. I thought someone had made a mistake—I couldn't get my head around it at all. Then I heard them saying that her death was the result of a bad flu, and I realised that nobody had discovered that she had had a baby. After she died, I was tormented about whether I should tell people that she had given birth to a baby. Maybe if we had left the village earlier or if I had made her go to the doctor after she gave birth, she might still be alive. I watched her parents at the funeral, and it was like they had grown elderly overnight. They were so weighed down by sadness. I would see them from afar in the village from time to time, and they were never the same again. For all these years I've questioned myself whether I did the right thing by saying nothing or if I could have done more for her. I was so torn, but I knew Della would never have wanted them to know. It was a scandalous thing to have a baby outside of marriage in those days—especially for a family like Della's who were held in high regard and so well respected in the village. I didn't want to tarnish her memory. That was all she had left, I couldn't take that away from her too, so for all these years I've kept our secret in my heart.'

'I'm so sorry, Albie,' Greg said. His heart ached for this man and the weight of grief he had carried for all these years.

'It seems so long ago now; it feels like a different life back then ... I'm sorry, Greg, for everything. I hope you will be able to find it in your heart to forgive us, but it seemed like the only option open to us back then ...'

'You have nothing to apologise for. You gave me the gift of a wonderful childhood. We'll never know what kind of a life I could have had with you and Della if circumstances were different, but I believe everything happens for a reason. I wouldn't have known my mom and dad if it wasn't for the sacrifice that you and Della made for me.'

'Thank you, Greg,' Albie said with tears misting his eyes. 'You don't know how much of a burden it has been on my mind for all these years.'

Greg looked at the man in front of him, confined to his wheelchair, and his heart broke for all he had gone through. He sat there thinking over it all. There was so much to get his head around now that he had found his father. Potentially he had half-brothers or sisters out there.

'Did you ever remarry? Have more children?' he ventured.

Albie shook his head sadly. 'Unfortunately not. I loved Della so much. I could have never loved another after her. When she died, she took my heart with her. I'm just so grateful that after all these years, I've finally found my son.' Tears fell down his face.

The door opened, and Fiona returned to the room. She took a look at Albie's tear-stained face. 'I think that's probably enough for one day, what do you think?' she said kindly.

Greg nodded in agreement. The last thing he wanted was to cause this man any more pain. They stood up to leave.

'Can I come visit you again tomorrow, Albie?' Greg asked.

'I'd like that very much, Greg.'

Chapter 50

Sarah drove them the short distance from Grovetown Hospital back towards her cottage. The wiper blades played a never-ending game of cat and mouse against the drizzle that was falling. It had been good to hear Albie's version of events. If he was honest, Greg had been scared of what he would discover once the truth finally came out. He had been so afraid that Della had been forced to give her baby up against her will. Although it was no doubt a tragic story, in many ways hearing Albie recount the events of that fateful September day had been a relief. Deep down Greg knew that his dad was a good person; he knew he would only have taken Della and Albie's baby if he felt the situation was desperate and there was no other option for them.

'Are you okay?' Sarah asked, pulling him out of his thoughts when they had stopped at traffic lights.

'Yeah,' he sighed. 'I'm just sad for Albie at how his life turned out. He never met anyone else again and has no family around to look after him. He seemed so shocked to have visitors. I guess he's sitting in that nursing home day in, day out and no one ever comes to see him ...'

'It's so sad,' Sarah agreed, pulling off again as the lights turned green. 'If Della and Albie had fallen in love a few decades later, their futures could have been so different. Society has changed so much in those forty-something years. It's heartbreaking when you think about it.'

Greg nodded at the tragedy of it all.

'MS can be a horrible illness,' Sarah said, shaking her head. 'I'm glad you got to meet him, Greg, for his sake and yours. Hopefully knowing his son's life turned out okay in the end will give him some peace.'

They both fell silent again, each lost in their own thoughts until they passed by the shipwreck and finally pulled up outside Sarah's cottage. The fresh sea breeze took their breath as they stepped out of the car into the rain. Sarah's long hair was whipped around her face as they walked up the small path. On days like this when Inishbeg Cove was being battered by the elements, it really felt as though they were standing on the precipice of Europe.

They went inside, and while Sarah made a pot of tea, Greg thought back to how heartbroken he had been leaving this cottage just a few hours earlier. In some ways it felt like eons ago, so much had happened since then. She handed him a steaming mug and flopped down onto the sofa beside him.

'What a day . . .' she said exhaling heavily.

He had to agree with her, he was physically and mentally exhausted, it had been one of the most emotionally draining days of his life.

'I never thanked you for coming after me,' he said.

She shook her head. 'I couldn't let you get on that plane if I knew there was even a tiny chance that Albie was your father,' she continued. 'I'm glad you came back, Greg.'

'I hated leaving you this morning,' he blurted. 'When I saw you running towards me in the airport, it was like a dream.'

'I don't know what kind of dreams you have because I'm pretty sure I resembled a howling banshee chasing you down.' She was being her usual self-deprecating self.

'Seriously, though, I feel like I've got a second chance.' It was true. He had a strange feeling akin to relief all afternoon. It was like he had narrowly avoided a death sentence—well, maybe not quite as dramatic as that—but he certainly felt very glad not to have stepped onto that plane.

'What do you mean?' Sarah asked, clasping her mug between both hands and bringing it towards her lips.

'I mean, I should be excited about going home and getting back to normality again, right? Even after my best vacations, I always looked forward to going home afterwards, but this time . . . I don't know—when I sat in that airport this morning waiting to board, I felt so deflated. I guess I just feel relieved not be going back today.'

'Well, even if it's only for a few more days, I'm happy you're here.' She put her mug in one hand, reached out and squeezed his hand with her free one.

'I've been doing a lot of thinking, Sarah—'

'What's wrong?' Her brow furrowed in concern.

'Well,' he said, taking a deep breath before saying out loud the words that had been swirling around inside his head all day long. The words that made him feel equal parts excited and terrified. He had tried rehearsing what he was going to say in his head, but now that he was here, standing in front of her, his mind had gone blank, and he wasn't sure how he was going to phrase what he wanted to say to her. 'Well . . . I was thinking . . . would it be so crazy if I . . . stayed here?' Was it really him, sensible Greg Klein the least impulsive person ever, saying these words? His heart was full of trepidation as he waited for her reaction.

'Stay? In Inishbeg Cove?' Her face read shocked.

'Well, yeah . . . I know it sounds insane.' He laughed a nervous laugh that didn't sound like it even came from him and only made him sound even more unhinged. 'Meeting you and Albie—everything really—I have so much to stay here for, and I don't want to leave. I feel excited every time I think about the life I could have in the village, whereas I feel sick to the pit of my stomach every time I think about going home. Albie doesn't have any family around, and now that I've found him, I can't run out on him. I owe it to him to try and make up for all the years he missed out on. I want to be here for him and get to know my father. I'll never know Della, but I can have a relationship with him.'

Her mouth hung open. 'But what about your job, your home, all your stuff?'

'What does "stuff" matter? If you're not actually happy, you're not really living. The old me was a workaholic; my life was completely unbalanced. I can now see I was trying to fill a void through work. Since I've arrived here in the village, I feel like I have a purpose again. I finally feel like I belong somewhere, and I haven't felt like that in a long time. Being in Inishbeg Cove has taught me so much about myself that I never knew before. I know now what I need and want, but it's not just Albie, Sarah, it's you too.' He reached across for her hand. 'I don't want to leave you again—I *can't* leave you again. I want to be with you, and if that means moving halfway across the world, then that's what I have to do.'

'But what will you do here? I don't know if you've noticed, but we're hardly *Law and Order*, we're not exactly crying out for attorneys here.'

He shrugged his shoulders. 'I don't know, but I'll figure it out. I have enough to get by for a while anyway.'

Sarah's face grew serious. 'Oh, Greg, as much as I'd love you to stay, what if you don't like it here? It's fine for holiday for a few weeks . . . but after a few months, you might hate the place—the weather is awful, and it's so far away from everywhere else—you might never forgive me if you give everything up to move here.'

'I have to take a chance. My dad always said you have to trust your gut, and every time I think about staying, it feels right. If I've learnt one thing from meeting Albie today, it's that life is precious—you get one shot. Della was the love of his life; he never met anyone else after her. None of us know how long we have left or what's around the corner, you have to make the most of today. When you find "the one", you have to hold on to them.' He took a deep breath before continuing and saying the words he had wanted to say for ages now. 'I love you, Sarah. From the first day I met you, my heart has been singing. I love your kindness and how you put everyone else before yourself. I love your positivity. You make me a better person, and this is the version of myself that I prefer. I was in a dark place before you came into my life. After my heart was splintered into tiny pieces, I never thought I'd be able to feel that way about anyone else ever again. Then you came along, pieced me back together and made me want to try again. You've taught me how to love again . . . home is wherever you are, Sarah.'

Sarah looked shocked by his admission, and he trailed off, suddenly feeling unsure of himself. Doubts began to infiltrate his mind. He hoped he hadn't scared her away. He knew she had feelings for him, but what if this was all too much for her and she felt he was coming on too strong?

Every second felt like a decade as he waited for her to say something. 'You don't know how much I've wanted to hear you say those words, Greg,' she whispered. 'I love you too.' They moved towards each other and kissed with the same passion as they had the night before. They were each enjoying this sweet moment, relieved that it didn't have to end. There was no time limit shadowing them or impending departure looming on the horizon.

Suddenly there was a knock at the door. They both groaned, and Sarah made to get up.

'Leave it,' Greg said, reaching for her hand and pulling her back down towards him.

'I can't, what if someone needs me?' She stood up again.

'You see, there you go again being all good.'

She laughed and walked over to the door, fixing her hair before opening it.

'Mrs Manning!' she exclaimed. 'Come on in, is everything okay?'

'I've been looking everywhere for you,' the old lady said, blustering in the door as fast as her walking stick would allow her. She spotted Greg and grinned. 'I thought you were supposed to be going home!'

'I was, but well . . . a lot has happened,' he said.

'I see.' She shook her head in exasperation. 'You young people seem to change your minds quicker than the weather! Well anyway, have you heard the news?'

'No, what is it?' Sarah asked, looking worried.

'It's the post office—'

Suddenly they both came crashing back to Earth. Sarah looked stricken.

'Oh no—'

Greg felt his heart sink. He jumped up and stood beside Sarah.

'Don't worry, dear, it's good news! The government have announced it is to be saved. It made the RTÉ News there and all.'

'Oh, Mrs Manning,' Sarah said, gripping the elderly lady

by her arm. 'Please say this isn't a joke? Are you sure?'

'I would never joke about something like that,' she said indignantly, digging her stick into the floor. 'Sure didn't the politicians arrive into the post office to announce it themselves. Timmy said they were practically beating one another out of the way to be the one to break the news! They'd do anything to get a bit of good publicity, but you were gone God knows where and there was poor Timmy trying to hold the fort!'

'Oh my God!' Sarah said as her hands flew up to her mouth. 'I forgot about poor Timmy! I just ran out of the post office and left him there. I never gave him the keys to lock up! I didn't expect him to stay and keep it open!' She laughed at the lunacy of it all. 'I'm sorry, Mrs Manning—I just can't believe it!'

'Well, I'm telling you it's true, they don't want the bad press in an election year. It seems people power has worked. We've told them loud and clear that Inishbeg Cove is not to be messed with!'

Greg lifted Sarah up and swung her around the room. 'It's the best news. Well done!'

She laughed and squealed with happiness. 'I couldn't have done it without you, Greg.' She beamed.

He put her down and kissed her on the lips. 'I'm so proud of you.'

'I'll be off and leave you two alone,' Mrs Manning said, excusing herself with a look of amusement on her face. 'Will I tell Timmy he can go on home then?'

Sarah grinned, and they pulled back from one another. 'Please, Mrs Manning.' Sarah gave the elderly lady the keys. 'Will you tell him to lock the door and I'll call up shortly to get them off him?'

'She must think I'm batty!' Sarah giggled in an adorably girlish manner. Her eyes were bright, reflecting the happiness that Greg felt in his heart.

He walked over and pulled her into his arms once more. He cupped her face in his hands and gazed at its beautiful contours. They were at the very beginning of something that he didn't really understand, something new and terrifying, but something his gut told him to trust. Finally, there was nothing between them, but the sound of their beating hearts. At last they could be together as one, without worries or trepidation about what the future held for them. He had imagined this moment a million times before, and it had always felt right. They were two broken souls who had found one another at last. Inishbeg Cove was the place to come when life got too overwhelming or the soul was in need of nourishment. Its people could revive even the most broken of spirits, and its beaches were a balm to a wounded heart. The warm blanket of a village had wrapped itself around him, and Greg knew he would never leave. Their mouths met once more as the start of something wonderful happened. It seemed the healing waters of Inishbeg Cove had worked their magic.

Author's Note

If you enjoyed The Secrets of Inishbeg Cove, then I would really appreciate if you could leave a review on Amazon. Reviews really help to get a book noticed by Amazon who will then promote it to new readers so they are hugely important to us authors. It doesn't have to be long – just one line will do – and I will be forever grateful.

Thank you x

Also by Izzy Bayliss

Lily McDermott Series

The Girl I was Before

Baked with Love

Inishbeg Cove Series

The Secrets of Inishbeg Cove

Coming Home to Inishbeg Cove

Acknowledgements

I wish to thank my ever-supportive family who put up with my daydreaming. Thank you for being so patient and my biggest cheerleaders.

I also owe a huge thank you to the amazingly supportive blogger community who have been so supportive of my books. I am always amazed at the enthusiasm you have and am grateful for all that you do helping us authors to spread the word.

I must also thank fellow author Janelle Brooke Harris and my fellow bunkerettes for their encouragement and advice. Najla Qamber who designed my cover, you have once against surpassed yourself with another brilliant jacket and also, Chrissy from EFC Services once again for your eagle eye.

Lastly, thank you to you the reader, from all the titles out there, thank you for choosing my book. I hope you enjoyed it!

Izzy xx

About the Author

Izzy Bayliss lives in Ireland with her husband and four young children. A romantic at heart, she loves nothing more than cosying up in front of the fire with a good book. She released The Girl I Was Before in 2016 and its sequel Baked with Love in 2018. The Secrets of Inishbeg Cove is her third novel and is the first book in the Inishbeg Cove series.

She can be found hanging about on Facebook @izzybaylissauthor or Twitter @izzybayliss.

If you would like to be the first to hear about Izzy's latest releases and other news then please subscribe to her newsletter on her website www.izzybayliss.com.

She also writes as Caroline Finnerty.

Made in United States
North Haven, CT
20 January 2022